I thought I'd gotten everything,

until my fingers brushed against something hard, wrapped in cloth, and oddly warm to the touch. I grabbed it and heaved myself out of the crate, then examined the bundle. It felt like a rock, heavy and solid. Most of the items in this crate were broken pottery shards, from vases and the like. Hard, maybe, but not heavy. Careful not to touch the item's surface, in case it was valuable after all, I turned it over and shook the covering loose.

Sure enough, it was a rock. Plain, gray, ordinary. About half the size of an American football, shaped like an irregular pyramid, with jagged edges and flat-but-rough surfaces. The only unusual thing about it was its warmth. Like Claude Rousseau. Which is maybe why, against my better judgment, I reached out and touched the very tip of the rock's pyramid.

And then it *shrieked* at me, the agony of centuries piercing my ears till I thought my skull would burst, electric shocks searing through my fingers, hand, arm, ripping through my whole body, gripping my lungs and squeezing until I couldn't breathe. I flung the rock away, covering my ears and dropping to the floor, shaking, gasping for air, while still it screamed, on and on and on and on, until I lay huddled on the concrete, red fire burning in my head, blackness filling my soul.

Then everything went silent.

Praise for Kerry Blaisdell

"*DEBRIEFING THE DEAD* is everything I want in a book: a smart, wise-cracking heroine on a witty, sexy, can't-guess-the-next-twist ride. Trust me, Kerry Blaisdell is your new obsession. I'm a huge fan!"

~*Lenora Bell, USA Today bestselling author*

~*~

"Filled with quirky characters, gorgeous locations and madcap mystery, it's easy to overlook that at the heart of Kerry Blasdell's delicious, rollicking romp of a story is a whip-smart protagonist whose love for her family leads her to strike a bargain with the angel of death. Archeology meets international intrigue in this dazzling debut by an author to watch."

~*Teri Brown, award-winning author*

Debriefing
the Dead

by

Kerry Blaisdell

Book One of The Dead Series

Debriefing the Dead

Cover Art by *Rae Monet, Inc. Design*

The Wild Rose Press, Inc.
PO Box 708
Adams Basin, NY 14410-0708
Visit us at www.thewildrosepress.com

Publishing History
First Black Rose Edition, 2018
Print ISBN 978-1-5092-2045-8
Digital ISBN 978-1-5092-2046-5

Book One of The Dead Series
Published in the United States of America

Dedication

This book is dedicated to my family, without whose
support I could never have written it:
~*~
To my husband,
you have been amazingly patient over the years,
even when it looked like all I ever did was sit and write.
~*~
To my children,
thanks for all the times you wore headphones,
or accepted yet another fend-for-yourself-night for
dinner, so I could get a few more words in.
~*~
To my mother,
who always said I could and should do
whatever I wanted, and then helped me figure out how.
~*~
And last but not least, to my father,
who wrote down those first stories for me,
until I could do it for myself.
I miss you every day and wish you could read
your little girl's stories now!

Chapter One

"Be sober, be vigilant; because your adversary the devil, as a roaring lion, walketh about, seeking whom he may devour."
~The Bible, 1 Peter 5:8

I smelled Death on the two men who walked into my shop that day. I should have listened to my nose.

Of course, death is an everyday part of my life, which is probably why I ignored it. I'm a dealer in rare artifacts, particularly those that haven't been acquired through, um, *normal* channels. Okay, I'm a fence, and before that, I robbed graves. But only those already being robbed, by "professional" archaeologists. And frankly, I know as much or more as they do about the care and preservation of ancient relics.

In any case, my shop, *Hyacinth Finch's Boutique des Antiquités,* now stocks items that are either stolen, or are being stolen back, by one or another of my usual clients, members of the Marseille elite who enjoy stabbing each other in the back, art-collection-wise. They pay well, and leave me to live my life the rest of the time, so I guess you'd call it a symbiotic relationship.

But these guys weren't from my client base. Until they arrived unannounced in my office above the shop, and sat, uninvited, in the chairs in front of my desk, I'd never seen them before. Which made their interest in this *exact* batch of goods even more suspect.

"Who are you again?" I asked, more to buy time than anything else.

The one on the left smiled genially. He was larger than his companion, not exactly fat, but taller and more…spread out, for lack of a better description. His dark blue eyes were rimmed with thick lashes, and his hair was oiled into a slick black shell. His tanned skin cracked and peeled in places, like he'd had one too many sunburns, and he had a heavy French accent, but as it was late August, and we were in southern France, neither was exactly remarkable. I myself spoke fluent French, but he'd begun in Franglish, and I hadn't corrected him.

"Mademoiselle Finch." He leaned forward, the flimsy wooden chair legs groaning and spreading under his bulk, making it look as if he had six legs instead of the usual two. "*Je vous assure,* nothing would please me more than to provide our *bona fides*. But the time, it is lacking." He glanced at his companion, equally dark and oily, but not as talkative. Oily Two smiled, close-mouthed, and gave a Gallic shrug. *We're all pals here, right?*

Yeah, right.

"Look," I said, suppressing a shiver of unease, despite the heat, "even if I wanted to, I'm not sure I could find this particular lot." I pretended to check a leather-covered log book I had open on my desk. "Where did you say it originated?"

"Turkey." Oily One's smile said he knew I knew that, his yellowed teeth big and sharp behind his dry, cracked lips.

I ran a finger down a column on the page. Look at me—organized, professional, absolutely-*not*-lying business woman extraordinaire. "Nope. Nothing's come in from Turkey."

His gaze flicked to the log, then around my office. Books filled wood-and-glass cases along the walls, and papers crowded the floor. The window stood open behind me, letting in the Mediterranean breeze and the slanted late afternoon sunlight. Also, *un fourmilion*—an antlion—a long, thin-bodied insect with lacy wings, that my seven-year-old nephew, Geordi, would have been fascinated by. He loves bugs. Me, not so much, but I'm a vegetarian, and a live-and-let-live kinda gal, and this guy wasn't doing anything besides buzzing lazily around my office, looking for ants to trap. At least, that's what Geordi says they do. I hate ants, so if there were any to chow on, more power to him.

Oily One and Two didn't seem bothered by him, but I rather wished they were, so we could hurry this along. The bell on the downstairs door had only rung once since lunch—when these two entered—and it seemed like a good day to close early. One of the perks of being an independent "art dealer" such as myself. The downside is, I can't afford to alienate potential clients. I have my regulars, but business ebbs and flows, and extra cash is always handy. Especially now.

I forced a smile of my own. "I want to help you—I do. But I have no idea where to find…something like this." Technically, this was true. I'm a big believer in technicalities.

Oily One leaned in closer, waistband straining, hands on his knees, palms up. Open. Friendly. I didn't buy it, but apparently, the antlion did. It landed on his

3

shoulder, black body silhouetted crisply as it crawled unnoticed over the expensive white of his suit.

He smiled again. "Surely a businesswoman of your reputation…?"

"Messieurs. I'm not sure what you've heard"—*or from whom*—"but I am merely a dealer. I buy. I sell. I don't find."

"Vous me surprenez. It is said you are *très accomplie* at these things."

I tilted back in my chair. "You flatter me. I've had good luck. And good clients. I can only sell what they bring in. Speaking of which—who did you say referred you?"

Touché. Point à moi. But he wasn't giving up. "A shipment from Colossae, in southwestern Turkey—*près de la rivière* Lycus. A region in which you specialize, *non?* Perhaps you have contacts. You will make some calls. We will, of course, reward your efforts."

He took out a business card and wrote on the back, the movement causing the antlion to take flight, hovering between him and his companion. Oily Two waved it away, then caught my eye and lifted a hand, as though asking if he should squash it. His full-lipped, sharp-toothed grin was creepier even than his friend's, and I shook my head hastily, noting that the insect—no dummy—was already out of reach.

His friend passed the card to me, and though our fingers never touched, I suddenly felt…*heat*…burning off him in sharp waves. I jerked my hand away, taking the card with me. It was as cool as paper usually is, and I gave a mental shake and glanced at the number he'd written, then had to hide my shock. This would be enough for me to take a year off—or pay for Geordi and his mother, my sister Lily, to get *really* far away from her ex. Some place where he could *never* hurt them, ever again.

I flipped the card over. *Les Rousseaux* was printed on it in plain type, with a cell number below. When I looked up, he smiled. Again.

"Claude Rousseau." He indicated Oily Two, who gave a slight bow. *"Mon frère,* Jacques. We are most pleased to make your acquaintance. If you hear of anything, you will call. Yes?"

"Yes," I said, the interview's end finally in sight. "Of course."

They rose to go, their tread surprisingly silent on the stairs, given their combined bulk. I waited until I heard the bell on the front door tinkle one last time. Then I ran down and shot the bolt. I flipped the sign in the window to read *Fermé,* then pulled down the shade. Next, I went to the back door and locked it as well. Only when I was alone in the dark store, so familiar and comforting in its clutter, did I take a deep breath and blow it out.

The whole experience bothered me on a number of levels, not the least of which was the timing. You see, I wasn't exactly upfront with the Rousseaux. Not only would I be able to locate the lot they wanted, I already *had* it—in storage, where it'd been for several months. The thing is, only two people should have known its origins.

One of them was me.

And the other was dead.

****

An hour later, I'd left the shop, wandering home via my usual circuitous route, past various markets,

5

plein air or otherwise, where I picked up the parts of my dinner. One of the reasons I prefer Europe to the States is the whole notion of buying your food the day you cook it. I'm not exactly a health nut, but I am a vegetarian, and a sucker for anything fresh.

Walking and shopping also gives me a chance to process my day. And today, I had a lot to process. It occurred to me the Rousseaux could be cops. La Boutique has been investigated a time or two, but I always come away clean. The thing is, if they were *les flics*, asking after *this* lot, then they already knew it was stolen. But it came from Colossae, a site which has never officially been excavated, so how could anyone know part of it was gone?

I'd "inherited" the catch from my business partner, Vadim, after he died in a boating accident. A lump rose in my throat, hot and sharp, and I swallowed it back down. Though we weren't "together" romantically, Vadim was more than a partner, he was my friend. His death was so unexpected; even half a year later, I still couldn't believe he was gone. I'd never even opened the crates he left me, just locked them up to deal with later. But…was my reluctance now because of my grief? Or were my instincts right and something was off?

Unlocking the iron gate leading to my building's interior stairwell, I saw my neighbor on his way down. Jason Jones is a little younger than me and a lot taller—at least a foot, and I'm five-five. He tends bar at one of the gay cabarets in Marseille, so he's frequently on his way out when I'm coming home. In theory, he moved here to pursue a theater career, but in practice, I think he likes the bar better. Rehearsals would mess too much with his "party all night, sleep all day" schedule.

"Hyacinth!"

He broke into a grin and finished coming down the steps, then gave a low theatrical bow and pretended to kiss my hand. He wore a black dress shirt, gray slacks, Italian leather shoes, and ridiculously large sunglasses that made him look like a very large insect hovering over my wrist. He can rock a pair of jeans, too, but today he was the perfect image of the playboy bartender, a look he cultivates with great care and uses to great advantage—and he has the tips to prove it. He's not actually gay, but he doesn't advertise the fact. However, he's never once tried to hit on me, which is not as insulting as you might think. I don't have the best track record with relationships, and with Lily and everything else, I had no desire to start one now.

As soon as I had the thought, I realized he was lingering over my wrist, turning it up and inhaling deeply. The heat of his breath tickled my skin, his fingers caressed my palm, and my knees wobbled. Apparently, I'm not immune to his charms after all.

He let go and straightened, examining my face. I couldn't read his expression behind the shiny glasses, but he must have seen something in mine that made him ask, "What's up? Something wrong at the shop?"

"It's nothing. Not really. Some new clients came in and wanted to chat. Actually…they might be a good fit for Vadim's last shipment."

He flipped the sunglasses up, blue eyes wide. He's never asked how I acquire my goods, and I've never asked what happens when he disappears for days with some girl he's met on the metro. He's entitled to his secrets, too. But he moved in right after Lily left her creepazoid husband and just before Vadim died. I couldn't burden Lily with my grief, and our parents died more than twenty years ago. If we have other family, I've never met them. I don't trust easily, but it turns out Jason has a strong, relatively safe shoulder to cry on, for which I'm eternally grateful.

That doesn't stop him from being opinionated about what I should do with my life. He gave a low whistle. "Are you going to sell it to them?"

"I…don't know." I moved up the steps, so I could look him in the eye without needing a chiropractor.

"You *have* to sell it. It's what Vadim wanted—why he *brought* it to you, for God's sake."

"I know. You're right. It's just—do I have to sell it to *these* guys?"

He planted his hands on his hips, glaring. "Hyacinth. It. Is. Time. *Let go.*"

His face was close, his breath warm, and despite it all, I found his earnestness vaguely attractive. He filled the narrow stairwell with his long, lean body, and I resisted the urge to back up another step.

"Okay, fine. I'll call them." He stood, unmoving, and I sighed. "What? I said I'd do it. Is something wrong?"

His gaze dropped to my sandals, then moved slowly up my legs, lingering on my hips, and from there over my chest and the sleeveless blouse that was all I could tolerate in this heat. By the time his gaze travelled up my throat to linger again at my mouth, before finally meeting my eyes, I had goose bumps in several inappropriate places, and was hoping the dark stairwell hid my blush.

His eyes flashed dark for a moment—almost

black—then he gave an odd little shake of his head and took a step back himself. He dropped the sunglasses over his eyes, and when he spoke, his tone was light and friendly as ever. "Just checking it's really you. You never agree with me in under five minutes."

Before I could gather my wits for a decent retort, he gave a mock salute, then buzzed the gate open and vanished up the block. I blew out a breath and finished the climb to my third-floor apartment—second, if you count European style.

Jason's only a little younger than me—late twenties or so—but I think he gets that whole *joie de vivre* thing better than I do. He's a hard worker, don't get me wrong. But he also plays hard, and flits from one activity to the next with an easy metamorphosis I admire. I didn't know what to make of his sudden inexplicable interest, but he had helped me feel better. And he was right. Holding onto Vadim's last catch wouldn't bring him back. It would only hold *me* back.

The apartment stairs lead to a short breezeway, open on both ends. There's one apartment on each corner, and mine's the first on the left. I unlocked the door and stepped in. My place is tiny, but less cluttered than the shop. In a complete reversal of the stereotypical antiques dealer, I am not a pack rat. Give me open space and tidy end tables and I'm a happy camper. Wood floors, throw rugs, small table and chairs in the dining nook. A kitchen that used to be a closet, as near as I can tell—only one person can stand in it at a time, and if the oven's open, nobody can. One window in the main room, another in the bedroom, and finally, a bathroom that's bigger than the kitchen, but not by much.

I have pretty basic needs, possibly due to growing up in foster care. But that's a whole other story, and I'm well-adjusted enough to know I can't blame all my idiosyncrasies on my parentless childhood. Some, but not all. The bottom line is I don't need a lot of junk to be happy. I do need a certain amount of cash, though. Lily's custody battle over Geordi wasn't only with her ex, Nick. It was with his entire family. And I do mean Family—as in organized, with a capital F. The Sicilian Mob. Which Lily swears she didn't know until after they were married, though how either of us were naïve enough to believe Nick was just "a" Dioguardi, and not one of *the* Dioguardis, is beyond me.

Worse, since Geordi's the first son of an *only* son, Nick's family weren't about to let him go, even if Lily found the one judge in Paris brave enough to side with her. It took serious guts for her to leave, and if I had any say in it, neither she nor Geordi would ever go back.

So, if the Oily Brothers' money could facilitate that, who was I to quibble?

****

The next day was Sunday, and not only is my shop closed, most of the other shops in my area are as well. I figured the Rousseaux could wait another day before I told them of the shipment. For one thing, it would lend credibility to my claim of needing to find it first. For another, as noted, I wasn't exactly anxious to call them.

But first thing Monday, I dragged myself out of bed, showered, and drove to the warehouse I rent at the docks, near the Bassin d'Arenc. I use it to store unsorted catches or big items I can't cram into the shop. Or, let's be honest, things I don't want out in plain sight.

Ordinarily I'd walk—it's only twenty blocks—but I had to move Vadim's stuff to the shop before calling the Rousseaux. Unfortunately, my car's a Peapod prototype, and about the size of a mini-Mini Cooper. It was a gift from a grateful client, and tops out at forty-five kilometers per hour, so no *autobahn* for me. But it's electric, costs around two cents a kilometer for gas, and is perfect for getting around town.

Not so perfect for hauling stuff.

I could've asked Claude and Jacques to meet me with a truck. Since the catch was currently in three large shipping crates, this would save tons of time and effort. But though I'd decided to unload the stuff, showing these guys where I kept my stock—or what I still had on hand—might not be the smartest idea. Besides, I was curious about the contents. Vadim had never told me what he'd found, and in our line of work, it could be anything from thousands-of-years-old "junk" to priceless relics. I was guessing at least some of the latter, or why would the Rousseaux care?

In order to find out, I'd have to move everything to smaller boxes, cart it to the store, go back to the warehouse, rinse, repeat. Part of me wondered if I should just hand it over as-is and be done.

I suppressed yet another twinge at the memory of yesterday's interview. Especially Jacques, sitting still and spider-like across from me. I had a feeling he didn't miss much and wondered what I might have unconsciously revealed while Claude distracted me.

I pulled into a parking space near my unit, and my cell rang, the cheery notes of Beethoven's *Für Élise* telling me Lily was calling for our weekly chat. For a second, I thought about answering. Lily might be Geordi's mother, but I have to say, he's pretty much the light of my life. Certainly, the best male relationship I've had, even counting Jason and Vadim. Who wouldn't love a guy who brings you dead bugs he's found in someone *else's* yard, then offers to split the last éclair because you're his "favoritest *tata* ever"? He's a smart kid, too. I'm his *only* auntie, and the flattery still works.

I sent the call to voicemail. It almost killed me, but it'd be hard enough opening the crates, knowing how excited Vadim was when he landed this catch. You can't get much fresher than an unexcavated site. If I spent even a half hour catching up with Lily and Geordi, I'd chicken out. And I had to know what was in those crates, or I'd never be able to let them, or Vadim, go.

I screwed up my courage, got out of the car, and unlocked the unit's roll door. Yep. Three large crates.

Very large.

I went back to the Peapod, opened the hatch, and extracted the paltry pile of produce boxes I'd scrounged from my favorite markets. I'd have to empty them again at the store for subsequent trips, or else go beg more boxes. This was ridiculous. But necessary.

Must let go. Must move on.

****

As is so often the case, once I got going, it wasn't so bad. Opening the first crate was tough, and I won't say I didn't cry at all. Vadim was a good partner, and a better friend. At least he'd died doing what he loved— sailing the Mediterranean, with a drink in his hand and two beautiful women at his side. He was a devout atheist, but if there's any kind of afterlife, I'd like to think he's still sailing and drinking, and looking for the next big catch.

I found a roll of paper towels on a shelf and blew my nose, then metaphorically rolled up my non-existent sleeves and dug in.

The more valuable items were wrapped in acid-free paper and sealed in airtight containers, which I didn't bother to open, because Vadim had helpfully labeled them. His clear, bold printing noted statuary and relics, both Pagan and Christian, from the ancient Phrygian city of Colossae, near what is now Denizli, in southwestern Turkey. The general period was the first century, so any Christian items were very early. While this fascinated me intellectually, and I did have some experience with artifacts from Turkey, it was mainly because Vadim brought them to me. My own interests lie more in the Egyptians, one of the reasons we'd complemented each other professionally. But it meant I had little personal experience with anything of this kind.

It took several trips to move the best items, and a few more for the midlevel stuff, plus getting more boxes. By the time I got to the third crate, the sun was well past its zenith, but I'd reached the dregs. Items down here were either unwrapped, loose in the packing straw, or else carelessly covered with rough cloth to prevent scratching.

This crate wasn't as full as the others, and it looked like I was on my final trip. Thank God. I'd had a quick lunch—veggies, hummus, cheese, and bread—but otherwise worked straight through. Lily'd called twice more, but I didn't pick up. I'd call her back over dinner, when we'd have time to chat, and I could tell her of my sudden windfall.

I plopped my last empty box on the warehouse floor, then hung over the side of the crate to excavate the bottom. I found a few more canvas bundles and pulled them out, setting them in the box, then went back once more.

I thought I'd gotten everything, until my fingers brushed against something hard, wrapped in cloth, and oddly warm to the touch. I grabbed it and heaved myself out of the crate, then examined the bundle. It felt like a rock, heavy and solid. Most of the items in this crate were broken pottery shards, from vases and the like. Hard, maybe, but not heavy. Careful not to touch the item's surface, in case it was valuable after all, I turned it over and shook the covering loose.

Sure enough, it was a rock. Plain, gray, ordinary. About half the size of an American football, shaped like an irregular pyramid, with jagged edges and flat-but-rough surfaces. The only unusual thing about it was its warmth. Like Claude Rousseau. Which is maybe why, against my better judgment, I reached out and touched the very tip of the rock's pyramid.

And then it *shrieked* at me, the agony of centuries piercing my ears till I thought my skull would burst, electric shocks searing through my fingers, hand, arm, ripping through my whole body, gripping my lungs and squeezing until I couldn't breathe. I flung the rock away, covering my ears and dropping to the floor, shaking, gasping for air, while still it screamed, on and on and on and on, until I lay huddled on the concrete, red fire burning in my head, blackness filling my soul.

Then everything went silent.

Chapter Two

"Then he forsook God which made him, and lightly esteemed the Rock of his salvation."
~*The Bible, Deuteronomy 32:15*

My heart thundered as it raced to restore oxygen to my brain and limbs. Slowly, I sat up and eyed the rock where it had landed a few feet away, next to the empty crate. It still looked totally uninteresting. It was also not screaming anymore. I took a shaky breath and tried to clear my head.

Had it screamed at all? Maybe a boat got too close to the docks, and what I'd heard was a warning blast from the harbor tower. And...I was weak from hunger, which would explain the whole "vibrate until you pass out" thing.

Yeah, that made sense. It was a rock. Rocks do not scream.

I crawled over and put out my hand. No heat came off it, and when I got up the nerve to touch it, it felt cool and hard. Nothing—not a peep—came from it, and I relaxed.

A little.

Still, I wondered how it got in the crate. Like most kids his age, Geordi's addicted to "edutainment" type TV shows, especially those sporting some version of the game, *Which of These Items Doesn't Belong?* Next to the bugs, he's never happier than when telling his onscreen "friends" that the fish does not, in fact, belong with the shoes, coat, pants, and shirt.

That's what this was like. Gold statues? Check. Ancient Phrygian vases? Check. Boring old rock with possible vocal prowess? Bing-*go.*

I grabbed the cloth and re-covered it. The fact that it *was* wrapped meant its inclusion was deliberate. And it was the same cloth Vadim used on all the other pieces, so it was likely him that included it. But why?

My cell phone buzzed, this time with a text from Lily: *Call me!!!*

I glanced at the clock, then out at the sinking sun. Damn. I'd wanted to hand the goods over to the Rousseaux before closing up shop for the day. Not that I'd ever opened. Another perk of sole proprietorship—the sign in my window reads "Approximate Hours," and I mean it. But I didn't want all this inventory sitting in the shop overnight, tempting Fate. Or, more likely, thieves. Plus, the longer I waited, the more time I had to change my mind.

Careful not to break the more expensive items, I set the rock in the last box and carried it to my car, closed the hatch, then locked up the storage unit. I got in the driver's seat, took out Claude's card, and dialed while backing out of the parking space. I was sure they'd want to meet right away, and I wasn't disappointed.

"Mais, c'est merveilleux!" Claude said when I told him I'd lucked out and "found" the shipment they wanted. I could almost hear him drooling across the line. "We will leave at once."

"Perfect. And, er, it'll be cash only."

Occasionally, I accept wire transfers to a Swiss

bank account, which I opened in mine and Lily's names a few months ago, after she filed for divorce from Nick. It sounds clichéd, but they're easy to get, and very…convenient, especially when hiding money from one's Mafia in-laws. I did it for Lily and Geordi, but it simplifies my, um, finances, also. In this case, however, I thought the Rousseaux, like the Dioguardis, might not be the best electronic business partners.

I half expected Claude to balk, since this was a *very* big price tag, but he said, *"Bien sûr.* That will not be a problem."

"Great. I'll be at the store in five minutes."

I hung up and pushed away another stab of unease. Jason was right. I needed to let go and begin the healing process. And when had I ever been this picky in the past? A few of my clients have questionable business practices—hell, *I* have them—but it's never bothered me before. Why now, when I didn't actually know anything bad about the Rousseaux?

Maybe the experience with the rock put me on edge. I didn't really believe I'd imagined it, and the false reassurance I got from pretending otherwise had worn off, partly because a low humming noise now came from the back of my car, faint, but noticeable, and having nothing to do with the engine. Which is in the front, in any case.

I reached the Rue de Lyon and made a snap decision. Instead of turning right toward the shop, I went left and aimed for my apartment. Vadim had included that rock in this shipment against all rational explanation. It was important to him, which made it important to me. Besides, those kiddie shows can't *all* be wrong: when an item doesn't belong, you take it out of the equation. I may be mixing my metaphors, but you get the drift.

My apartment building is tucked away off a side street, off another couple of side streets, in the Quartier Saint Louis. It's an older, quiet neighborhood, and my building's no exception. Jason's probably the loudest tenant, and his main offense is listening to jazz until nine at night. Today as I ran upstairs, the lack of noise felt oppressive. Or maybe it was a rare attack of conscience. I'd agreed to sell the *whole* shipment, and the rock was clearly part of it. But the Rousseaux wouldn't want a boring old rock, would they?

My conscience piped up, *If they know it screams, they sure as hell will.*

Yeah, that would do it.

I unlocked my door, then stepped into the dim interior. I needed to be fast, but I couldn't just drop the rock on the floor. Luckily, I am a smart and savvy businesswoman, with a healthy suspicion of non-Swiss banks, who had a wall safe installed a while back.

Okay, I'm not that smart—I hid it behind a painting over the futon, because that's the only interior wall. And I felt kind of stupid, hiding a rock in a concealed, fireproof safe. Like using a machete on mushrooms. But I had the safe, and the rock, so I went with it.

The rock still hummed—a slight disturbance, barely detectable in the atmosphere. It wasn't exactly unpleasant. More persistent, and somehow urgent. It had started to feel warm again, and I had no desire to touch it and accidentally set off another round of screams. Careful to keep the wrapping intact, I placed it inside the safe with my stash of cash.

I make a comfortable living, both from the shop and my "extra-curricular" activities. The safe was small, but fairly full. I could tap into my resources and live the high life, like my clients do, but it's not my style. Besides, I get a lot less attention from *les autorités* this way.

My cell buzzed with another text from Lily: *Where r u?* Which was weird, because she's one of those texters who spell out every word, no matter what.

I'm not. I texted back, *Call u l8r. Bg sale!!!* Then I locked the apartment and ran downstairs, passing Jason on his way up. He still wore his clothes from Saturday, including the shades, and looked like he'd been up since then, too. His dark hair stood out at all angles from his head, and two days' stubble gave him a feral look.

"Hi," he said on a yawn. "Where're you off to?"

"Shop—meeting the buyers for Vadim's stuff."

"Sounds nice." He took off the sunglasses, then squinted blearily. "Have fun."

I gave him a once over. "Looks like you had fun last night."

"Yeah—you should've been there." His gaze flicked to my mouth, eyes darkening, and I resisted the urge to fan myself.

Abruptly, he seemed to become aware of what he was doing. An odd look crossed his face—regret?—and he turned and stumbled toward his door. Maybe he was just a little drunk. Yeah, that made more sense than that he would suddenly start flirting with me. I have to say, though, I've only ever seen him tipsy once or twice, and never drunk. Being a bartender, he knows how to keep his hands off the merchandise, so to speak.

I started to move past, but he turned and reached for my arm. "Wait—something came for you on Saturday, before I left. It's a letter, for Lily."

We have mailboxes on the ground floor, but anything too big or needing a signature is supposed to be brought to our doors. It's a six-story building, though, with no elevator, and lately *la poste* has a tendency to make it up one flight to Jason's door, then stop. He doesn't seem to mind, though. He says it gives him an excuse to be neighborly, and I have to admit, he knows every other tenant by name, age, and occupation, which is more than I can say.

"Oh—okay," I said. "I'll get it when I come back."

"Sure." He held my arm a moment, searching my face. I don't know for what, or if he found anything, but for a fraction of a second, he looked stone-cold sober, and more than a little worried. I opened my mouth to ask what was wrong, but then he released my arm and looked all bleary and tipsy again, and I was sure I'd imagined it.

Then a new question popped into my head. "You mean *from* Lily, right?"

Jason looked up from fumbling his key at his lock and grinned. "Hyacinth. Last night was fun, but not *that* fun. Plain white envelope with *To Lily Finch* on it, care of your address. No return, but the postmark was Paris."

Shit. No wonder Lily'd been calling me. *Shit, shit, shit.* "You're sure it was Paris?"

"Positive." He'd finally gotten his door open. "I can get it for you. Only take a sec."

The sun was even lower now, and the Rousseaux probably wondered where the hell I was. "I've got to get to the shop before I blow this sale. Can you slide it under my door?"

"'Kay."

That's Jason. Sometimes he's so laid-back, I'm afraid he'll melt. Unlike me. I'm not laid-back. Especially when it comes to letters *for* Lily, *from* Paris, sent to *my* address.

Shit. Damn. *Merde.*

I can swear creatively in a number of languages. When you drift around Europe and Africa for a decade or so, you pick up a lot. But sometimes the feeling is just too much. I *had* to get to the shop, now more than ever. I needed that cash, and what was in my safe, and I needed to find Lily. Because the letter could only mean one thing.

She'd lost custody of Geordi. Which wasn't surprising. If there's a judge in France who's not in the Dioguardis' pocket, it's because said judge hasn't been "informed" yet on which side the bread gets buttered. But Lily wouldn't let a judge or anyone else stop her. She'd snatched Geordi—the letter was our prearranged signal, telling me where to meet her. She must have been frantic when she didn't hear from me. She wouldn't say or text anything on her phone, though, in case Nick had it bugged.

It hardly mattered. No matter how big her head start, he'd be right behind. And if he found her, he wouldn't let her or Geordi go, ever.

Not alive, anyway.

****

I made it to my rendezvous with the Rousseaux in record time, luckily not passing any *flics* because I drove way over the speed limit. Which in my car is a rare feat.

A black Maybach 62 sedan was parked in front of my shop, looking like an expensive beetle with dead, unlit eyes. I only know the make because Nick coveted one, but couldn't afford the half-mil price tag, despite his nefarious "business dealings." The thing took up half the narrow street, and behind it, a good-sized box truck took up the rest. Even in my cracker-box Peapod, I had to jump the curb to get by, and then there was barely room to park.

The Maybach's windows were so dark I couldn't see anyone inside except the chauffeur, a stone-faced thug I wouldn't want to meet alone after dark. Or before, for that matter. The driver of the truck wasn't much better—or maybe it was the huge black cockroach painted on the side panel, surrounded by spidery lettering that read *Les Rousseaux— Exterminateurs*. At least now I knew how the brothers earned their keep. The knowledge wasn't reassuring.

Good thing Jason knew I was here and would notice if I didn't come back. Remembering his inebriated state, I tacked on an "eventually," and hoped it wouldn't come to that.

I climbed out of my car, opened the hatch, and unloaded the last of the filled produce boxes. The Rousseaux got out of the Maybach, oily as ever, and I felt another twinge of anxiety. Evidently Claude was still the spokesman.

"Mademoiselle Finch. We had begun to doubt you were coming."

"Sorry—got stuck in a construction zone. Let's get this over with. You have the cash?"

"Mais oui." If he was put off by my bluntness, he didn't show it. He also didn't whip out the cash. Not

that I really expected him to. "I am sure you will not object if we verify the merchandise?"

"Of course. My, um, contact assures me this is the entire lot. But feel free to take a look."

Claude signaled the truck driver and the chauffeur, who got out of their respective vehicles and grabbed a box each off the curb. The whole Band of Creepy Men waited while I unlocked the shop, then filed in behind me. My *this-is-not-right* feeling ratcheted up another notch, but what could I do? Inside or out, I was no match for four large men. Hell, one of them alone could "exterminate" me and dump my body off the Vieux Port into the Bay, without breaking a sweat.

I'd pushed back the display cases and shelves that took up the bulk of my floor space, to make room for the dozen neatly stacked boxes the shipping crates had dispersed to. The truck driver had a box cutter, while the chauffeur produced a pocket knife, and they went to work, slicing the boxes open and rummaging through them. So much for my careful packaging.

Like Jacques, neither spoke, their faces devoid of emotion in the dim light. They hardly seemed human, their movements robotic: slice the box open, lift an item, hold for inspection, drop it carelessly into a new box, turn back. They obviously didn't know what they were looking for and didn't care. As soon as Claude or Jacques gave a negative shake of the head, the item ceased to matter, and I winced as several relics cracked on impact. More and more it seemed the money I already had was enough to keep Lily and Geordi safe. But I'd made a deal.

As each box was emptied, Claude's expression grew grimmer. They wanted the rock. I knew it. The question was, what would they do when they realized it was missing?

Jacques' expression was impassive, worse than Claude's frowns. That silent offer to kill the antlion still creeped me out, and now I knew how the poor bug felt.

When the two thugs had tossed their way through the last box, Claude turned on me, all pretense of civility gone. *"Putain!"* He shoved me so hard, my side slammed into the counter's sharp metal corner. I wheezed and doubled over, but he yanked me up by my shirt and shook me hard. *"Where is it?"*

"Where is what?" I managed, fighting for breath, and he backhanded me across the cheek, pain exploding in my jaw, blood filling my mouth. My vision grayed, and I swayed, grabbing the counter, then gave up and slid to the floor, my back against a display case. Through my pain-red haze, I saw Jacques murmuring to his brother, and I thought, *so he* can *speak.*

It's funny what the mind does in dire circumstances. For one thing, who the hell cared if Jacques spoke or not? For another, when he glanced at me, I could swear his eyes glowed black, like coals in the deepest pit of a fire. Then Claude punched me between the eyes, white hot pain splitting my forehead, my skull bouncing off the cabinet, cracking the glass, blood trickling behind my ears. Dull throbbing from the back of my head pulsed forward to meet the sharp pain between my eyes, and when Claude raised his fist again, I held up my hands.

"Wait. Stop. I'll get it."

I'm not proud of the fact, but I'm basically a wimp. A rock—even a talking one—isn't worth dying over. I only hoped the Rousseaux would let me live once they got it back. I wasn't at all sure they would.

"Bon. You see reason." Claude released the fist and instead hauled me to my feet. "Where is it?"

"Somewhere safe. I'll bring it to you."

His laugh was utterly without mirth, his voice hollow. *"Ça me doute.* You will not get a second chance to cheat us. I will come with you, and if you try anything, I will kill you."

The last thing I wanted was them knowing where I lived, but I had no choice. He shoved me, and I stumbled to the door just as it opened, the bell tinkling cheerily.

"Tata Hyhy!" squealed my nephew, running inside and flinging his arms around my aching side.

Chapter Three

*"When my father and my mother forsake me,
then the Lord will take me up."*
~*The Bible, Psalm 27:10*

Geordi smelled sweet and boyish and so-so *good,* and it was so-so *wrong* that he was in the middle of this. I inhaled the earthy scent of him, my heart freezing even as I clutched him close and prayed for a way to get him back out. He looked up from under curly black bangs, blue eyes hopeful. He's the spitting image of his father, except where Nick is the Devil Incarnate, Geordi's a little angel. Even when he's trying to get something from me.

"Tata Hyhy—do you have any sugary slugs?"

Apricot delight is his favorite treat, but when I first offered him one, he was highly suspicious. Knowing his bug obsession, I'd made up the moniker, and to this day, I doubt he knows their real name.

"Maybe in my car," I said, thinking fast. If I got him outside, maybe the Rousseaux would let him go.

Then Lily came in, her eyes clearly not adjusted from the bright, low sun to the dim of the shop. Her light hair was pulled back in a messy ponytail, and her jeans and white blouse looked like they'd been slept in. Geordi sported his favorite Spider-Man backpack, and Lily wheeled an overstuffed pink carry-on behind her.

Whatever safe haven she'd counted on, Nick must have found it.

"Hey, sis—sorry to barge in on your sale. We tried to wait in the cab, but we're low on cash, and Geordi has to go potty."

Even with everything going on, I heard the strain in her voice. Lily and I are close, but not a lot alike, except for the blue-gray of our eyes. She's blonde and willowy, where I'm a brunette and more solid. Not fat by any stretch, but I'll never be a size two. On a good day I'm an eight, after a pint of ice cream, a ten, and I'm okay with that.

I tried unsuccessfully to dislodge Geordi. I had to get them out of here before the Rousseaux went ballistic or Lily noticed anything was up.

Too late. She caught sight of my battered face. "Oh my God! Hyacinth—what happened?"

"Get out of here!" I yelled, pushing Geordi at her, but at a signal from Jacques, the truck driver yanked Lily into the shop and slammed the door while Claude snatched Geordi and held him in an iron grip. Geordi's eyes widened in terror, and he used all his seven-year-old strength, trying to get to his mother. Lily gouged the truck driver's arm with her nails and kicked his shins, which only pissed him off. He outweighed her by at least a hundred pounds, and looked ready to choke her in a heartbeat.

Claude yanked Geordi's head back to examine his face. *"Qu'est-ce qu'y a?"*

Geordi shrieked and Lily flailed harder, and the driver pulled a big-ass gun out of his waistband, aiming it at her head. The soft *click* as he cocked it was almost inaudible over the racket in the shop, but it did the trick for me.

"Wait!" I shouted. "Stop! Lily—calm down!" I moved forward to reassure Geordi, but the chauffeur's hands clamped down on my shoulders. "Let me go! I won't do anything, I swear—at least let Geordi go to his mother—*please.*"

Claude's grip on Geordi tightened, and he exchanged a look with his brother. Jacques lifted a shoulder negligently, as if to say *the child is unimportant—don't bother me with details.*

Claude pursed his lips, but all he said was, "By all means, the child and his mother may go. When you have returned what you stole from us."

I hadn't thought anything could be worse than Claude invading my apartment, but I was wrong. Lily's eyes were huge. Geordi'd stopped shrieking and trembled miserably in Claude's grasp. And through it all, the two thugs stood silent and unblinking.

"Okay," I said. "All right. You don't have to do this—I said I'd get it."

Claude pushed Geordi at Lily, so that the driver could train the gun on them both at the same time. "A little security, to ensure your cooperation. I will still accompany you, of course."

Lily clutched Geordi tight and looked at me. "Hyacinth—what is this? What's going on?"

"I'll explain later." I tried to keep my voice calm, to make myself believe there'd *be* a later—that I'd hand over the rock, and Claude and his entourage would crawl back to whatever maggot-infested lair they came from, letting me and my family go. But deep down, I didn't believe it. Here I'd thought Lily's biggest danger was from Nick, when in fact, it was from me.

"Just do what they say," I said. "I have to get something from the apartment. We'll be back in fifteen minutes. It'll be okay."

Lily gave a quick nod, and Claude held the door open. Outside, the day was still hot. After the chaos of the shop, it was surreal to find the rest of the world running along like normal. Claude followed me to the Peapod and got in, his bulk out of place in the small car. I didn't like the proximity. He smelled...*off*. Not unclean—elementally rotten. He had no gun or knife, but it didn't matter. Lily and Geordi were all he needed to make me comply with his every demand.

I'd like to say I had a plan—that I knew a place where I could speed up and kick him out of the car, to fall off a cliff and never be seen again. Or a panic button to call one of my shadier clients to my rescue. But I didn't. Not a damn thing. So, I made a tight K-turn and drove to my apartment, all the while trying to stop my heart from beating out of my chest, my stomach from kicking up my lunch.

Claude was silent, which was good, because it took everything I had to grip the wheel and force myself to drive. The route from my shop to home gives glimpses of the ocean, and by the time we reached my street, the sun rested on the horizon.

We got out, and Claude waited while I unlocked the gate, then trailed me up the stairs. Jason's door was shut. I longed for him to stick his head out, so I could see his face. He couldn't help me—even if he overpowered Claude, Lily and Geordi were still in Jacques' control. But maybe on the way out I could get a message to him, to call the cops. As we climbed to the second landing, I felt a glimmer of hope. I wouldn't give up—I *couldn't* give up.

My burst of resolve lasted until I reached the top of the stairs and saw the man standing by my door, pointing a gun at us.

"Nick," I said, strangely unsurprised. Somehow, it made sense on this utterly horrific day.

He was so close I smelled his expensive aftershave. He was lean and muscled, wearing a Swiss watch, French jeans, and Italian shoes, with a black tee under his leather coat. His wavy dark hair had been cropped, but his hard-blue eyes were the same. He still wore his family's signet ring on his right hand, a big gold sucker I recognized from the falcon imprint it left on Lily's cheek the last time he hit her. He also still wore his wedding ring. Since the Dioguardis are strict Catholics who simply ignore pesky little things like divorce papers, this didn't surprise me.

He would *not* take Geordi. I would never let that happen. But at the moment, it wasn't up to me. Frying pan, meet fire. And where did that leave me?

"Where the *hell* is my son?" Nick demanded. He was as pissed as the last time I'd seen him, running after my car, shooting at Lily, Geordi, and me on the day she left him. His gaze landed on Claude. "And who the hell is your boyfriend?"

Claude only smiled. *"Mais, c'est merveilleux.* You must be Geordi's father."

Nicholas Dioguardi is pretty much a tool, and a violent one at that. He brought the gun up and pressed it between Claude's eyes. "You know my son. Tell me where the fuck he is or I shoot."

Not very creative, but it got the point across. It didn't faze Claude, though. His tone was conversational, even with the gun making a dent in his too-dark tan. *"Mais bien sûr je le connais.* A charming child. He waits with his mother, at the shop."

"Lily's there?" Nick frowned, considering, then lowered the gun.

Damn. I didn't know what Claude's game was, but in a non-weaponed fight, my money was on the Rousseaux. The Dioguardis are bad, don't get me wrong. But by now I'd finally decided to trust my instincts, which screamed that the Rousseaux were flat out *evil.* Even though the Dioguardis were currently up one, thanks to the gun, Claude was smarter than Nick, so I held my breath and waited, trying to figure out some way this wouldn't end with all of us dead, or maimed, or any of a hundred other unpleasant scenarios running rampant through my head.

Meanwhile, Nick decided Claude had something— or some*one*—he wanted. "Take me there. Now."

"Of course." Claude put a hand on my shoulder, squeezing possessively as though I really were his girlfriend. His fingers were hot, the light contact scalding, and I fought back a gasp while he continued genially, "We will be happy to reunite you with your son. Please—we had forgotten something and returned to retrieve it. Allow us to get it, and we will be on our way."

Nick frowned again. "What is it?"

Claude shrugged. "Nothing of great import. A rock—it has sentimental value, that is all."

Nick might be a cog in the great Dioguardi wheel, but he wasn't entirely stupid. "Why do you need it *now?"*

"It is our anniversary." Claude turned and smiled

into my eyes. "The rock is from the place where we had our first date, is it not, *chérie?*"

To Nick, I'm sure it appeared we were lovers, sharing a private moment. But I could see Claude's eyes—so completely devoid of...*anything*...that a shudder passed through me. They held no emotion, no anger, just...emptiness. I looked away to find Nick watching us.

"Yes," I managed, the searing pressure of Claude's fingers reminding me that my first priority was getting the rock back. "That's right. The rock is from the...beach...where we had our first date."

Nick, creep though he was, thought himself a romantic. It was how he justified beating Lily up—he "loved her too much." Disgusting, but today, it worked in my favor. His gaze took in the bruises covering my face, and he shot Claude an approving look. Claude smiled and shrugged, and I tried not to vomit.

"Fine," Nick said. "You can get it. But only that, and I'll shoot if you try anything."

I nodded, then unlocked my door and led our little trio inside. I removed the painting from in front of the safe, ignoring the *I-can't-believe-you're-this-dumb* looks from both Claude and Nick. In another life, they might've been pals. And wasn't that frightening?

I dialed the combination and took out the rock, careful not to unwrap it. Not only did it feel warm again, it seemed *agitated.* Frightened or upset or—I can't explain it. I just got this vibe that something was wrong in Rockville. I had my own troubles, though. I'd tried to be surreptitious while opening the safe, but Nick got suspicious and shoved me aside.

"Well, well. Guess the antiques business pays

better than I thought. You won't mind helping your brother-in-law out, will you?" He reached inside and started stuffing his coat pockets with my hard-earned cash.

"No!" I grabbed his arm, but he laughed and shook me off.

"Now, now, *chérie.*" Claude pulled me firmly away. "It is good to share with family. We have our…souvenir. Let your charming *beau-frère* take his due."

I'd had about enough of him, but I had to play along. Lily and Geordi were more important than the cash, and besides, there was still the Swiss account.

When Nick had cleaned me out, he gestured with the gun and we all paraded back to the landing and down the stairs, me clutching the wrapped, jittery rock, Nick with wads of cash bulging out of his pockets, and Claude acting like we were out for a stroll in the park.

Of course, that's when Jason decided to poke his head out and say hi. His gaze took in my split lip and the shiner I was sure blossomed between my eyes, then moved to Claude and Nick, grouped behind me like bodyguards. I don't think he saw the gun, as Nick had it pressed into my back, but he suddenly drew back into the shadow of his doorway, looking a little stunned.

Surely, he'd guessed something was up. If my face wasn't enough, I rarely have men up to my place, and never two at a time. I needed help, but if he confronted Claude or Nick directly, he'd be shot. He looked at me uncertainly, and I stared back hard, willing him to call the cops, not try to be a hero himself.

"What're you up to?" he asked at last, still keeping back, as though hoping no one else would notice him.

"Nothing." I slowed, but Nick wasn't having any, and pushed the gun harder into my spine, scowling at Jason.

For some reason, neither Jason nor the gun bothered Claude. He smiled casually at Jason and walked alongside Nick, neither helping nor hindering his quest to kidnap us.

We were at the top of the stairs—I had to do something. Desperately I twisted around. "Jason! Thanks again—for dropping that package off at the shop."

His eyebrows rose, and I'm sure Claude knew what I was up to. But whatever his plan, he clearly thought he had it in the bag. Nick ignored my outburst, using his whole body to herd me onto the stairs.

"No problem," Jason called as we disappeared into the stairwell. I didn't know if he got that I wanted him to call the cops, but surely he knew I'd tried to tell him *something*.

Now that I had two badasses, instead of one, dragging me all over Marseille, there was no way we'd fit in the Peapod. In theory, it's a four-seater, but in reality, the only person who fits in the back is Geordi, and at seven, even he's getting too big. Luckily, Nick had a decent-sized BMW. Not as nice as the Maybach, but big enough for Claude to sit in the back while Nick drove one-handed, training the gun on me in the passenger seat. Mr. Macho.

Of course he'd popped for the leather interior. Besides not eating meat, I also don't wear animals, or support making them into furniture. Nick's coat was bad enough, but at least I wasn't forced to touch it. Luckily, the trip was short, and I didn't get too nauseous. Unluckily, no *flics* with lights flashing and sirens blaring magically appeared along the route, so either Jason didn't get the message, or the cops didn't believe him.

Which left me with…nothing.

I got out of Nick's car, retrieving the rock from the floor, and Nick and Claude followed me into the shop. Jacques looked up when he heard the bell, his impassive black gaze immediately going to the canvas bundle clutched in my hands. As near as I could tell, the two drivers were in the exact same positions as when we'd left thirty minutes ago, but Lily and Geordi had moved, now huddling against the front of the counter, quiet if not calm. Relief washed over Lily's face when she saw me, and Geordi sat up straighter, trying to be brave.

My heart broke to see them. Surely the Rousseaux could let us go—I hadn't witnessed anything illegal and wouldn't call the police if I had. But my limited knowledge of "evil" was that it annihilated first and asked questions, well, never.

"We found it," Claude announced. "And something else."

"Hi, honey, I'm home," Nick growled, hot on Claude's heels.

Apparently, he was stupider than I thought. He walked right into the shop, with no idea what the situation was, gun out, thinking he'd grab Lily and Geordi and go. Lily had other ideas. She took one look at him, screamed louder than the rock had, then grabbed Geordi and dove behind the counter.

Nick roared and dove after them as they scrambled toward the back of the store. Neither the Rousseaux nor their thugs seemed disturbed by any of this. Jacques walked to me and gently removed my burden. He shook the covering loose, careful not to touch the rock's surface with his thin, elegant fingers, then exhaled sharply.

For my part, I felt a strange regret—an emptiness that the rock was no longer mine. I thought I heard it give a faint wail, as though it missed me.

Lily and Geordi rounded the counter, Nick close behind, and without looking up, Jacques murmured to no one in particular, *"Tuez-les."*

Kill them.

The truck driver aimed and fired at Nick's head, killing him instantly, his body dropping to the floor. Lily screamed and hid Geordi's face, and I ran to them, shouting, *"Go*—out the back! *Now!"*

I pushed and shoved, herding them forward, knowing the driver must be taking aim again. If I could get them out the door, maybe they'd be safe. Lily wrenched the knob open—improbably, Jason was on the other side.

"Take him!" she shrieked, shoving a frantic Geordi into his arms.

Jason took one look at us and scooped Geordi up, then hauled ass down the alley and around the corner. Lily was out the door, me right behind, and still no other shots were fired.

We started to run, and I realized why we weren't shot inside. There, it was crowded and dark. Out here, even in the waning light, we were sitting—or running—ducks.

We'd made it about halfway up the block when I finally heard the gun's silencer go off. A bullet whizzed past my cheek and hit Lily's leg. She started to fall, and another went into the back of her head. I screamed and then something hit my own back, between my shoulder blades.

I'd like to tell you what I felt or saw or thought in that instant, but I don't remember much. I don't think there was any pain, but I did know I was shot. I might even have seen the bullet exiting through my chest, but I could be imagining that part.

All I know is suddenly my legs didn't work. They felt heavy and rubbery, and no matter how I focused, I couldn't control them. My arms were next, then my vision dimmed. Then all thought started to drain away like liquid from a broken vessel. I crumpled to the ground but didn't feel the impact. I lay there a moment, maybe two, while my heart pumped blood through arteries that could no longer contain it.

And then…

I died.

Chapter Four

"Call no man happy 'til he is dead."
                    ~Aeschylus, Agamemnon, *458 BCE*

I don't know how long I was unconscious. I use that term because now I know it applies to Death as much as Life. Apparently, you can be dead and still conscious. But I wasn't for a while, and when I came to, I was seriously disoriented.

For one thing, everything was white. Bright white. So that part's true, at least. Except it wasn't a tunnel. It was a square room. Floor, ceiling, walls, all white. So white, it hurt to look at, and I had to shut my eyes again.

Plus, my head throbbed with a nauseous, pounding ache made worse by a sweet fragrance in the air, a floral scent I couldn't place. It wasn't exactly heavy or unpleasant, but in my current state, anything stronger than plain air cloyed my nostrils and made me gag.

I thought when you died, physical suffering stopped.

Guess not.

I pushed up onto my knees, then wished I hadn't. Bitter, hot bile burned up my throat, my head swam, and my limbs wobbled, and I dropped back onto my stomach, forehead on the floor. My mouth was so parched, I could barely force the bile down, and I curled into myself, burying my head in my arms, trying to shut out the buzzing in my ears.

Eventually it receded, and I became aware I wasn't alone. Voices murmured nearby, one deep, one higher, a man and a woman. Slowly I lifted my head, blinking hard against the searing brightness. I forced one lid to stay open, and when that eye quit burning, tried the other.

Two forms stood a few feet away, facing each other. The first was clearly male, and larger than the second—not just taller, but broader, built like a souped-up American wrestler.

Or, based on his costume, an ancient warrior. He wore a gray metal chest plate, dull and dinged-up from use, extending around his back and leaving his enormous arms bare. Underneath was a sleeveless tunic that might have been white once, but now was only marginally less gray than his armor. It ended midway down his tree-trunk thighs, above brown leather sandals whose straps snaked up around his hard calves. A heavy leather belt completed the ensemble, sporting a massive sword and various other nasty-and-sharp metal objects. His mass of curly brown hair hung loose down his back, crowned by a thin metal band at his forehead. Except for his thick beard, the whole effect was vaguely Roman, but somehow, I knew it was far older.

Despite his violent getup, he spoke in a low, soothing voice to the other figure, a woman with blonde hair, wearing a white blouse and jeans.

Lily.

Memory flooded back, and I sat up, ignoring the pain in my head, like a shovel pounding the back of my skull. Lily was dead—shot right in front of me. *I* was dead. I knew that, but seeing her here made it much more real. On the heels of that realization came another.

Geordi.

If Lily and I were dead, the Dioguardis would get him. With Nick gone, Geordi was now the only son of the *deceased* only son. Without him, the Dioguardis would die out and be replaced—by the Lefevres, or the Buonfiglios, or whoever. They'd never let that happen—in a fast five minutes, the Rousseaux had turned my nephew into the Holy Grail of Dioguardi-dom.

I would *not* let them get him, no matter how dead I was.

The unknown warrior said something to Lily. It had a ring of finality, like heavy swords clanging at the last stroke of battle, and she smiled and took his hand. They moved away as bright light began leaking through chinks in the far wall. Eventually these linked together in small chains, then larger ones, until finally, the edges of two white doors were carved out by clear, golden light. The one on the left opened of its own accord, showing a white metal staircase leading up, up, as far as I could see. Still holding Lily's hand gently in his gigantic one, the warrior led her through the door.

"No…" I croaked through dry, cracked lips, but they didn't hear. I tried to crawl after them, but my limbs wouldn't support me, like a vine too weak to bear its own fruit. "Lily—Geordi—"

The room swallowed my voice, and Lily's gaze was focused away from me, on whatever waited above. Was that the door to Heaven, then? And did the other lead to Hell?

Wherever they led, I knew that once Lily passed

through, she'd never be back. I had to stop her—we *couldn't* abandon Geordi. My stomach woozed, and my head throbbed, but I inched forward, trying to make her hear me. It was as though I wasn't in the room with them. I felt a happiness resonate from Lily, a sense of peace and understanding.

It was useless. I lifted a hand, but they were through the door. The room felt diminished without her in it, smaller, the light less bright, the air less sweet. Lily gazed up as she stepped onto the first stair, the warrior holding her hand, his own gaze trained lovingly on her face. Another step, then another. The door began to close. I wanted to cry.

Geordi—nooooo…

The door shut. My head sank to the floor. Lily was gone.

****

The next time I became aware of myself, I knew immediately I wasn't alone. I smelled him first, the metallic scent of him, crisp and tangy and not at all nauseating. The floral fragrance was gone, perhaps pushed out by his heavy presence, which enveloped me. His energy seemed to caress my skin, and his breathing was a soft hum, like a lullaby. A golden glow warmed the backs of my eyelids, and when I tried to swallow, my tongue tasted dirt and minerals and the iron-metal blood of ancient battles. It was as though I *felt* him with every sense I had, if you could call them "senses" when, technically, there was no brain to interpret them. Yet I still processed everything as though I had a brain.

And a body. I lifted my head, waiting to see if the nausea came back. When it didn't, I pushed up onto my knees, willing my limbs to cooperate.

"You will get used to that," said a voice, deep as cast iron, behind me.

I twisted in a crouch to face him. He stood several feet away, stance casual, hands clasped in front of his tools-of-torture belt as though waiting on something. Probably me.

"Or rather, you will get used to your new form, its limitations and advantages. But it will take time."

Time. *Geordi*—

I scrambled up, swaying, and planted my feet wide to keep from falling. "No."

His brown eyes widened, gaze dropping to my trembling legs. "I am impressed. Most souls take much longer to regain the use of their non-corporeal limbs."

"No," I repeated. "I can't die—I can't be dead. You have to send me back."

He stared like I'd sprouted horns. Then he burst into loud, booming guffaws that cannoned off the walls of the small room.

"Child," he said at last, wheezing with mirth, "you are already dead. 'Tis not a choice. Come. We must decide where you are going." He indicated the two doors still outlined behind him, and I shook my head.

"Neither. I have to get back."

I turned and sure enough, the edges of a single door shone bright in the wall opposite the other two. I ran to it, but there was no handle. I slid my fingers around it, scrabbling to find the mechanism that would open it and let me go back to Earth and my terrified nephew.

The creak of worn leather, the jangle of armor and weapons, came from behind me, and his gentle voice said, "Child."

The sound compelled me to face him. His

42

expression was sad and glad and understanding all at once, and I saw how Lily could have been reassured and gone with him. Though his skin was as battle-scarred as his armor, he exuded Peace, the warm brown of his eyes calming me and pulling me in. I felt myself letting go, forgetting my life on Earth, the people there, turning my thoughts to whatever came After.

"No." I shook my head, blinking and backing up until I bumped the door. "I won't go with you—I have a nephew, a little boy who's *seven.* You can't make me leave him. You *can't."*

He seemed surprised by my outburst. Or maybe by the fact that I'd resisted his wiles. "Child. He is not alone. There is his father's family."

"Exactly! Do you know what they're like? Do you have *any* idea what they'll do to him? They'll raise him to a life of hate, to kill and steal and cheat, to beat women, to crush anyone weaker, until someone crushes him."

My gaze landed on the right-hand door in the far wall. I stepped forward and grabbed his shoulders—they felt surprisingly solid to my touch. That I could feel his skin through his tunic—feel it as though through my *own* skin—was even stranger. His muscles rippled with tension and his dark brows rose in shock. I don't think many souls touched him.

"Geordi's father," I said, gripping him harder. "He was here, wasn't he? Nick Dioguardi. You sent him through the right-hand door—I know you did. Without me, that's where Geordi will go—down, not up. After a lifetime of hate and cruelty and torture. You can't let that happen—you *have* to send me back."

He disengaged himself, expression patronizing.

"Do you know who I am, child?" His voice was soft but commanding, filling me with the urge to obey, to comply, to make him happy.

Sadly, I'd have to disappoint him. Though our parents were Catholic, and Lily's adoptive family raised her to be as well, my religious education was spotty at best. Too many foster families, from too many religions. I made it through First Communion and have vague notions of Heaven and Hell. But my travels have exposed me to so many different cultures that I'm not sure any one group has it *all* locked down.

I shook my head, and his smile warmed. "I thought not. Perhaps I should introduce myself. I am Michael."

It took a moment to take root, and then I got it after all. *"The* Michael? Archangel Michael? Highest of the high, defender of the universe, and all that?"

His laugh rang out richly again. "The same. Although you've laid it on a bit thick."

I'm glad I entertained him, at least. I frowned at his armor and weaponry. "I thought angels had wings. The paintings always show them—you—with wings."

"Some do have wings, yes." He shrugged. "Angels, especially archangels, have a different function than the Living understand, and we cannot control how we are portrayed."

I thought of the museums I'd haunted during my early years in Europe. The paintings and sculptures and illuminated manuscripts that formed the heart and soul of my self-education. "You drove Satan out of Heaven. You have a lifelong battle with him—older than Christianity—older than almost anything."

He inclined his head. "That is one of my jobs, yes. Satan and his minions walk the Earth, and I do what I can to defeat them."

"Then you understand—the Dioguardis must be stopped."

"I am sorry, child. You are right. The Dioguardis are evil. But they are human. I can do nothing against them, until they die."

"But you said—"

He looked suddenly tired. "Come. We have a few moments." He lowered his massive form to the floor, the heaviness of his gear weighing him down and making it hard for him to bend. Once settled against the wall, he patted the space next to him.

I shook my head. "Geordi—"

"Is in no immediate danger."

He indicated the floor again, and since I didn't have a lot of other options, I joined him. But my heart or soul or whatever I still had cried out for my nephew, and if there was a God—which seemed likely, under the circumstances—I prayed harder than I ever had in my life that Jason had gotten Geordi to safety and would keep him there.

"There are bad people in the world," Michael said. "They do terrible things, often at Satan's bidding. But I have no power over the Living. Think, child. What do they call me?"

Feeling like this was a pop quiz, and unsure what I'd get if I passed or failed, I said, "Saint Michael. The Angel of Death."

"Precisely—although in truth, I was never canonized. And I am certainly no saint. My primary function is to lead souls from the Earth, to deliver them to Heaven, and Saint Peter, or to Satan's door in Hell. But only once they have died. I try to be at every sick bed, every fatal accident, to reassure and guide them from the moment they have passed on."

"Shouldn't you be somewhere now, then? Don't millions of people die every day?"

"Time is a strange and relative thing. You are in limbo now—a place between times. A space in which to…adapt…to your new circumstances."

I didn't bother telling him I wasn't going to adapt, because I was *not* leaving Geordi. Partly from interest, and partly to buy time to find an angle to get me out of this, I asked, "Still, that's a lot of souls. How do you manage it?"

He waved a dismissive hand. "Christians, Muslims, Jews, yes. But other faiths have other guides." His rapier-sharp gaze penetrated mine. He knew damn well what I was up to. "You are dead, child. There is nothing I can do, except guide you where you are going. Perhaps you will see your nephew again, perhaps not. It depends on which door is his, and which one is yours."

He stood, leather creaking and weapons jangling again, and my panic came back. Although how I could feel my pulse race and my head spin, when in theory I no longer had either, I had no clue.

I jumped up. "Wait—you keep saying I'm dead, but there's still time. How dead am I?"

"If you are worried about which door is yours—"

"I'm not." In truth, *that* concern hadn't crossed my mind. With my, er, career choices, there was a good chance I'd go through the right-hand door. But an eternity in Hell paled in comparison to Nick's family getting Geordi. "You said I'm in limbo. So, my body's still back on Earth, right? I could be resuscitated— maybe I'm not *totally* dead yet."

"Child, despite what you appear to think, I am not omnipotent."

He hadn't actually said he couldn't do it, though, and I pressed my advantage, moving toward him, pleading my case. *"I'll do anything you want—go straight to Hell—later. Please let me go back, long enough to see that Geordi's safe."*

I was in his space again, and he didn't like it. He frowned, stepping back, but the room was small, and he had nowhere to go.

"Look," I said. "I've made mistakes. Plenty of them." I grabbed his hand, holding tight when he tried to pull away. Do *not* ask me how I had the chutzpah to touch the Angel of Death a second time. By now I acted purely on instinct. This was my last shot, and I had nothing to lose. Nothing except an innocent, sweet little boy, whose very life depended on whatever happened in the next few seconds. *"Please*—don't let Geordi live a life of Hell on Earth just because I was stupid enough to take a talking rock from the Rousseau brothers."

Michael froze. Literally. He paled, and I *felt* the shock ripple through him. He yanked his hand from my grasp and gripped my shoulders. His massive body shook like a bomb about to detonate, which meant *I* shook, too.

"What did you say?"

"I—I don't know."

"You found a *talking* rock—and tried to keep it from Jacques Rousseau?"

"Yes—in a batch of goods from Turkey. Denizli—or, east of there. Colossae."

If possible, Michael looked even more shocked. Abruptly he let me go and I staggered, trying to regain the use of my "non-corporeal limbs" with the after effects of adrenaline still spiking through me. What the hell is the point of being dead, if you can still feel all the yucky crap you felt while alive?

"Impossible," he muttered, then shot me a curious look. "And yet…"

He stepped toward me, and I skittered back. It was a reflex—I didn't think he'd hurt me, but something about *me* rattled the Head Angel, the baddest of the, er, Good—the dude who fought Satan and *won.* And that was pretty damned unnerving.

Michael lifted a hand as though to touch my cheek, then let it drop. "Tell me." His voice was soft, but there was no doubt it was a command.

So, I told him. Everything. About Vadim, the Rousseaux, and the rock. How I couldn't give the rock to the Rousseaux, and hid it before meeting them, and then about Lily and Geordi's arrival, and Nick, and how the Rousseaux got the rock after all.

When I finished, Michael was silent, staring at me, his expression filled with wonder. "Why?" he asked at last. "Why did you keep it? You must have known Jacques would want it."

I shook my head, trying to pinpoint what the deciding factor was. Greed? Did I think it was so unusual that I could sell it? I really had no idea. "I suppose I felt…sorry for it. Whatever the Rousseaux wanted it for, it couldn't be good."

"It did not frighten you?"

"Maybe at first. But later on, no. It sounded upset, mainly. Lost. Not scary."

"When—how—did it speak to you?"

Something in his tone made me think this might

have the most bearing on my fate. Unfortunately, I had no idea what the angle was. I don't lie *all* the time, but I have to admit, I'm more of a fudger than a straight-up honest kind of gal. This had to be a personal record— fifteen limbo-minutes without a single lie.

"It screamed," I said. "When I touched it."

"Did you hear it at any other time?"

"Yes. I could hear it humming sometimes, even under its wrappings. And I could feel it."

His gaze sharpened. "You felt it? When you were not touching it?"

I nodded. "It gave off a warmth. Claude did, too. I don't know about Jacques—I was never close enough to him to tell." I paused, remembering. "The rock also sort of vibrated. Like a tuning fork." The next part would sound even weirder, but I had to tell him. "I got the sense it was…excited…to have found me. Like maybe it hadn't had anyone to talk to in a long time."

"It hadn't," Michael said slowly. "Unless… Do you know why your partner took it? If it spoke to him, as well?"

"I wish I did. He never said, and the crates have been in storage for six months. I just opened them today." Literally, a lifetime ago.

Michael shook his head, and went back to staring at me, expression unreadable. I waited. What else could I do, when the Angel of Death held my fate in his hands?

Finally, he blew out a heavy breath. "Very well, Hyacinth Marie Finch. You may have your life back."

Chapter Five

"Your lost friends are not dead, but gone before,
Advanced a stage or two upon that road
Which you must travel in the steps they trod."
                    ~Aristophanes (448-350 BCE)

It was my turn to stare. When an archangel grants your dearest wish, it's probably best not to argue. But I had a million questions, such as *Why? How?* And most important, *When?*

Before I asked any of them, Michael turned and began pacing the room, its size far too small to contain his bulk. He was excited and tense, like a bowstring pulled taut, almost to breaking, and I added two more questions to my list: *How hard would this be for him to accomplish?* And, *What's in it for him?*

For the former, I had no idea. For the latter, he told me right away. He stopped in front of me, bushy brows drawn, eyes flashing. "This is a temporary grant only. You will not be alive, per se, only visiting the Earth to make arrangements for your nephew. And there is one condition. I need that rock back. Get it for me."

"What?"

"You are…resourceful. I do not know everything about every soul. But I am given enough information to know which door to choose. You are well-travelled. You speak several languages. And you are adept at, shall we say, removing things without their owners' notice."

"Why *me,* though? I'm not the only person with those, um, skills. If it's so important, why not send an angel or something?"

"There are others with your talents, yes. But no one—not a single soul in thousands of years—has ever sensed the rock's abilities. To them, it is ordinary. To you, it speaks."

No wonder he was so shocked. "You've been searching for this rock for thousands of years? Why?"

"This one, and many more like it. As to why—suffice it to say that if I lose it, your nephew will not be the only one subjected to 'Hell on Earth.' Find it, and you may live long enough to settle Geordi. Refuse, and I will lead you to your door."

In truth, I was intrigued. After all, I got into the stolen artifact business because I love art, history and archaeology, but not so much authority or playing by the rules. Then I thought of Claude and Jacques, and their soulless helpers, and shivered.

"But the Rousseaux—I have no idea where they went. They could be anywhere by now."

"In that, I can help. I believe they will go to Colossae—to the rock's place of origin."

"Why?"

"There is a ritual they wish to perform. You must get the rock back before they succeed."

"Why not do it here, right away, if it's so important?"

"The ritual must occur at the very site where the shard was split from the original slab. They intend to send the shard to Hell—to Satan."

"To *Satan?* As in, the *Devil?* The Prince of Darkness, the—"

"Yes, Satan." He hesitated, then shook his head. "We have no time. Though you are in limbo, the longer we wait, the harder it will be to restore your life. You must decide."

"If this is all so important, why can't *you* get it back?"

"I wish it were so simple. As you pointed out, a great many deaths occur each day, and I must attend a goodly portion of them. Then there are Satan's more pressing acts of evil, which I also must prevent. I have been so busy, I did not realize this shard had been found."

He was an archangel, and something of this magnitude slipped his notice? Sheesh. He must be overworked.

I stared at him, thinking hard. Geordi was out there, hopefully with Jason. But he'd only met Jason once, and had to be beyond terrified by everything he'd seen and heard today. Michael would let me go back long enough to comfort him and hide him from the Dioguardis. No matter how impossible getting the rock back seemed, I had to try. What choice did I have?

"Okay," I said finally. "I'll do it."

Michael's relief was palpable. Whatever the rock's origins, its significance was enough to make him doubt my compliance, which should have scared me even more.

"Excellent. I will send you back."

"Just like that? Don't you have to get clearance or something?"

His rich laugh rang out. "Child, I *am* your

clearance. Come." He moved to the single door, which had started leaking natural light around the edges, and now crumbled and receded, eroding before our eyes. "When you pass through, you will feel as though you are falling. You will land in your body, but the impact will be jarring. You will most likely lose consciousness."

"How much time will have passed? You know— since I was shot."

"You will arrive after the immediate danger to your person is past."

Good. I'd been a little worried I'd wake up while the truck driver was making sure I was really dead. *Oops! Surprise!* Which reminded me…

"What about my wound? Will I still have it?"

"Yes. And no. The wound will be healed, not erased. It will be as though you have spent time in a hospital, recovering. You will still feel its effects. There may be pain. You may feel weak and tired. You will need to take it easy, as they say."

"Great. I have to find my nephew, travel to Turkey, and stop the Rousseaux, all with a sucking chest wound." That brought up another thought. "Can I die? I mean, again?"

"You are not immortal, nor are you immune to injury. But you may find you suffer less or heal more quickly in the event you *are* wounded again." He searched his memory. "As you may imagine, I have not done this often. There may be other side effects to death and rebirth, but I do not know what they are. I would advise you to avoid getting hurt as much as possible."

Well, duh. I did that anyway. "How will I find you again?"

"I will find you. Once you have the rock, think of me, and I will be there. Perhaps I will check your progress from time to time, as well."

An unsubtle reminder that, if I didn't do my job, he'd come for me. Of course, I still didn't know what consequences he risked, for sending me back in the first place. I suppose a few surprise inspections were to be expected.

The door had fully dissolved, revealing an unblemished blue atmosphere that extended, unbroken, in all directions. Apparently, we were suspended in the air, or in another dimension or something. I peeped out. No stairs here. What was the deal with that? Heaven got stairs, maybe Hell, too. I guess most folks floated up here and never went back. Heights aren't my strong suit. But hey, I was already dead. What's the worst that could happen?

"One more thing," Michael said as he positioned me at the edge. That sure was a long drop into nothing—literally, no end in sight. I just wanted the whole thing over, not to hear more instructions. On the other hand, I should probably pay attention, since I'd done this even less than he had.

Michael's voice was serious. "Remember when I said that Satan's minions walk the Earth, but the Dioguardis are only human?"

"Yes."

"The Rousseaux are not."

I twisted to face him. "What are you saying?"

"Jacques and Claude Rousseau are Demons of the Last Circle of Hell. They live—if you can call it that—and breathe and die for Satan's whims, and Satan wants this rock as much as I do. If the Rousseaux catch you, they will torture and obliterate you, body *and* soul. You will not go to Heaven or Hell. You will end. And I will be unable to stop them. Be very careful, Hyacinth. Especially of Jacques."

With that, he pushed me out.

****

If you're wondering, he was right about the impact, wrong about the consciousness. I almost wished I *had* passed out. At least then there'd be a respite from the shock of reentry.

Hel-*lo* street.

"Ow."

I think I said it out loud. My throat felt funny and my ears echoed—hell, my whole body felt odd, worse than when I'd woken up dead. I tried to push myself up, but my "real" limbs stretched and wobbled and slid out from under me just as my non-corporeal ones had, so I gave up and lay there, catching my breath. Luckily, the alley behind my shop is too tight for cars—even mine—and there was no sign of the Devil's minions or their, er, minions.

My car. *Merde.* It was still at my apartment. Normally, walking wasn't a problem, but if my legs didn't shape up, I wouldn't make it one block, let alone twenty.

One thing at a time. When my head quit spinning, I brought a cautious hand to my chest. My arm decided to obey and my fingers, though tingling, wiggled as directed. I poked around. No wound, no blood, just dirt and grime from the street on my top.

I levered myself up and looked around. The sun was down but the twilight revealed Lily's body a few feet away.

Why didn't you fight to stay alive?

I choked down the tears and looked away. I couldn't afford to grieve. Not when Geordi was out there somewhere, terrified, wondering where his mother and I were.

Judging by the light, it was ten or fifteen minutes at most since we'd died. Thanks to the gun's silencer, no one in the surrounding buildings heard the shots. Most of the other shops were long closed, and the inhabitants of the apartments above had no reason to look out their back windows at the grimy street.

Still, someone would notice Lily's body eventually, and I didn't want to hang around and risk bumping into the cops. Or the Rousseaux, if they forgot something and came back. They were bad enough in daylight. Demons after dark? I don't think so.

Especially Jacques. It's always the quiet ones.

My legs felt a little more normal, so I tried them out in a kneel, then got myself up to standing. Only problem was I didn't exactly have a plan. I had to get Geordi, then get to Turkey. But first, I needed cash. In this at least, I knew where I might find some.

I turned from Lily and moved up the dark alley, then poked my head through the still-open rear door of the shop. I *thought* everyone had left, but I wasn't quite as dumb as Nick. Everything was silent, and it's not a big room. Long, but narrow. The shelves and cases were still pushed aside, and in the gloom, I was fairly certain no one was there.

No one vertical, anyway.

I closed the door and tiptoed past Nick's prone form, avoiding the pooled, coagulating blood, then quickly lowered the shades on the cluttered front window cases and the door. I doubted anyone would walk by, but to be safe, I skipped the overhead light and turned on the reading lamp I keep on the counter. To be thorough, I made a quick check of my office upstairs, which was thankfully vacant and undisturbed, before returning to the shop.

Then I took a deep breath, pretending I wasn't about to do what I was about to do, and knelt to touch Nick's neck. No pulse. Not that I'd thought he'd survive a bullet to the brain, but good to check. Another breath. I reached for his coat pockets, searching for the cash he took from my safe.

It was gone.

Merde. Merde, merde, merde.

Jacques or Claude or the drivers must've taken it. Maybe they wanted it to look like a robbery—although I wondered why they didn't just use their demon magic to make us all disappear. I suppose since they hadn't found the rock on their own, and had clearly tried to "pass" as humans, there must be some limit to their powers. Or maybe it had to do with their master being imprisoned in Hell. Maybe with him incarcerated, they had to tone it down for now.

I checked the register. Most of the day's take goes in my safe, but I leave some change in the drawer. The bastards took that, too. I looked for my purse, which I'd tossed on the counter seemingly eons ago. Gone. Naturally. I expected nothing less from the meticulous Rousseaux.

So, not only did I have no cash, not one single euro, I also didn't have checks, credit cards or ID. Fat lot of good a Swiss bank account did me if I couldn't withdraw the money. I'd straighten it out eventually, but that would take time. Meanwhile, I was screwed.

Plus, there was the small matter of my keys. For my apartment, I could go to the landlady on the ground floor and ask for a spare. But for my car, sad to say, I don't have one. It's been on my to do list, most of which I haven't gotten to in the many years since I started it.

Right about then, I remembered Nick's Beamer.

I turned to look at him. Yep, still dead. I'd hated him for what he did to Lily, but I have to say, in death, he looked pathetic. Not that peaceful, sleeping crap people talk about. Just empty and gray, like the dead, papery skin shed by the world's biggest snake. The thought of touching him again was icky to say the least. But he didn't need his car, and I did, and every second I dithered brought me closer to a run-in with *les flics*.

I dropped to my knees and gingerly patted him down. Sure enough, the keys were there, in the front left pocket of his jeans. His very tight jeans. Why couldn't he have put them in his loose-fitting and easily-accessible jacket pocket?

Earlier, when I said death was an everyday part of my life, I meant *old* death—mummies and tombs and sarcophagi. This was my first experience up close and personal with a new corpse. Besides my own, which didn't count as I wasn't technically dead. I think. Or was it the other way around, and I wasn't technically alive?

In any case, I'd managed to check Nick's pulse and hunt for my cash without touching him too much. But to get those keys, I'd have to dig in. At least dead, I wouldn't need to worry about the, um, region I'd be fiddling with.

The jeans were snug, but with some wiggling I got the keys out and quickly let his body go. I tried to feel sadness at his death, but I couldn't. He'd been too cruel. Maybe once he was sweet and innocent, like his son, but I'd never seen it. Still, the moment needed something, so before I thought about how ridiculous it was—after all, I already knew where he'd gone—I made the sign of the cross over his body.

Then I rose and peered out the door. It was full-on night, but I could see the silver BMW parked right where Nick left it. I slipped out the door and locked it behind me, then stood on the stoop, scanning the deserted street. The air was warm and dark, filled with the scent of the clematis vines growing from planters on either side of my door. They formed an arch over my head, and I felt safer under their protection, their honey-sweet aroma familiar and reassuring.

At some point, the cops would come for me. I mean, dead brother-in-law in my shop, dead sister behind it, and a missing mob heir last seen in my company? *I'd* want to question me.

My best bet was to pretend I wasn't here when it all went down, and hope Jason and Geordi played along. With luck, I'd buy enough time to escape and retrieve the rock, but I wasn't holding my breath. If worse came to worst, though, I did have options. My clients appreciate me. Maybe not enough to bribe a judge, but enough to get me a really good lawyer. One client, in particular, might be helpful in finding Geordi a home.

Ugh. Bad idea. Don't think of Geordi, living with strangers, alone, scared, missing his mother and auntie. Michael had given me a chance to save him from the

Dioguardis, for which I should be grateful. And I was. But first, I had to *find* him, which wouldn't happen by hiding on the stoop. Plus, the street wasn't getting any emptier.

I moved to the Beamer, pressed the unlock button on the key fob, opened the door, and got in. Of course, I'd ridden in the car on the drive over, but sitting in the driver's seat was a whole other experience. The engine fired right up, and I could tell immediately it had a ton more horsepower than the Peapod. Nice. If I had to steal a dead creep's car, at least it'd be fun to drive.

I noticed something else, though. Something…odd. The first time I got in, I was disgusted by all the leather, trying not to touch it or think about it too much. But now it felt almost…good.

No, not almost. If I'm being honest, it did feel good. Really good.

It smelled even better. I took a deep sniff, and the sensation almost overwhelmed me, the way I imagine getting high would be like. I did feel high—awake and sharp and *alive.*

And starving. Like my appetite woke up and said, *Hey, you, you might be dead, but you need to eat. Pronto.* I'd have to raid Jason's refrigerator, since I'd missed today's trip to the markets, and there wasn't time to look for an all-night convenience store.

I flipped a quick U-turn and drove to my apartment, assuming Jason would head home. He didn't have a car, but with his long legs he'd be pretty fast, even carrying Geordi. By my best guess, about forty minutes had passed since Lily shoved Geordi at him and they took off. Enough time to run to his apartment and hole in, but hopefully not enough for Geordi to freak out.

I shuddered. How the hell was I supposed to tell a seven-year-old his mother was dead? And his father. It occurred to me that Lily and he both had their backs to Nick when he was shot, so Geordi might have escaped that horror at least. Then there was my death, too, but I couldn't explain that to myself, let alone anyone else.

I found a parking space and got out of the car. From a nearby window came the scent of bacon frying, and my mouth watered, and my stomach growled. I ignored it and ran for the stairs. On the first landing, I hesitated. Jason's door was shut, the curtains closed. Every fiber in me screamed that I needed to get to Geordi *now*. But I had to get ready to leave, which would be a thousand times harder after I'd told him about Lily.

I forced myself to keep going up to my apartment. I'd grab what I needed, so we could take off right away. I wasn't even sure how we'd get to Turkey. The simplest would be by train or ship. From Vadim, I knew that Colossae is inland, near the city of Denizli, but Marmaris has a decent-sized port, from which I could rent a car and drive the remaining 150 kilometers.

The first problem with that was the money. As noted, I didn't have any. Second, if I hoped to stay under the radar, then waltzing down to the train station or the docks to buy a ticket would defeat the purpose. Unless I used a fake ID, which, believe it or not, I have no idea how to get. I might be a thief, but I've always travelled under my own name. Plus, I'm pretty sure you have to pay for fake documents, so, back to the money.

Option two would be to drive, but not in my car. It's three thousand kilometers from Marseille to

Colossae by land, and at the Peapod's speed, I'd probably get run over by anyone too impatient to pass me. I could take Nick's car, but stealing it to drive home was one thing. Crossing international borders in it would net much higher jail time.

Another option would be to beg a private flight from one of my clients, at least half of whom have jets. But I was reluctant to take anyone into my confidence. Let's face it—people who make a game out of stealing from their peers probably aren't all that trustworthy. Wistfully I thought of Vadim's boat, which he'd left me in his will, and which I'd been keeping tied up at the slip he rented—largely because I had no clue how to drive it. So, back to square one.

Feeling depressed and trying not to miss Lily even more, I crested the landing and abruptly realized I'd forgotten to stop by the landlady's for a key. Which didn't matter after all, because right then I noticed my door was open. *What the...?*

I was positive I'd locked it when I left with Claude and Nick. Not only am I anal about these things, but I remember them standing around, two big creepy thugs, waiting for me to turn the deadbolt on the barn after the horse—a.k.a., my "liquid assets"—was already gone.

I looked around, but the breezeway was deserted. The lady across from me travels a lot, and the two other tenants on our floor rarely have visitors. Call me stupid, but I tiptoed to my door and pushed it in. I was already dead, my sister was gone, I had the Devil's minions to track, and the Angel of Death to please. It didn't make me invincible, but it gave me a helluva lot less to lose.

I stepped inside, then paused as my eyes adjusted. The apartment was dark and quiet, but something felt off. Then I heard it—the soft breathing of someone nearby, waiting, watching me.

Two someones. I smelled fear and adrenaline, as though my nose, like my ears, was hyper-tuned to my surroundings.

I whirled on instinct, but before I made it back out the door, someone grabbed me from behind, a large hand smothering my mouth and nose, cutting off all air, and I was dragged, kicking and scratching, backward into the apartment.

Chapter Six

"The idea is to die young as late as possible."
~Ashley Montagu (1905-1999)

The Dioguardis had found me. Somehow, they knew already that Nick was dead, and they'd come for me.

I jabbed back, hard, with my elbow, and tried to stomp on his instep, but my attacker was taller and stronger, and lack of oxygen rendered me weak. Michael was right. I'd been running on adrenaline, and suddenly, I wanted to give up. Wouldn't it be simpler to follow Lily, to forget about rocks and Michael and Satan? Even the threat that I'd go through door number two didn't seem like a big enough reason to fight. My captor kicked the door shut, trapping us inside, and I sagged, exhausted, prepared to die for the second time today. Then I heard a boyish shriek, reminding me that all I needed was one small, seven-year-old reason to stay alive.

"Tata Hyhy! Let her go! *Let her* GO!"

Geordi tackled us with a heavy *thwump!* and my attacker let go. We all fell hard on the floor in a tangle of flailing limbs, and I scrabbled to get away.

Geordi.

I *couldn't* let Nick's family get him. Panic shot through me, and I snatched the first thing that came to hand, a stone statue I use as a doorstop. It shows Inanna, the Sumerian goddess of sex and warfare, standing astride two lions atop a large square base carved with sharply-pointed stars. Twisting to stand, I flipped on the light and brought the statue up, head pointing down, the heavy stone base aimed like a club, ready to bludgeon whichever Dioguardi peon lay before me.

Instead, I came face to face with Jason, flat on the floor, panting under my struggling nephew. Geordi launched himself off Jason's stomach, making Jason grunt in pain, and hurled himself into my arms. I dropped the statue with a heavy *clunk* and hugged Geordi tight, inhaling his earthy scent and relishing the warmth of his safe, living little body.

Jason sat up, still breathing hard, eyes dark with shock. "Hyacinth…? *Hyacinth?* Holy shit—you were *dead.* I saw you—I checked your pulse for Chrissake, and you bloody well *didn't have one!* What the *hell* is going on?"

Well, hell. Here was something I hadn't banked on. Not that *any* part of today was planned. But it never occurred to me Jason would stick around to see if Lily and I were safe. Oh, God—

"You didn't—*Geordi* didn't—"

Jason gave a quick shake of his head, his mane of dark hair damp with sweat. "We hid in some bushes until those men left, then I ran back. Alone. When you didn't follow me out of the alley…" He shook his head again, this time in denial. "I saw you. *I saw you.*"

He was haggard, like he'd been to Hell and crawled back out. But he was also…different. I couldn't put my finger on it, other than to say he came off more serious than I'd seen him before, not even remotely the debonair playboy I'd come to know. Given the circumstances, maybe that wasn't surprising.

I gave Geordi another squeeze, and tried to figure out what to tell them. Every good liar knows it's best to stick to the truth as much as possible. I wasn't about to tell Jason the whole dead-not-dead thing, but I thought I could safely go partway there.

"I tripped—must've passed out when I hit the ground, and the guy thought he'd shot me. Maybe you were nervous, and missed my pulse." Okay, that sounded lame, even to me. And I hadn't explained away the blood that must have been leaking out of me, and wasn't anymore, but I couldn't change my story now.

Jason's eyes narrowed. He examined my face, searching for the truth of my words. Then abruptly he pushed off the floor and grabbed my shoulders, pulling me under the light and staring at me hard, Geordi trapped between us.

"You were all beat up—bruised and shit! What the *hell* happened to your face?"

Merde. I turned to the mirror I keep on the wall by the door. He was right—not a single bruise or cut was left of the beating Claude gave me. Damn, damn, damn. Michael had said I would heal faster, but I didn't know he meant *this* fast.

Jason's hands rested on my shoulders, his gaze boring into mine in the mirror. He towered over me and Geordi, looking madder than a stirred-up hornet. I suppose having a seven-year-old dumped on him, then thinking Lily and I were dead, and then having me magically reappear, alive and, quite literally, kicking, was as good a reason as any for getting pissed off.

I shrugged helplessly. I couldn't even come up with a half-lie for this one. "Jason, I know none of this makes sense, but please—I can't explain it right now."

He glanced down at Geordi, whose face was buried in my abdomen, then looked back at me and mouthed, *Lily?*

I shook my head. And suddenly I couldn't hold it in any more. The tears welled up and before I knew it, Jason turned me around and pulled me close, cupping my head to his shoulder, not saying anything, just holding me while I cried and held Geordi. I'd never had a hugging relationship with Jason, but now, in this moment, it felt natural. He was tall and strong and warm, smelling of sweat and dirt and *life*. It was the first time I'd felt safe since I met the Rousseaux at the shop, and I let the sobs overtake me, clinging to my nephew and letting the one friend I had left cradle me close.

When I came back to myself, Jason's shirt was wet from my tears, his arms were tight around my waist, and he muttered into my hair, "Jesus Christ. You sure know how to scare a guy."

Geordi squirmed to get out from between us, reminding me I wasn't done with the hard stuff. Lost in my own grief, the monumental task of telling him about his mother had slipped my mind. I let him go, and Jason let me go, and I stood there, unsure what to say. To either of them.

In the end, Geordi solved the problem for me. He looked me in the eye and asked solemnly, "Did Mommy go up to Heaven?"

"Yes," I said, the sheer relief of *knowing* I was

right making the hardest thing I've ever had to do a tiny bit easier. "I'm sorry, honey. I'm so-so sorry." I choked back a new wave of grief and waited, letting him guide the conversation.

"Oh. Did she want to leave me?"

His voice was small, and my answer came out thick with tears. "No, sweetie. She wanted more than anything to stay. But she had to go, and I know she's up in Heaven, sending all her love to you right now."

"Will there be sugary slugs up there?"

"Yes. So many, she can eat them all day long."

Geordi thought about that. "What about my dad? Did he go to Heaven, too?"

This was trickier. I was pretty sure scumbag Nick took the down stairs, but I couldn't tell Geordi that. "I'm sure he did," I said at last. Over his head, I met Jason's steady blue gaze, and he gave a slight nod of approval. What else could I say?

Then Geordi asked the worst question ever. "Will you die?"

"Oh, honey." I dropped to the floor and cupped his small, serious face in my hands. "I don't expect to die for a long time. I'm going to take care of you as long as you need me." God help me for the lie. The thought of leaving him, ever, broke me in a million pieces. But Michael had made it clear this was a temporary fix, just to get Geordi settled.

Which reminded me of my task. "Sweetie, we have to get out of here. There are some people who might be looking for us, and there's something I have to do. It might be a little scary, but I'm going to keep you safe. I promise. Will you come with me?"

I held my breath and waited, and after a minute,

Geordi nodded. He was trying so hard to be brave, when everything about today had to be even more terrifying for him than it was for me.

Then Jason said, "I'm coming, too."

"No!" I shot up. "I have to do this alone."

"Why?"

That stumped me. Michael had never said I had to find the rock by myself. In fact, he hadn't said much at all about my parameters.

I countered, "Why do you want to come? You don't even know where I'm going or what I'm doing." *Ha.* Score one for my side.

Jason looked profoundly uncomfortable, and I knew he was trying to figure out a way to lie, or at least, to flit around the truth. Good liars recognize a kindred soul. But instead of the expected whopper, he sucker-punched me with logic.

"Let's just say, some of the people who are looking for you, might come looking for me." He glanced pointedly down at Geordi, then met my gaze again.

Damn. He had a point. I was pretty sure that, to the Rousseaux, we were about as significant as dirt. I mean, what could I do? Tell the world demons existed and…what? They'd stolen a talking rock? Yeah, that'd go over well.

The Dioguardis, on the other hand, had every reason to want me dead—plus anyone who helped me. Sure, they could run me to ground, take Geordi, and leave it at that. But I was Lily's sister, Geordi's closest blood relative, able to make a fair claim for custody. Unless I was dead, I'd be a constant thorn in their side. At least, I'd try to be. Jason they'd squash like an ant out of spite. Or to keep him from making trouble after I showed up dead. But would he be safer if he came with me? Or in worse danger? For that matter, would Geordi?

I looked at my nephew, so young, so small, plucked from everything good in his life, cast off, rootless and adrift on the winds of Fate.

I'm doing this for you, so I can keep you safe.

I had to do it, and I had to take him with me. I had no choice.

Jason saw the direction of my gaze and said, "Look, wherever you're going, if it involves the kind of men you were with today, you'll need backup. Or at least a babysitter."

He put a hand on Geordi, who seemed to readily accept him. Not just accept—Jason's touch seemed to physically ground Geordi, anchoring him in place, in a good way. Geordi took a small breath and stood a little taller, and watched me with solemn eyes. But should I base a decision of this magnitude on the feelings of a traumatized child?

"I—"

Nothing came to mind. No argument for or against Jason tagging along. Other than my own innate caution and general mistrust of my fellow man. Especially respectfully distant "best friend" neighbor-types who had suddenly begun flirting with me.

I wished I could put my finger on what was different about him. His eyes, dark with unnamed emotion a minute ago, had returned to their normal baby blue. Maybe it was the clothes. I was used to seeing him all duded up for gay bar work, or heading out on a date, not looking all manly and attractive in muscle-revealing shorts and short sleeves.

"What about your job?" I asked. "I can close the shop for a while, and call it a holiday. But won't you be fired if you just take off?"

His mouth tightened, like I'd hit a nerve. "Someone else can cover for me. I put in my time—they owe me this."

I got the feeling he meant something other than the bar. What did I really know about him, anyway? He'd said he was from the States, and certainly sounded American, but that hardly proved anything. Look at my own affinity for languages. I knew he worked at the bar, because I'd dropped in on him there. But…was that his only job? Where *did* he disappear to so often, and was it really with a girl? Or was it for something more sinister?

I was probably being paranoid. I'd only told him bits and pieces about *my* life. Did I have the right to expect more from him?

Secrets. Don't ask, don't tell.

Like Michael, I wouldn't have to tell Jason everything. But I would have to let down my guard a little. Could I do that? After so many years of confiding only in Lily or Vadim? I had no one else. But was *that* a reason to throw my trust at Jason?

Jason glared at me, as though reading my mind, which made him look much more like his old self, and I gave up. Why the hell not? He was the only real friend I had and going it alone would be beyond overwhelming. Besides, if he'd wanted to hurt me, he could've done it in the last fifteen minutes. And though Michael had said I wasn't immune to dying again, rebirth did give me a certain feeling of empowerment. Or maybe it was stupidity.

"Fine," I said at last. "Can you drive a boat?"
****

Not only could Jason drive Vadim's boat—the best news I'd had all day, other than finding Geordi safe— he also had cash. Not a lot, but enough to last a while. When I finally asked what he was doing in my apartment, he said he'd thought Geordi would be more comfortable here, which was true. In all the commotion, I'd forgotten Jason also has a key. I've got one for his place, too, for those late-night returns when he doesn't want to wake the landlady.

When I told him I had to get to Turkey, his eyebrows rose, but he didn't ask why. I'd have to tell him eventually, but for now, the fact that he let me have my secrets bolstered me. I only hoped that whatever his own secrets were, they weren't as bad as mine.

I did take him aside, away from Geordi, to tell him the Rousseaux had killed Lily and Nick. It occurred to me he might think the Dioguardis did it—that Nick killed Lily, and someone else shot him. I also wanted Jason to know the Rousseaux were worse than Nick's family. I just didn't tell him they were—technically— demons.

I must have impressed on him how horrible the Dioguardis were, because he actually looked relieved to hear Geordi's father hadn't done the deed. Of course, given enough time, Nick probably would have, but what the hey.

Geordi sat quietly on the futon while Jason ran down to his apartment to pack, and I rushed around doing the same. I know kids process grief differently, but watching Geordi sit, staring into space, was ten times worse than if he'd thrown a tantrum. For the first time, I fully understood why Lily used to say that Geordi throwing a fit meant he felt safe.

Packing didn't take long. Turkey would be warmer even than here, and tanks and shorts don't take up much space. I grabbed my "dig" boots from my grave-robbing days and tossed in some toiletries. Luckily Nick had left my passport in the safe, so at least I had one form of ID.

Briefly I considered a side trip to Switzerland, to get my own cash. I might be able to do it over the phone, but since my bank cards had been stolen, and I was shortly to be wanted by *les flics*—maybe even by Interpol—going in person would be less messy. But Jason assured me he had funds, and since he's as cautious about money as I am, I believed him.

While I was in the safe, I grabbed Vadim's will, in case I needed to prove ownership of the boat. According to Jason, the harbor permit should be on the boat itself, and once at sea, he could plot a course for Marmaris. If one of his deep dark secrets turned out to be an affinity for sea navigation, I wasn't about to argue.

Meanwhile, my stomach was growling, and as expected, my cupboards were bare. I had everything I needed for the trip in one small bag, so I took Geordi outside, locked the apartment, and went down to Jason's, to find him just locking his own door.

"Food?" I asked.

Jason knows my eclectic eating habits, and bless him, he held out a bag filled with bread and cheese, juice boxes, apples, and a container of roast beef for Geordi. I grabbed a hunk of cheese and doled out a juice box and some meat to Geordi. Everything smelled heavenly, and I licked the residual beef taste off my fingers, earning an odd look from Jason.

He'd changed into a clean t-shirt, so tight it formed a thin white shell over his hard chest, and khaki shorts that showed off his long, lean legs. I did another double-take. I mean, I knew he worked out, but I didn't know he looked *this* good. It had to be my hormones. He'd saved my nephew, and offered me aid, so I'd transformed him into my knight in shining armor, when in reality, he was the same old Jason. I hoped.

He shouldered his own bag and said, "All set? Where to?"

"The shop. I'm hoping Geordi's passport is in Lily's stuff."

"Walk or drive?"

I thought a minute. We didn't have much to carry, and I was already nervous about driving Nick's car. On the other hand, it was probably better to leave it at the shop with his body, instead of here. "Drive. We can walk to the docks from the shop."

"Okey-doke."

We hurried down to the ground floor and checked the street, which was mostly deserted. A twenty-something guy meandered along the sidewalk, looking confused, but I didn't think he was a threat. Indigent or a drug-addict, or both. The climate here is so nice, we get a lot of Europe's leftovers, the folks with nowhere else to go. Even after dark, the air was still warm, and the landlady's maroon Mystery Night lilies gave off a pungent perfume, both sweet and somehow sad.

Jason knelt to rummage in his bag for something, and I waited for the man to go by. As he passed, he looked up and met my gaze. Shock lit his face and he turned to me.

"Tu me vois?" he demanded hoarsely. *"Qu'est-ce qui se passe?"*

You see me? What is happening here?

Normally I ignore the local loonies, but though his clothes were dirty, there was a clarity in his manner that begged me to respond. "I'm sorry. I don't know."

Jason looked up at me. "What did you say?"

"Nothing, I was talking to that guy."

"What guy?"

I turned back to the street, but the man was gone, and there was no sign of him up the block. "Never mind. Let's go."

I'm not a big night person. After dinner, I like to curl up and spend a quiet evening at home. Jason, by contrast, thrives when the sun goes down. Plus, he sees better in the dark than anyone I know, so after we strapped Geordi in, I gave Jason the keys and let him take the wheel.

"Nice," he said when the engine roared awake. He pulled out of the parking space, pointed the car toward the store, and gunned it.

I'd never been in a car with him driving. I had to say, if he drove the boat like he drove the Beamer, we'd get to Turkey in no time. When we screeched to a stop in front of the shop, he killed the engine and reached for the door, but instinctively I threw a hand across his chest.

"Wait. Something's wrong."

He froze. "What?"

"I'm not sure." I examined the storefront, the gut feelings I'd ignored with the Rousseaux now tingling again like gangbusters. The door was still shut, and the stoop and the bushes on either side looked undisturbed. I glanced at the windows. The shades on the right were askew. Had I done that, in my haste to close them? Or had someone been here after I left?

If so, it wasn't the cops. That was obvious from the total lack of flood lights, crime scene tape, and forensics specialists. If the bodies had been discovered, there'd be a news crew or two as well. I unbuckled my seatbelt and started to get out, but this time, Jason stopped *me*.

"You can't go in there by yourself!"

I threw a pointed look at Geordi, who stared out the window at the street. I don't know if he avoided looking at the shop on purpose, or if the direction of his gaze was random. Regardless, it would be way too traumatic for him to come inside.

"Someone has to stay here," I said.

Jason nodded. "Yep. You." He pinched the shop keys from my grasp and got out of the car, then locked us in, saying through the closed window, "Be right back."

He was gone a minute or two at most, but they were some of the longest, most agonizing minutes of my life. Geordi still wasn't talking, and I didn't have the energy to try. Maybe being quiet was best for him anyway. If he needed to talk, I'd be here, and if nothing came out by tomorrow, I'd push him. Not tonight, though.

From a few blocks away, I heard the normal sounds of traffic on busy cross streets. Engines gunned, horns honked, the drivers of *les taxis* shouted at pedestrians and cyclists. A man ran by on the sidewalk, stumbling a little as he passed us. He flung his arms out for balance, looking like a bird about to take flight, then regained his stride and ran on. He hadn't even glanced our way, and I felt the tears welling up. Here in the car, in front of the shop where Geordi'd lost his parents, and I'd lost half my family, I felt isolated, removed from everything real or normal or good.

Then Geordi made a soft sound, like a sniffle he tried to hide, and I reached back and found his hand. The connection was instantaneous, like a completed electrical circuit. He squeezed my fingers, and we held on for dear life, not talking, but communicating all the same.

When Jason finally came out, he was empty-handed, but his expression said something was very wrong. He jumped in the car and locked the door again, then turned to me.

"They're gone."

At first his words didn't register. "Who's gone? The Rousseaux? They left hours ago."

"Not them." He glanced in the rearview mirror at Geordi, listening solemnly from the back seat. "The...*others*...who were here when you left. *They're* gone."

And then I got it, and I fell back in my seat, too stunned to speak. When I found my voice, all I could ask was, "How?"

"I don't know. But the shop's empty." He paused, and I knew he didn't want to tell me the rest. He took a deep breath, choosing his words, whether for my benefit or Geordi's, I didn't know. "I checked the back, too. *There's nothing there*. Someone took them away— both of them—then cleaned the shop and the alley. It's like nothing ever happened."

Chapter Seven

*"For we brought nothing into this world,
and it is certain we can carry nothing out."*
                              ~The Bible, 1 Timothy 6:7

I had to see for myself. Jason tried to stop me, but I argued the point and eventually he gave in. I don't even know what good I thought it would do. But it was *my* shop, *my* scumbag ex-brother-in-law, *my* sister, that someone had "cleaned up."

My first guess was the Rousseaux. Maybe they'd changed their minds about blending in and had decided to wiggle their fingers after all, to cover up the crime scene. The giant hole in that guess was, though, why not do it immediately? Why leave and come back, after I'd had time to be reborn, search Nick, and steal his car?

But…if not the Rousseaux, then who?

Whoever did it even put back my shelves and counter. The discolorations on the floor must've told them where everything went. I poked around, but other than the fact that they'd done a thorough cleaning job— much better than I do—I learned nothing else.

Steeling myself, I went out the back. Not that I *wanted* to see Lily's body. But she was my sister, and I didn't like the idea that someone had messed with her. At least if *les flics* found her, she'd eventually get a burial or whatever she'd specified in her will. She was a much better Catholic than I—my own preference would be cremation.

Which reminded me, I didn't have a will. Maybe I could have one drawn up before Michael took me away again.

Shoving that thought away, I stepped into the alley. It was a good thing I already knew where Lily went— the real Lily—her soul or whatever you want to call her essence. Because here again, Jason was right. Though I'd never call the alley "clean," there was no sign of Lily, her blood, or my own. Or of anything else indicating our deaths had occurred here mere hours ago—just trash and dirt, graffiti on the buildings, and the faint scent of potted flowers mixed with the lingering meat and grease smells of the day's cooking, wafting down from the kitchen windows above.

There was also a tenant from the apartments across the alley, standing by the dumpster. Monsieur Lebeau had to be ninety at least. I'd met him a few years ago while taking out the trash. We struck up a conversation, discovered a mutual love of travel and faraway places, and he'd been a regular visitor to La Boutique ever since.

It had to be way past his bedtime. But then, I left the shop by four most afternoons, so what did I know of his nocturnal habits?

"Monsieur Lebeau?" I walked toward him. "What are you doing out here?"

He glanced around agitatedly, as though searching for something. *"Je suis ici?* I do not know which way to go. They do not tell one what to do."

His mind was usually nice and sharp, but it was

awfully late. He wore a robe over pajamas, so maybe he was sleepwalking. Jason and Geordi waited in the car, but I couldn't just leave him.

"Would you like me to help you?" I asked.

He turned sharply, looking frightened, then relaxed when he saw me. "Hyacinth! I did not know it was you." He regarded me for a moment, then nodded once. *"Mais bien sûr—tu le sais.* You know. Would you be so kind as to show me the way?"

"Of course."

I took his elbow and led him to the back entrance of his building, which consisted of a grimy metal door flanked by two withering purple Moonflowers planted in dry, caked soil. Their dying vines had crept up the building wall, taking hold in the cracks and chinks of the old yellow bricks. A few tenacious blooms still clung to life, perfuming the night air with their heady scent, as though leaving the world something to remember them by.

Like the plants, Monsieur Lebeau seemed frail and old, barely hanging on, and a pang of loss swept through me. Then I chided myself. He wasn't dead yet—*I* was. Which only made the pang worse. I gave myself a mental shake. *You're here for Geordi. Stay focused, help* him*, and worry about the rest later.*

I wasn't sure which floor Monsieur Lebeau lived on, only that it wasn't street level. When I opened the rusty door, I saw a hall with stairs going up to the left, down to the right. Since there were no apartments below ground, only storage, I steered him toward the left.

He paused uncertainly. *"Vraiment? Celui-ci?"*

Whether due to my melancholy over Lily's death

and my own, or because the stairs reminded me of the room I'd been in with Michael, I don't know, but I had an incredible urge to reassure Monsieur Lebeau. He'd been so nice over the years, bringing snacks and companionship when I needed them most.

I took his hand and gave it a squeeze. "Yes. This one. This is where you should go."

His skin was surprisingly warm, and at the contact, he drew a shaky breath, then blew it out, becoming instantly calmer. He gave my hand a squeeze back, then withdrew from my grasp. *"Merci beaucoup,* Hyacinth. I am glad you were here."

"I can walk you up, if you like."

"Non, merci. I know the way now. You have been a great help."

He grasped the railing in one arthritic hand, putting a slippered foot on the stairs. I fought down the sudden lump in my throat, thinking this might be the last time I ever saw him, but he turned and smiled, and I knew he'd be okay.

The question was, would I?

I watched his laborious progress until he turned at the first landing and disappeared from sight. Then I went back into the shop, locking the alley door behind me. I'd learned nothing about whoever removed Lily and Nick, but I had the oddest sense that I was supposed to be there, for Monsieur Lebeau. I'm not the best Good Samaritan. Too much fend-for-yourself foster care. But I have a soft spot for the elderly who, in my opinion, get the shaft more than the rest of us. I was glad Monsieur Lebeau was safe, and even more happy I'd helped speed him on his way.

In fact, the whole episode made me feel better

about things, like maybe I could handle this after all. It's amazing what one small accomplishment can do for your self-esteem.

The warm fuzzies lasted for the thirty seconds it took me to walk through the dark shop and out the front door, where I spied Jason and Geordi several yards away on the sidewalk, their backs to me. Jason took a step forward, looking at something on the ground, then beckoned Geordi closer, and my heart leapt into my throat.

Jason was taking Geordi. I'd totally misjudged him—he had no intention of helping me—he only came along so he could snatch my nephew.

And…do what with him? Ransom him to the Dioguardis?

It was completely irrational. I knew that. But the fear was there, palpable, souring my gut, dizzying in its perniciousness. Was this how it would be from now on? I'd always loved Geordi, but now I was his parent. All at once, a bone-deep need to keep him safe vibrated from my hair down to my toes. With sudden clarity I knew if a bus came barreling at him, I'd throw myself in front of it—or face down a whole pack of demons— just to save him.

There'd be no point in letting Jason come to Turkey with us if I didn't trust him. But the thing about suspicions is, once you have them, they tend to stick. And the bottom line was, I knew almost nothing about Jason's past, his present, or his future plans.

Except that he had cash, could drive a boat, and would schlep me and Geordi across the Mediterranean at the drop of a hat. Which pretty much all worked in my favor, and didn't have an apparent benefit for him, besides maybe hiding him from the Dioguardis. Who'd only be interested in him because of *me.*

I blew out a breath. They heard me and turned, Geordi looking solemn as ever, Jason with a big grin lighting his face.

"Look what we found!" He held up something small and rectangular, and as I got closer, I realized what it was.

"Geordi's passport! Where was it?"

Jason rested his other hand on Geordi's shoulder, looming behind him like some sort of bizarrely protective bird of prey. Geordi let him, and a little more tension eased out of me.

Jason said, "When you didn't come back, we men decided to stretch our legs. Then Geordi here needed to answer the call of nature."

"I peed in the bushes," Geordi piped up, startling me.

He'd been so quiet, but now he had that look little boys get when allowed to pee outside. Like he'd gotten away with something, and the fact that it involved a body part girls didn't have made it even more special. Of course, I have a commode in the shop, but why spoil his fun? He looked almost normal for a second.

"Cool," I said, earning an actual smile, which warmed me even more.

"Anyway," Jason said, "the passport was out here on the sidewalk. Lily probably dropped it in all the commotion."

This was a stroke of luck. Without the passport, my complicated existence would be even more of a pain. I took it from Jason and flipped it open. Thank God. As soon as she left Nick, Lily'd gone back to Finch, and the passport listed that as Geordi's surname. If asked, I could either explain he was my nephew, or pretend he was my son. I didn't know exactly how far-reaching the Dioguardis were, but my thought was, *very far*. Maybe even in Turkey. Flashing the passport of Geordi Dioguardi around could set off a bunch of red flags.

Though I suppose Nick's family would know Lily's maiden name and add "Geordi Finch" to their list of seven-year-olds to track down. Duh. Maybe I should have used a fake name after all.

Maybe I should start now.

I turned to Jason. "Do you know anything about getting fake ID's?"

He looked a lot less offended by the question than I would've liked. "I don't. But I know someone who does." He paused, then added casually, "He can take care of Nick's car, too."

Great. I think.

****

We drove back to my place, and Geordi and I switched to the Peapod. I still didn't have my keys, but I added "hot-wiring a car" to Jason's list of previously unknown talents, and we followed as he drove the Beamer to his friend's place.

I didn't ask what "taking care of" the car meant, but it sounded smart. For one thing, it had a GPS unit, and if the Dioguardis didn't already know Nick was missing, they would soon, and would put a trace on his car. For another, it now seemed politic *not* to leave my psycho ex-brother-in-law's car at a crime scene about which I, once again, planned to pretend total ignorance. Not that there was any "scene" left, but still.

Physically, I felt better and better, like I'd never

been dead. Except I was *starving.* The cheese had evaporated long ago, and my stomach was about to digest itself if I didn't eat again soon. When it growled, Geordi giggled, and I marveled at the adaptability of children. Lily's death would hit him hard, but right now he was in survival mode. So was I.

Could I really track down the Rousseaux and take the rock? Michael had called me resourceful, but this was out of my depth. Where *does* one get the experience needed to defeat Satan's minions? I didn't even go to Mass regularly. Okay, at all. The extent of my knowledge of Good and Evil was that—hopefully—Good won. But I had no clue how to make that happen.

And before I could defeat the Rousseaux, I had to find them. Another monumental task. Turkey isn't exactly small, and I didn't know the first thing about tracking people down.

Maybe Jason did.

And...back to my suspicions. Just because he'd played the playboy, and had suddenly dropped the act, didn't mean *everything* was a lie. Twice now he'd offered me unconditional friendship, right when I needed it. I'd leaned on him when Vadim died, and wanted to lean on him now. Who else did I have, besides Geordi? And *he* needed *me* to be strong.

I glanced in the rearview mirror. Forget Monsieur Lebeau's bedtime. It was long past Geordi's. And mine. At least he didn't have to drive. He'd fallen asleep with his head on his backpack, looking sweet and troubled and about to break my heart.

How could I ever leave him? How had Lily?

How had she left me?

Ahead of us, Jason turned right onto a side street,

and two blocks later, stopped near a dark tenement fronted by a tiny weed patch of a yard, which was mostly taken up by an old, rusty American Eagle motorcycle parked on the dead grass. Another car had turned off the main route behind us, but disappeared around the first corner, leaving us alone on the deserted street. We'd been driving for twenty minutes, and I had no clue where we were. Smart. If I planned to defeat badass demons, I should pay more attention to what I was doing.

Jason got out and came toward us. I put the car in neutral—I didn't want to shut it off, in case we couldn't start it again—then opened the window.

He held out a hand. "Passports?" I gave him ours, and he glanced at Geordi, sacked out in the back, then said, "Wait here. It won't take long."

Which was fine, except I had no idea where "here" was. This didn't look like the greatest neighborhood, but then, people who faked passports and "took care of" dead creeps' cars probably didn't live the high life. Or maybe I was prejudiced by the rundown apartment buildings, wash lines linking them window to window, like a bizarre multi-level spiderweb. Or by the quantity of stripped down cars on the street, many up on blocks and missing essential parts, like wheels or engines.

Across the street, someone had attempted to turn their building's weed patch into a garden, and the hope implicit in the miniature roses and half-stunted marigolds bordering the walk heartened me. Maybe in daylight, this was a very nice middle-class *quartier,* like my own.

Yeah, right.

"Hurry back," I said to Jason.

He flashed a quick grin, then was gone.

We'd been waiting about five minutes when I heard the first sirens wailing from the main street behind us, followed shortly by a second set, then a third. Something big was going down, and I held my breath, praying they wouldn't come this way. They passed our street and instead turned off a block or two farther along, and I let out my breath in relief.

This was good for two reasons. First, it meant whatever crime was committed hadn't happened *right here*, allowing me to maintain my illusion of safety. Second, *les flics* wouldn't be swarming around, noticing a stolen BMW in a non-Beamer neighborhood, with the missing mafia owner's ex-sister-in-law parked behind it. And, oh-by-the-way, Mr. Mafia's kidnapped son in the backseat.

A cool breeze brought the spicy sent of the roses from across the way into the car, and Geordi let out a soft *whuff!* and shifted in his sleep. I turned to power the window up, then stifled a shriek when I saw the man *right* beside the car, glaring at me. Why hadn't I heard him run up? His chest heaved with large, gasping breaths, and sweat darkened his clothes.

Not sweat—I looked closer and saw blood. Lots of blood.

"Police—aidez-moi!"

He gripped the car door, filling the window. His light-colored shirt was shredded, his chest sporting a gaping, ragged hole—probably a gunshot. From my limited knowledge of physics, and my own recent experience, it looked like an exit wound, and appeared to be right where his heart should be. He shouldn't have been able to stand, let alone threaten me. His eyes were wild, and heat rolled off him in waves. Plus, the stench was awful, acrid and metallic and sickly sour-sweet, and a wave of nausea clawed my gut.

"Aidez-moi!"

I scanned the block. Where was Jason? Even from a few blocks away, the cops might hear if I honked or screamed, but I didn't want to involve them if I didn't have to.

"I'll help you," I said to the man. "But please, step away so I can get out. I can't do anything, stuck in the car."

The man's eyes focused on my face for an intense moment. The corded tendons in his hands stood out in sharp relief, and his knuckles, white from his hold on the doorframe, were scraped and dirty. Maybe he'd been in a fight before he got shot. We stared at each other, and I willed my heart rate down, forcing my expression to stay neutral. After what seemed like hours, he released the door and stepped back.

The second he moved, I put the car in gear and floored it.

Or, I tried to. The downside to eco-friendly cars— or at least, to *my* eco-friendly car—is they only go sixty minutes on a charge. Normally, this isn't a problem, as I only drive a few miles a day, and charge it overnight. But today I'd driven it all day, back and forth between the shop and the docks, then my apartment, and now the long trip here, never thinking to plug it in.

So instead of the dramatic, low-speed getaway I'd planned, the car wheezed once and died. But not before the man figured out what I was up to. He snarled, baring his teeth, and reached through the window. I tried to raise it, but he got an arm in and wrenched the door open, then pulled me out by my shirt, lifting me off my feet.

"Aidez-moi!" he demanded, shaking me until my teeth rattled. *"Help me!"*

"All right!" I gasped. "I'll help you—what do you want?"

Our faces were inches apart, and some of his blood probably smeared my shirt. He searched my face, looking for something, and then abruptly let go. I fell hard on my knees, scraping them and my palms on the pavement.

"Tu le sais. Qu'est-ce qui se passe?"

I froze. What the hell? The same thing the man at my building had asked: *What's going on here?* And like Monsieur Lebeau, this new guy had also said, *you know.*

What did I know?

I shivered. He'd said *"police"*, and I'd thought he was asking me to call them. But—was it the cops who shot him? Or someone else? I never could distinguish the different types of sirens, but I hoped at least one of the emergency vehicles I'd heard was an ambulance.

"You need a doctor," I said, trying to sound calm. I rose and took a step toward him. He didn't appear to be armed and getting him away from Geordi was still my main goal.

He shook his head, more sorrowful now than anything else. *"Trop tard. Où dois-j'aller?"*

Too late? Where should he go? How the hell should I know?

And yet… Again, the same question posed by Monsieur Lebeau.

"Hyacinth—why are you standing in the middle of

the street?"

I turned. "Jason! Thank God! This man needs an ambulance. I heard one a couple blocks away—can you take him?"

Jason frowned. "Are you feeling okay?"

"I'm fine. *He's* the one in trouble." I gestured at Mr. Shot, who swayed on his feet.

Jason stared right at the man, then back at me. "Who's in trouble? Hyacinth, you aren't making any sense. Let's get you back in the car." He moved toward me and I jerked back.

What the *hell* was going on?

I turned to Mr. Shot. The wildness was gone from his eyes, replaced by resignation. He lifted a shoulder, looking even sadder than before. *"Il voit pas. Seulement toi. J'suis mort."*

His words hit like the proverbial ton of bricks and it all came together. The man on my street who Jason hadn't seen. Monsieur Lebeau, wanting to know if he should go up or down. And now this man.

No wonder nothing he said or did woke Geordi. No wonder Jason was confused.

He doesn't see me. Only you. I am dead.

Holy shit.

Chapter Eight

"The wise man's eyes are in his head; but the fool walketh in darkness; and I myself perceived also that one event happeneth to them all."
~*The Bible, Ecclesiastes 2:14*

Holy shit, holy shit, holy *shit*.

"Hyacinth?" Jason's tone said he thought I'd had one too many shocks, thereby losing the ability to distinguish reality from insanity. I turned back to my new friend, who shrugged again.

"*Tu m'vois.* You are here. You must know what it is I should do."

"But I don't," I said helplessly, earning another look from Jason.

Why *was* I here? Not here, on this street. Why was I here, where this man could see me? Why could I see, hear, smell—even *touch*—him?

And Monsieur Lebeau. Sadness swept through me. He must have been dead, after all. Of course, so was I. For *some* reason, I kept forgetting that. Talk about denial.

But maybe therein lay the explanation. I was dead, but reborn. Michael had said I wouldn't be "alive per se." Did that mean I was literally more dead than alive? That other dead people sensed a connection and sought me out? But why? For what purpose?

And why did they all think I *knew* something?

My impression from Michael was that he needed to be at the deathbed of every newly dead soul, except those who didn't believe in him. But if another guide never showed up...did those nonbelievers hang around on Earth forever? Monsieur Lebeau was Catholic, but we'd had more than one discussion about what really happens after death. Maybe he was still uncertain, and I'd reassured him, helping him decide to go up after all.

There were no stairs here, and I got no strong sense whether this guy should go up or down, or nowhere at all. It wasn't my job to shepherd lost souls anyway.

I did get a sense from Jason's tense form a few feet away that if I didn't start acting sane soon, he'd take matters into his own hands.

"I'm fine," I said to him. "Really. I...thought I saw something. Must've been my imagination. Let's go."

Jason nodded with obvious relief and moved to the passenger side of the car. I started to get back in the driver's seat, but the dead guy reached out an imploring hand.

"Please. Tell me where I should go."

Jason crammed himself into the tiny front seat and turned away to check on Geordi, so I shook my head at the guy and said under my breath, "Sorry. Can't help. Gotta go."

"You cannot."

"I'm sorry. I have to."

"Non. Tu comprends pas. You *cannot* leave—your car won't start."

Well, hell. Trust a dead guy to have a better memory than me.

Jason faced forward again and watched me through

the windshield. "I dropped an earring," I said, then turned away before he told me to forget it. I pretended to search the street while saying in a low voice to the dead man, "I still can't help you. I don't know what to do."

"That makes two of us."

His tone was so ironic I looked up, startled. Now that I wasn't afraid of him—largely because he'd stopped manhandling me—I noticed he was actually pretty good-looking. About six feet tall, with a compact build—solid-looking shoulders, lean through the abdomen, or at least, what was left of it, and narrow hips. The bullet that killed him had ruined his pale blue dress shirt, but his tan slacks and shoes were relatively clean. He looked to be in his mid-to-late thirties, so not much older than me, with medium-blond hair just long enough to tousle. His jaw was firm, his nose angled, as though it had been broken a time or two, and there was a slight worry crease between his brows. It was too dark to determine the color of his eyes, but I thought they might be a light hazel.

"What's your name?" I asked.

He hesitated, then must have decided I was okay, or at least unable to harm him further.

"Eric."

I noticed he gave no last name, but then, he was dead, and we stood on an empty street in the dark of night. First names probably sufficed.

"Hyacinth," I said and held out my hand.

He shook it, his skin warm, like Monsieur Lebeau's. If I'd thought of it at all, I'd assumed the dead were cold. But so far, that wasn't the case. Of course, I'd only touched two souls so far, both newly dead. Maybe the cold came on later, when life was farther away.

"What happened?" I asked, indicating his chest.

He looked down and frowned, as though he'd forgotten what killed him. Then he gave a sad half-smile. "Wrong place, wrong time. I was caught in the crossfire."

"I'm sorry."

"De rien."

I didn't have much time. Jason was already impatient, and we had to get moving. But I'm not a hardass, and being recently dead myself, I had some inkling of how upsetting this might be.

"Look, I really wish I could help. But I don't know what to do. And we—my friends and I—really have to go now."

"Take me with you."

"What? Why?"

He only shrugged. He knew even less about my situation than Jason, and I was starting to feel like Dorothy on her way to Oz, skipping along the Yellow Brick Road, collecting strays.

"You're dead," I said. "I can't have a dead guy trailing around after me."

"Look," he said reasonably, "I have nowhere to go. You are here, you see me. Perhaps you are to guide me somewhere. *Je t'assure*—the first exit I see, I will take. *Eh bien,* I will not get in your way or ask what it is you are doing. Who knows? Perhaps I can help you."

He looked so hopeful. I mean, I know men need a purpose. But he was dead. Wasn't that a big enough challenge? He seemed so lost, though. Could I really walk away?

No. No lost puppy dogs—or cute dead guys.

I turned to the Peapod just as Jason got out, scowling at me. "Hyacinth—we have to go. *Now.*"

Shit. I'd forgotten again. "The car won't start. The charge ran down."

"I have a car," Eric said, and I turned sharply back to him.

"Where?"

Jason came around the car and grabbed my arm. "Forget the damn earring. We'll move everything back to the BMW and take it to the docks after all."

"That yours?" Eric asked, gesturing at Nick's car.

"Kind of," I said, hoping Jason was too engrossed in pulling me along to hear.

Eric grimaced. "That is the one they are looking for. I recognize the plates."

"What?" I stopped and yanked my arm out of Jason's grasp, turning away and lowering my voice as much as I could. "Who's looking for it?"

"The Dioguardis."

"How the hell do you know about them?"

"Everyone in France knows the Dioguardis."

He had a point. I glanced at Jason, who'd opened the Peapod's hatch and stuck his head inside, then I turned back and gestured for Eric to continue.

"*Alors*—they tracked the GPS to here, but were…sidetracked. You heard the sirens? The police chased them. As I have said, I was caught in the crossfire."

I was so stunned, I didn't even think to ask how he knew any of that. "Shit!" I turned to Jason. "Get Geordi out of the car—*now!*"

He jerked out from under the hatch and glared at

me. "That's what I'm doing. Jeez."

"No! You don't understand—the Dioguardis are coming. The sirens I heard are for them. They'll be here any second!" Even in the dark I saw the shock on Jason's face, and I hurried on. "We can't take the BMW—they're tracking it. We have to run."

Eric said, "My car is in the next block. Take me with you, and I will show you the keys."

I hesitated for a second. But once again, what choice did I have? "Deal."

Eric grinned, and I held up a hand. Luckily, Jason was now frantically getting Geordi and our stuff out of the car and didn't notice me still talking to no one.

"I'm not guiding you anywhere," I said to Eric. "I'm going to Turkey. You can tag along if you want, but don't get in the way. Especially on the boat. It's pretty small."

The grin vanished. "Boat?"

"Yes, boat." I grabbed my bag, which Jason had tossed onto the street. He hefted a barely-awake Geordi in one arm and grabbed his own bag in the other, and I picked up Geordi's backpack.

Eric swallowed nervously. "I don't like boats."

"Then don't come," I snapped.

Jason shot me another glare. "Of course I'm coming. Let's go!"

I turned my back on him and mouthed to Eric, *Which way?*

He blew out a breath and straightened his shoulders. I never knew dead folks acted so much like live ones. Except for me, of course.

"This way." He headed down the block, and I followed, Jason right behind. If Jason wondered why I went that way, he didn't ask, just held Geordi tight and still managed to run.

It occurred to me I knew even less about Eric than I did about Jason. On the other hand, Eric was dead, so it seemed like the worst he could do was lead us straight into whatever police battle had killed him. I was starting to wonder if that was, indeed, his plan, when at the next intersection he veered in the opposite direction. We were just out of sight of the block with Nick's car when I heard shouts behind us.

"Là! Cette auto—c'est à lui!"

They'd spotted the Beamer. If I could hear their shouts, could they hear the pounding of our feet as we tried to escape? We ran harder, and I kept thinking, *I don't want to die again. Don't let them get Geordi—please!*

Eric started to lag. Of course, he was already dead, and no one but me knew he was there. Still, I felt responsible for him. I'd agreed to help, though I had no idea how I could. Souls weren't usually depicted as old and decrepit, or covered in the evidence of what killed them. Would Eric regain his original form eventually? Or did that only happen after passing out of this world, into the next? What if you never passed through?

Death had clearly taken a lot out of him. Halfway up the block, he stopped and doubled over, wheezing. He pointed to a black Fiat. "That one." Then he indicated a spot in the street a few feet away. "Keys…by curb."

I came abreast of the car, pretending to kick the keys as I ran, then scooped them up. I turned to Jason. "Look!" I made a show of searching the parked cars for a likely candidate.

"Remote…lock," Eric managed between gasps. "Gray…button."

I clicked the middle button of the remote and the car's lights flashed twice, and the locks popped open. Bless Jason—once again he acted unquestioningly. He tossed Geordi in the backseat with our bags, then grabbed the keys from me and got in the driver's seat. Eric shot him a dirty look. I don't think he liked another guy driving his wheels.

"He drives faster than me," I said and ran to the passenger side, and Eric somehow got in the back without opening the doors. When I'd touched him, he felt solid enough. But of course, he wasn't. He was a spirit, without a body, and I guess they really can pass through objects. I couldn't. But then, I wasn't exactly dead *or* alive.

What was I thinking? I couldn't find Satan's minions, or be a guide for dead people. I couldn't even care for Geordi, because I wasn't really alive myself. And now I'd dragged Jason deeper into danger. He deserved better—so did Geordi, but I *had* to bring him. I couldn't leave him behind, until I'd found a loving, safe family for him. Even then, I didn't know how I'd do it.

I turned to Jason as he started the car. "You don't have to do this. You can give me the keys, and Geordi and I can drive to Denizli."

"Yes!" Eric said weakly from the back. "Please—I really hate boats."

I ignored him. "Jason—seriously—the Dioguardis are bad, bad folks. If you walk away now, they'll leave you alone." I glanced at Geordi behind me. He was fully awake, but quiet, and gave no sign that he sensed

Eric next to him. I half-hoped Geordi *could* see him, so I wouldn't feel so freakishly alone.

Jason also glanced at Geordi, reaching over the seat to ruffle his hair. Then he turned back to me. "I'm not leaving you. There's still your Rousseaux friends to worry about. And if you need to get to Turkey, the boat is faster."

I still hadn't told Jason I was actually going to Turkey to *find* the Rousseaux, but now didn't seem like the time. "If you're sure…"

"Positive. To the docks!"

Jason put the car in gear and peeled out of the space, and Eric groaned. "Tell him to go easy on the clutch!"

I shot him a repressive look, and he glared at me. Then he closed his eyes and leaned back in the seat, muttering, "Really, really, *really* hate boats."

Geordi caught the direction of my gaze and looked curiously at Eric's seat, then at me. Damn. I'd have to be more careful about my actions. And my words. If, God forbid, Geordi did end up in the clutches of the Dioguardis, I didn't want him more scared than he already was. In truth, as a child, they'd treat him like royalty. He'd want for nothing, from food, clothes, and toys, to the best education money could buy. It's what they'd expect of him as an adult that sent shudders down my spine and panic through my heart.

We turned onto the main drag, and Jason hit the accelerator and shifted up a gear. "Nice car. Guy's got a police scanner." He pointed to a fancy walkie-talkie type thing on the dash.

I'm no expert, but it looked expensive. It certainly had enough buttons and switches. Luckily, it was off, but still. Just what I needed. Either Eric was a nut-job ambulance chaser, or he had more sinister reasons for monitoring police channels. I threw him a surreptitious glare over my shoulder and he shrugged.

"I like to stay informed."

I couldn't say anything back, of course, and I faced forward, suppressing my frustration. At least it explained how he knew the Dioguardis were near. What it didn't explain was why he cared. Or why he'd left his perfectly safe car to run *to* them, thereby getting himself killed.

Jason glanced at me and frowned. "You okay? You've been acting a little…weird."

"I know. I'm sorry." Even this late, traffic was fairly loud around us, and I thought if I kept my voice low, Geordi wouldn't hear. I said to Jason, "Promise me something. If Nick's family comes for Geordi, and I can't stop them, you'll take him. Keep him safe."

"Hyacinth," Jason said calmly. "Nothing's going to happen to you. I won't let it."

I felt a bubble of hysteria, because of course something already *had* happened. And no, Jason had not been able to prevent it. Whoever he was, I doubted he'd be much protection against Demons from the Last Circle of Hell.

The offer was nice, though. I touched his arm, and he shot me an intense look, his eyes dark in the unlit car. Quickly I took my hand away. "Just promise me. Please?"

He was silent for a long time, staring at the road. Finally, he nodded. "From what I've seen of the Dioguardi empire, it's no place for Geordi. I'll do anything I can to keep him safe."

"Thank you," I said, feeling like at least one load had been lifted.

It wasn't until a long while later that it occurred to me to wonder at his word choice. Eric was right—everyone in France knew *of* the Dioguardis. But exactly how much had Jason *seen* of their empire? And…when?

But by then we were at the docks, parking near the slip where Vadim's boat was tied, and once again, immediate survival took precedence. After all, Jason could drive the boat. I couldn't, and Eric's apparent "hatred" of them—not to mention his ghostliness—made him an unlikely captain. I had to trust Jason at least until we made it to Marmaris. After that, it was open season.

Geordi and Eric followed us out of the car. Geordi shouldered his own backpack and tried to look stoic as we boarded. Eric looked a bit green in the dock's floodlights, but he avoided my gaze and took a seat near the back. Except for when he'd gotten into the car, he seemed to move around like a live person. He'd left the car through an open door, and his feet even appeared to touch the gang plank. Why couldn't he just float everywhere?

I pushed the thought away. What difference did it make? I'd find out eventually, when my own death became official.

I don't know much about boats. Vadim's wasn't big, maybe ten meters long, but it did have a room below deck, with a table nailed to the floor and bench seats that converted to beds when folded out. It also sported a functioning toilet and a kitchenette. Above deck was open except for a small windscreen. There was a clear vinyl top that could be hooked on if the weather turned bad. It wasn't much, but it helped.

Geordi ran around, exploring, while Jason went straight to the controls and began flipping switches and checking gauges. A short while later, the engine roared on. At which point, Eric leaned over the back and hurled his dinner into the harbor. I use the term "hurl" loosely, since he was dead, and nothing actually came out. But the retching was real enough, and I could see why he hated boats, if he got this sick before we even left the dock.

Oblivious to Eric's plight—or, for that matter, to Eric—Jason looked at me and grinned. "Your friend Vadim knew what he was doing."

I joined him at the wheel, sliding into the cushy passenger seat. I'd only been on the boat a few times for day jaunts, but I knew Vadim had customized it for his "business trips."

"Why do you say that?" I asked, looking at the confusing array of dials and displays.

"This is a nice cruiser. Inboard engine with a Volvo Penta IPS joystick." I stared at him blankly. "Never mind. Here's the really great part." He pointed to two identical gauges. "Hundred-liter fuel tank—that's about fifty gallons—*and* a spare."

"Is that good?"

He rolled his eyes. "Very good. With two tanks, we should only have to refuel once, and we'll be there in about two days. If we go fast."

"Does this boat go fast?"

"Oh, yeah," Jason said, and revved the engine.

"Excellent," Eric muttered, and leaned over the side again.

Chapter Nine

"Die (verb): To stop sinning suddenly."
~Elbert Hubbard (1856-1915)

And that, kiddos, is how I found myself traveling to Turkey with the seven-year-old heir to the Dioguardi mafia empire, my own self-proclaimed babysitter-cum-bodyguard, and a seasick dead guy with nowhere else to go. At least my life-after-death was interesting.

Except that suddenly, I couldn't *do* anything about any of it. Ever since I'd found the rock, I'd been zipping from one crisis to the next. Once Jason got us out onto open water, I went from being in charge, making—literally—life or death decisions every five minutes, to sitting on a cramped boat with nothing to do but wait. Eric sat in the back, hunched over the railing, clearly wanting to be left alone. Jason did all the driving, refusing all offers of help. And even Geordi was occupied, exploring the boat and asking Jason about all the instruments.

It was like going from ninety to zero in seconds flat, and it gave me way too much time to think. And remember. Geordi might be excited to be on the boat, but I knew plenty was going on under the surface. When the harbor lights had winked out of sight and I was reasonably certain no seaborne Mafiosi were on our trail, I went to find him. He'd taken a seat on the boat's starboard side, looking away from his homeland. I could totally sympathize with that.

I sat down next to him. "Hey."

He didn't respond, and for a few minutes, neither of us spoke. We watched the black waters slip by, the chug-chug of the boat's engine the only real proof we made any progress through the dark night.

The truth was, I still had no clue what to say to him. He'd given me a pass earlier, when he brought up Lily's death himself. But at some point, I had to learn how to parent him. Of course, if I waited long enough, I might *not* have to figure it out. I shoved the thought away. Better to plan on staying permanently.

With that in mind, I cleared my throat and tried again. "How's it going?"

He shrugged, staring studiously at the horizon. I glanced away to find Jason watching us. I raised my hands in a helpless gesture, but Jason jerked his head toward Geordi. His message was clear: *Giving up is not an option.* Tactfully, he then went back to steering the boat, and I gave an inward sigh and reached for Geordi's head, ruffling his hair.

"This has been a lot," I said. He didn't pull away, so I stroked his head, much as I would have stroked Monsieur Lebeau's cat, who had also regularly visited the back door of my shop, until she died last year. "It's been really upsetting, for both of us."

He shrugged again and all at once, I couldn't keep the tears back. Lily would have known what to say, how to fix it. I couldn't fix this—I couldn't fix anything. I was just as lost and confused as Geordi. I wanted someone, anyone, to tell me what to say, what to do, how to feel.

And then it hit me.

I stopped stroking his head and dropped my hands to his shoulders, turning him to face me. "It's okay, sweetie," I said softly, looking into his eyes, which were unreadable black pools in the night. "It's okay if you don't know what to feel right now. It's horrible and awful and confusing. But you don't have to have it all figured out tonight. I don't have it figured out yet, either. But it's going to be okay. I'm going to make sure it's okay, for both of us."

There was a pause as my words sank in, and then he nodded, a jerky, quick movement, eyes shining with tears, before I pulled him in for a fierce hug. His arms wrapped me tight and we held each other for I don't know how long. Eventually, I let him go. I smoothed his black hair off his forehead and smiled, and he smiled back, tentatively.

I drew a shaky breath. However, much I might prefer to forget large chunks of today, he had a right to know. "Do you have any questions for me?"

He thought a minute, then looked at the wide-open sea. "Where are we going?"

I exhaled. Practicalities. Those I could handle. "Turkey."

He faced me again. "Tonight?"

Ah. Even more practical than I'd first thought.

There was a soft step behind us, and Jason came to sit on Geordi's other side on the bench. "I think I can answer that for you, buddy. Thanks to your aunt's friend, we've got two big fuel tanks. I'm pretty sure we can make it to Malta at least before we need gas." He sent me a questioning look over Geordi's head. "Unless your aunt would rather stop somewhere else?"

Geordi glanced at me, checking my response. I thought a minute, calling up a mental map of the Mediterranean and its various islands and coastlines. If memory served, stopping on Malta would get us almost exactly halfway to Turkey. Sardinia was bigger, but also nearer to France, which might necessitate a second fuel stop later. Not only did I not want to take the time, I didn't want to risk showing our fake ID's more than I had to. We were now the Leclerc family, traveling abroad from our home in Paris, but Jason's friend had essentially lifted our photos from our old passports and pasted them, seals and all, into new documents. If anyone looked too closely, we wouldn't pass muster.

As if reading my mind, Jason said, "There are a few other ports, but one advantage to Malta is it's smaller, maybe not as...stringent." He shifted on the seat. "Or there's Sicily...?"

My eyebrows shot up. He couldn't be serious—take Geordi *to* Sicily, straight into Dioguardi Central? I shook my head. "No. Absolutely not."

"Why, Tata?" Geordi asked, looking anxiously from one to the other of us.

"Good question," I said, glaring at Jason. "Why? Why would you suggest such a thing?"

He shrugged and glanced up at the stars. Maybe he was checking our course. Or avoiding my gaze. After a moment he said, "Not everyone in Sicily is...unsympathetic."

I waited, but he didn't elaborate, and I wondered again what his connection to all this was. It had to be more than just fearing the Dioguardis would kill him, to make him give up everything to tag along with me. But with Geordi between us, I couldn't ask.

When I didn't respond he met my gaze again, his expression unreadable. "Or there's Tunisia. The Leclercs are French, so like Turkey, we wouldn't need visas."

I didn't even have to think about it. "Not a good idea. I've been there a few times on, um, business, and found the government to be a little…restrictive."

"But would Madame Leclerc have any problems?"

"They might recognize me, from a, er, photo they *might* have lying around."

"Ah," Jason said. "Malta it is."

"Have you been there before?" I asked, glad to have the focus off me and my questionable past, and back on Jason. He nodded, and I wished it still surprised me that he got around so much.

"There are three ports. I suggest we go to Marsaxlokk, down south. It's a little out of the way, but not as much of a tourist stop as Valletta. We can refuel, stretch our legs, and stock up."

"Can we make it that far without stopping?"

He smiled, looking much more like the Jason I'd always known. "If not, we'll be close enough to the coast to radio for help. They can send a tug to bring us in. We'll be fine—trust me."

He got up and returned to the wheel, and Geordi went back to staring at the unchanging horizon. I suppressed a shiver, glancing up at the bright stars dotting the oppressive black sky. Something about the dark water below and all around us, with the limitless sky above, made me feel small and vulnerable.

Or maybe it was the sudden thought I'd had, sparked by Jason's offhand remark about radioing for help. If we could be picked up by coast guard radar, or

107

whatever aid system the Maltese had in place, couldn't the demons sense me coming from miles away?

Call me clueless, but just because I *thought* Claude and Jacques didn't give two figs if I lived or died didn't mean they *actually* didn't. What if they were using their demon magic, or whatever it was, right now, tracking me like a blip on their radar? What if the only reason they hadn't come back to obliterate me once and for all was because they wanted to obliterate the rock first? If I got too close, didn't it stand to reason they'd come for me after all?

Come for me—and for my nephew, my friend, my ghostly acquaintance, all of whom were now my responsibility. The sky, the sea, Geordi's loss, my own, all of it weighed on me. Hot tears slid down my cheeks, and I prayed neither Geordi nor Jason would see as I silently shook, all alone on a boat so small, I had nowhere to go to be by myself.

****

In the morning, as per usual, things looked a little brighter, and we established a routine. Jason showed me how to take charge of the boat in case of emergency, but mostly, he put it on auto-pilot and sat with Geordi near the front, telling him stories about Malta. Of which he knew quite a few. Geordi was fascinated and began to anticipate our first stop with excitement. Who could blame him? A seven-year-old boy trapped for an entire day on a small boat, with nowhere to go, and nothing to do—I'd want to go "'sploring," too.

Meanwhile, I managed to surreptitiously check on Eric every few hours. Even though he was dead, I could still sense everything about him, including the smell after he'd barfed dead vomit over the side for the umpteenth time. I mean really—how could a dead guy barf so much? He wasn't eating anything. Unlike me. I was ravenous, all the time, to the point that we might run out of food before we ran out of fuel. Jason shot me some odd looks as I stuffed my face, since he knows my appetite is generally much smaller. But I pretended to laugh it off.

"Must be the sea air," I said, and though I could tell he wasn't convinced, he let it go. For myself, I assumed being half-dead took a lot out of me. It didn't explain why I had to eat *all* the time, but there wasn't much I could do about it either way.

Meanwhile, Eric stagnated. When night fell after our first full day on the water, I offered to take the first watch, specifically so I could make a more in-depth assessment of his condition, without fear of being overheard.

As soon as Jason and Geordi vanished below decks, I rounded on him. "How are you feeling?"

He gave a half-laugh, which turned into a coughing fit, though no blood or anything came out. When he finished wheezing, he looked at me and lifted an ironic brow. "As well as I look."

"That bad?"

He really did look terrible. Even in the dim light of the battery-powered lantern, he was pale and green at the same time. From what I could see beneath his ripped shirt, his wound was exactly the same. I'm not sure what I expected. Unlike me, he didn't have a body that could heal. But somehow, I'd thought he'd get "more dead," and the wound would fade or even disappear.

Like Lily's. When Michael led her away, she had

no blood on her whatsoever—even a single drop of red would have stood out in that white-white room. And speaking of Michael, shouldn't he have been at Eric's death anyway, to guide him wherever he needed to go?

"Are you a Christian?" I asked, and Eric's eyes narrowed. "Sorry. I don't mean to pry. It might explain why you're still here."

"Catholic," he said slowly. "Mass every week. And confession." I raised an eyebrow, and he shrugged. "I had much to confess."

I was right about his eyes. They were gray-green, like old jade, and regarded me now with a slight cynicism. Quickly, before I lost my nerve, I scooted close and reached for his shirt.

"Hé!" He jerked upright, but the wall at his back prevented his escape. Apparently.

I unbuttoned the torn shirt and pushed it aside—ghost fabric felt as "real" as ghosts did—and I took a look. Then wished I hadn't. Yep. Big hole in his otherwise very nice chest. Lots of blood and grossness, some of it red, angry, and fresh, other bits black and starting to fester. Ugh.

I reached out and touched his skin above the wound, and he made a noise like sucking in a breath, then caught my hand and lifted it away. *"Mon Dieu—* my God, what are you doing?"

"I'm *trying* to help."

Even with his wound, his grip was strong, and I could swear I felt his warm breath on my face, which was ridiculous, because he didn't breathe. He became aware of how close we were at the same time I did, but he didn't let go, just stared at me intently.

"How is it that you see me? How can I speak to

you?" He brought my hand up and, still holding it, brushed my cheek with his knuckles. His voice was low, hoarse. "And how can you feel my touch?"

Hoo, boy. A bunch of my female parts that hadn't had much to do in a while suddenly woke up. *Way* up.

Bad idea. I was not in a position to get involved with anyone, least of all him. For one thing, he was dead. For another, *so was I.* But even with his face puke-green, he was still awful-damn cute.

"I don't know." I shook my head, helplessly, then blurted, "Why can't you fly?"

His fingers tightened on mine, and he studied my face. After a moment, he released my hand and fell back against the wall. "I do not know. Believe me, I have tried. Something holds me back. It is like a weight, attaching me to the Earth."

"But you went *through* the car. You dematerialized or something. Didn't you…?"

He seemed amused by my word choice. "I did. I will not do so again soon. It was…unpleasant."

"Oh."

I must have looked disappointed, because all at once he smiled. It transformed his face, and his dark, moody eyes lit with laughter. The spark was momentary, though, and he sobered again. "When I first realized you saw me, it gave me hope. I do not know what I thought would happen when I died, but I did not think it would be this."

Him and me, both.

Should I tell him I wasn't really alive myself? What harm could there be? He couldn't tell anyone, except other dead people, who, as far as I knew, also couldn't tell the Living. Then again, just because I couldn't think of a reason not to, didn't mean telling him was a good idea.

Eric watched me, and I wondered what he saw. The circle of light cast by the lantern barely encircled us, giving a sense of intimacy to our conversation. But other than his dislike of boats, he was pretty good at hiding his feelings. I had a sudden urge to lean farther back, out of the light, where my own secrets would be safer.

Then he said, "I tried to speak with your nephew."

"What? He's a child—he just lost his parents. He doesn't need Casper or any other ghosts right now!"

"Ne te fâche pas—do not anger yourself. I said I *tried.* I did not say I succeeded." He lifted a shoulder negligently, making him look supremely French. "For a moment, I thought he heard. But I was mistaken."

"I'm sorry," I said, surprising him. "I am. Obviously, I don't want Geordi seeing dead people. But it must be lonely for you, with only me to talk to."

One side of his mouth quirked up. *"Mais mademoiselle—t'es très belle."*

I snorted. "If you're well enough to flirt, tell me how you got your wound."

He hesitated, holding my gaze, and I knew he was trying to decide how much to share. At last he said, *"Ça ne fait rien.* It is not important."

"It might help." Not that I knew what to do for a real wound, let alone an ephemeral one, but it seemed important to try.

"You will not let it go, will you?"

I raised my hands, palms out, and he gave an exaggerated sigh.

"Comme j'ai dit—I was driving when I heard on

the scanner that the Dioguardis were near. I stopped to see what was happening, and…here I am."

Which told me absolutely nothing new or important. "But *why* did you get involved? A normal person would've booked it the hell out of there when the Dioguardis showed up."

He shrugged. "I had to stop. *C'est tout.*"

"No, that's *not* all." I tried a different tack. "Why were you in the neighborhood in the first place?" He opened his mouth, and I held up a hand. "Don't give me any crap about living there. Your car is way too nice for you to live in *or* visit that slum, without a very good reason."

"I was…following up on something." His expression was carefully blank, and I felt the first twinge of real unease. What, exactly, was he hiding?

I said lightly, "Don't like answering questions much, do you?"

His gaze searched mine. "Do you?"

Heat crept up my face, and I resisted the urge to look away. "We're not talking about me."

"Perhaps we should." He straightened, looking suddenly more…alive, for lack of a better word. Purposeful. Authoritative. "*Bon.* Tell me—why were *you* in that neighborhood, parked behind a BMW registered to *l'heir apparent des* Dioguardis? Why are you on this boat, carrying a fake passport, traveling with *that* man?"

His contempt of Jason seemed to extend beyond a mere manly defense of his car, but I had no time to ask about it, or about how he knew the Beamer belonged to Nick. He leaned closer, eyes gleaming in the lantern light, voice soft, urging me to trust him.

"Let me help you. Tell me—what is it you are running from…or to?"

I crossed my arms, unable to keep from leaning back, putting distance between us. "Jeez. What are you, a cop?"

He froze. Then the tension eased out of him and he sank back against the rail, looking haggard and drained. "*Ouais.* Until last night." He inclined his head. "Eric Guilliot, *Officier de Police Judiciaire, à ton service.*"

Chapter Ten

"There is no such thing as death,
In nature, nothing dies:
From each sad moment of decay
Some forms of life arise."
~*Charles Mackay (1814-1889)*

Before dawn on the second day, Jason steered us to a quiet area in St. George's Bay, Birżebbuġa, Malta, which is a little south of Marsaxlokk. We'd picked the area specifically because it's mainly used by small pleasure craft, and our little boat would blend right in with the hundreds of others tied up to the slips. While Jason hopped off to secure the ropes, I made sure Geordi wasn't looking, then knelt beside Eric.

"I'm going to get some breakfast. Will you be okay until we get back?"

One corner of his mouth twisted in a half-smile. "I believe *l'ordre du jour* is utterly free of appointments. I am at your disposal and will await your return with bated breath."

After his Big Reveal of the night before, I'd beat a hasty retreat to the cabin below. I think I mumbled something along the lines of *pleased to meetcha, gotta go,* then turned and escaped, waking Jason to take over the watch. I wasn't sure if the knowing laughter in Eric's eyes stemmed from any actual intel he had on me, or if he assumed my skittishness was what even the most law-abiding citizens experienced when faced with the cops. Either way, I was too chicken to deal with it at the time.

I still couldn't process it—Eric was *un flic.* I'd unwittingly brought a *cop* on what was sure to be my most questionable "business venture" yet.

Okay, he was a dead cop, but still. As noted, *les flics* and I don't always see eye to eye, and uneasily, I wondered if he'd ever investigated me. Today he looked incapable of much beyond lying in a heap, and I went back to worrying about his ghostly health, instead of what he'd do when he discovered my moral failings.

"Tata Hyhy!" Geordi called from the boat's ramp. "Let's go! I'm hungry!"

"I'll be there in a minute," I called back. "I'm, er, looking for something." I pretended to poke around in a pile of rigging, whispering to Eric, "Seriously—you'll be okay?"

He lifted a shoulder, then winced, which wasn't exactly reassuring. All he said was, *"Frais et dispo.* Go—eat your fill. I am not going anywhere."

Reluctantly I left him, and Geordi and I headed down the ramp to the pier, where Jason joined us. "I asked around. We should be able to find a breakfast place in the commercial district a few blocks north of here, and then a grocery market in the same area for supplies."

English is the second language here, so at least that wouldn't be a problem. We walked briskly in the direction Jason indicated, Geordi's young legs taking two steps for every one of Jason's. He badgered Jason with more questions about Malta, and I walked behind them, enjoying his excitement. If not for the whole searching-for-demons thing, we might actually have been the happy Leclercs, out for an early breakfast before touring the country.

In fact, I gathered from Geordi's chatter that he wanted to spend some time here before getting back on the boat. I didn't blame him. The sun was rising on our right over the harbor, the breeze was warm, and it would be so easy to forget about demons, the rock, and everything else.

And yet, I couldn't.

I watched the passersby, feeling their eyes on me. Did we really stand out? Or was it Jason's reference last night to tracking radar, making me paranoid? At this hour, there weren't many people out, a dozen or so at most, but I couldn't decide if I'd feel safer in a crowd, or if I'd just never feel safe again, until I gave the rock to Michael.

Maybe not even then.

Jason turned to see why I'd lagged behind, lifting his eyebrows in an unspoken question. I forced a smile and sped to catch up. "I'm fine. Just hungry."

"Okay," he said, then glanced at the rapidly filling streets himself, gaze flicking from one person to the next. Catching my eye, he shrugged. "Doesn't hurt to be cautious."

Geordi tugged my hand, and we resumed walking. Birżebbuġa is a resort town of about ten thousand residents. The buildings are yellow or tan brick, and the feeling is of a large fishing village that's mushroomed with the tourist trade. Commercial industry is near the water, as are hotels, parks, and beaches, with residences, markets, and local hangouts farther inland.

We followed a wide street for two blocks, then turned north, away from the bay toward the heart of town. After a block, we found an open-air café whose owner was just lifting chairs off the tops of the metal tables and arranging them on the ground. He happily let us choose seats with a view of the bay, then bustled off to start the grill. When he came back, Jason and I ordered coffee, while Geordi got hot cocoa. Then Jason flattered the man by asking him to make us whatever he thought we'd like, and he beamed and vanished into the kitchen.

While we waited, Jason hailed a street vendor and bought a copy of the *Times of Malta*. He turned to the World News, handing *les bandes dessinées* to Geordi so he could color over the comics with crayons from his backpack. I don't read the paper much, but Jason seemed engrossed, frowning at something on page two. With nothing else to do, I decided to check in with my nephew again. Since our chat on the boat, he was doing better, but he still wasn't opening up about his grief. In the interest of practicing good parenting, I thought I'd poke around.

I peered over his shoulder, seeing he'd chosen the crossword as his canvas. He worked quickly with a brown crayon, filling in a series of squares in the shape of a squat pyramid.

"Whatcha working on?" I asked.

"A map."

"Of what?"

"The mountain." He switched to a blue crayon, coloring in more squares starting near the top of the "mountain" and descending its side in a narrow triangle. "That's the river." He set down the blue crayon, then used a black one to make a smaller triangle at the base of the blue one, overlaying it so that one blue side was straight, while the other angled to the right.

"What's this?" I asked, pointing to it.

"The river goes in two."

"Oh—you mean like a fork?"

He looked up at me, blue eyes solemn. "Yes. Only it wasn't always like that. It was big and strong, but the bad men came and tried to stop it. So the other man broke it apart to save it."

Ouch.

Okay, maybe he wasn't talking much, but he sure was processing. He picked up a white crayon and filled in squares at the top of the puzzle, in a seemingly random configuration.

"That's the Cotton Castle," he said, laying the crayon down.

This was actually a relief. Good to know it wasn't all ink blots and Rorschach tests. "That's a really nice picture. Can I have it?"

He nodded, and I reached for the page as the café owner returned, bearing platters overflowing with tasty goodness. He set them down with a flourish, then went back for more. It was heavenly. He started us off with cream cheese pies and honey pastries with more cheese inside—and it only got better after that. Dates deep fried in golden-brown dough, two spicy stews, plates of kebabs, and at least four kinds of pasta. I don't remember picking up my fork, I only remember the tastes exploding on my tongue, rich and varied, thick textures and juicy bursts of cool crispness that both satisfied and made me crave them more.

Every now and then, I looked up to find Jason watching intently. At first, he seemed surprised, but as the meal progressed, so did his expression, moving from concern to a full-blown frown. By the time we got to the fourth course—the owner'd really outdone himself—I'd had it.

I threw down my fork. "What? Is there sauce on my face? Why are you staring at me?"

He lifted his hands defensively. "Nothing. No biggie. I've just never seen you eat meat."

"What?"

I looked at my plate. It was true. Lost in the amazing tastes, and the feeling of finally getting the food I needed—the *right* food—I hadn't paid attention to what I ate. The evidence lay before me, in the bits and pieces I hadn't gotten to yet. I saw steak, and sausage, and—*bacon.* I hadn't eaten bacon in fifteen years. And yet, looking at the scraps, I wanted *more.* My body craved it with a ferocity I couldn't control.

God help me but I wanted to lick my plate.

I shoved my chair back and ran out to the sidewalk, then stopped, drawing in deep breaths of the cool morning air. I stared at the street and the ocean beyond. I'd been so focused on checking in with Geordi and Eric, I hadn't checked on *myself.*

Since smacking back into my body, I'd been really pushing myself. I'm not exactly "driven"—that's more Lily's style. But when I have a goal, I stick to it. I'd done one or two quick check-ins amid the chaos, but now I did a thorough self-examination.

My wound really did feel totally healed. There was no pain, no shortness of breath or signs of weakness like I'd noted in Eric. In fact, I had none of the outward symptoms of rebirth that Michael had warned me about. But on the inside—on a much deeper level than even my wounds went—I realized I'd been feeling weak. Disoriented. Not fully alive. If I'd thought about it, I'd put it down to not *being* alive.

With my stomach now full, of meat, I *did* feel alive. Totally, completely, one hundred percent. The obvious conclusion was that, in order to recover from death, I needed meat. Red meat. In all its cholesterol-rich, animal-protein-and-iron gory glory. As a vegetarian, I'm careful to eat iron-rich plant foods, and take supplements. But I gravitate more toward dairy. A great source of protein, but the calcium interferes with iron absorption.

In a *well-duh* moment, I realized if I was going to regenerate a dead body into a live one, it made sense I'd need iron for new blood, to replace all I'd lost. And animal protein had to be better at repairing tissue and bone than legumes. I may not eat meat, but I do recognize that humans evolved on that model.

Damn Michael and his "side effects." I ignored the fact that I'd badgered him into sending me back. Much easier to get pissed that he hadn't known I'd be a magnet for dead folks, and would need the very food I loathed, to keep myself going.

I turned around to find Jason and Geordi watching me worriedly from the table. It must have taken a lot for Jason not to run out after me, and I was grateful he'd stayed with Geordi. I took a deep breath and returned to my seat.

"I'm fine," I said. "I guess all the stress just got to me."

"Okay," Jason said, but I'm not sure he or Geordi

believed me.

****

A short while later we paid the bill—thank God for the euro—and left the café. Breakfast was like a mini-vacation, but now I had to face reality. Unfortunately, my reality involved hunting demons and snatching their new best toy out of their very own sandbox. All while a giant clock ticked over my head, counting the seconds until I had to abandon Geordi.

Jason must have seen something in my face because as we started down the road, he pointed to a small street on the right. "I think if we cut over here, we'll save about ten minutes."

"Thanks," I said gratefully, and Geordi perked up when he realized he'd get to see more of the island.

We turned onto the street, but after a block, the pavement petered out, T-ing into a dirt track running roughly east-west. To the right, it went another hundred and fifty meters or so, before ending in a clump of low, leafy trees. To the left, it edged an expanse of rich brown soil, also dotted with trees, then curved south, hugging a high brick wall. Behind this appeared to be the backyards of the residences we had passed on our way in to the town, and at the track's end, I could see a narrow swathe of the main drag leading back to the harbor.

Jason and I turned toward it, when Geordi cried out, "Look, Tata!"

I faced the direction he pointed but didn't see anything worthy of a seven-year-old's interest, unless it was the potential for bugs in the trees. "What is it, sweetie?"

"There—next to that church! Can we go look? Can

we?"

I squinted, but beyond a misshapen pile of pale yellow boulders near the largest clump of trees, I hadn't the faintest clue what he meant. "What church? What are you talking about?"

"In the cave—the stones are the church, and there's a cave. Jason told me about the caves on Malta. Didn't you Jason?" Without waiting for an answer, he tugged my hand. "Some of them go on and on forever, and no one's ever found the end. Let's go—can we? Please?"

Of course I'd encountered standing stones throughout my travels. Generally, they marked the entrances to caves or tombs, or sometimes, they served as religious structures. Had Jason told Geordi anything like that? Was that why he called them a church?

Though the sun was at our backs, I felt heat rolling toward us, as though it reflected off the boulders. It must be later than I'd thought. A movement caught my eye, and a man appeared from behind the largest boulder, moving toward the track. He wore work clothes, heavy boots, and a dark knit cap, pulled low. Probably the farmer who owned the field to the left, or perhaps someone who lived in the houses nearby.

Except... Suddenly he bent low, pawing through the grass in front of the stones, looking for all the world like a giant furry caterpillar, hunched over and hunting for something on the ground. Maybe it was the skull cap. It looked wildly out of place in the sub-Saharan heat.

"I think that's private property," I said uneasily. "We can't just explore someone's farm."

"No," Geordi said. He widened his stance and planted his feet on the ground, and I recognized the stubborn set his jaw got when he was about to mutiny. "It's a church, not a farm."

"Sweetie, there's no church there. There's not even a building."

"Jason said we could explore! Didn't you, Jason? You promised!"

Jason looked at me, then ruffled Geordi's hair. "Not today, kiddo. Maybe we'll come back when your aunt's finished her, er, job."

"NO—I want to go now!"

He darted up the track, but Jason caught him and held tight, ignoring Geordi's flailing limbs. It was a good thing he'd come along, because I doubted I was strong enough to restrain a really determined seven-year-old.

I glanced at the man by the stones, and found he'd caught sight of us. He still squatted, but now with a spiderlike stillness, very predatory, and a cold chill pricked my skin.

"Let's get out of here."

I walked quickly away, and Jason fell into step behind me, Geordi still windmilling in all directions, despite Jason's iron grip around his midsection.

"What is it?" Jason asked between huffs.

"Nothing. I…just got a creepy feeling."

I looked back. The man had risen and moved further up the track, studying us intently. Even over this distance, I knew his gaze was unblinking, recording everything about us. Maybe we were just trespassing. Or maybe I should have listened to my instincts back when they said *get the hell away from the Rousseaux*. Fool me once, and all that. I quickened my pace, and Jason somehow managed to keep up, even lugging

Geordi.

"Hyacinth, it's just a farmer." Nevertheless, he cast an uneasy glance over his shoulder, then tightened his hold on my nephew.

"Uh-huh." From behind us, I felt…*something*…a disturbance, like the breeze, only it crackled as it came closer. The air shimmered, and heat burned, as if we were on the plains of Africa. My skin crawled, and I started to run as fast as I could for the busy street ahead.

"Hyacinth—wait!"

I ignored Jason, and though I heard him blow out an exasperated breath, I also heard his sneakers on the rocky dirt, picking up the pace. My heart pounded—his had to be about ready to explode. The heat wavered around us—I could actually *see* it now, shiny and bright and deadly. It felt like the heat that had rolled off Claude, which scared the crap out of me.

We'd almost reached the corner—somehow, I knew we had to get around it, out of sight of the man—

I heard a *thump!* followed by the sound of gravel skittering. "*Hyacinth!*"

I skidded and looked back—oh God—Jason had tripped, landing on Geordi, clouds of dust kicked up around them. He started to lift himself up, then glanced over his shoulder at the farmer, who didn't seem to have moved. Without knowing why, I opened my mouth to scream, to tell them to *run!* But I was paralyzed—my lungs seared by hot smoke—I couldn't make a sound. I stood rooted to the spot, watching in horror as the roiling air raced forward.

NO!

As though the thought forced them down, Jason curled back over Geordi. There was so much dust—I couldn't see—it looked like he was shielding Geordi with his body.

I don't know where it came from, but suddenly I had a vision of a cold clear wall surrounding them. Instinctively, I concentrated, *thinking* it stronger. If I'd had time, I would have felt foolish, like a kid using "the Force" on a heavy object. But I didn't have time to think, only to *do*—the energy crackled faster, closing in on the two people I cared most about. I zeroed in on them, picturing the wall, feeling its strength, protecting them with everything I had.

And then the energy hit them. I registered something like a sonic *boom!* and the shimmer, the heat, the crackle, everything exploded into a million shiny shards of light, the force hitting me in the face and knocking me flat. I coughed and gagged, clouds of dust swarming over me like millions of minuscule bugs. I pushed up, staring hard down the track. As the dust dissipated Jason and Geordi sat up, coughing, but looking none the worse for wear, and my heart started beating again.

Thank God.

I looked farther along, to where I'd last seen the man standing. He was gone. There was absolutely no sign of him. Which should have been a relief, except that I didn't know where he'd gone, or if he'd come back, or even who—*what*—he was.

Had I killed him? Or imagined the whole thing?

Was he a demon? In league with the Rousseaux, or working on his own? Had he known something about me specifically, or was he picking up on my "radar"?

And if I *had* killed him, how had I done it? That's certainly not what I was going for, demon or not. I looked at my hands, my arms, my body. Where had that clear wall come from? I hadn't consciously created it, and yet, I'd seen it, known I could manipulate it. But I didn't know *how* I'd manipulated it.

Which made me more than a little scared...of myself.

What the hell had I done?

Chapter Eleven

"If this is dying, I don't think much of it."
~Lytton Strachey (1880-1932)

We made record time back to the boat. Lucky for me, Jason and Geordi apparently didn't feel the energy field or whatever it was, or the bubble wall that deflected it. When Jason quit coughing from all the dust, he stood and offered Geordi a hand. He did look once more to where the farmer had been, but his back was to me, and I couldn't tell if he thought anything unusual had happened or if it was just curiosity.

Meanwhile, Geordi'd given up on the tantrum. I guess being hauled kicking and screaming down the track, then landing hard on the gravel with six and a half feet of Jason squashing him, was enough excitement for one morning. He accepted Jason's help up but walked the rest of the way under his own steam.

I had a hard time not running. I kept looking over my shoulder, and when we hit the main drag, every person we passed, and every honking car made me jump. Jason shot me some odd looks, but mercifully didn't say anything. Probably because he didn't want to worry Geordi.

As it was, I speed-walked. Jason had no trouble keeping up, but Geordi's short legs meant he had to jog. When I got to the pier, and it was obvious no one—or no *thing*—was in hot pursuit, I relaxed somewhat. I still had no clue what exactly I'd done back there, but I wasn't about to look a gift like that in the mouth.

Jason gave Geordi a push up the gangplank, watching until he was safely on the boat. Then he leaned against a nearby joist, breathing hard. "Jesus, Hyacinth. What's the rush?"

His tone was casual, but I detected an edge to it, like something about the incident upset him. Probably me and my crazy-ass flight from a harmless farmer.

But I can be casual, too, when it's called for. "We need to get going."

He pressed his lips together, then drew in a deep breath and exhaled slowly. "Hyacinth. We have all day to get to Turkey, and we still need supplies. What was that about? Would another thirty minutes have made that much difference?"

Crap. I'd forgotten about the supplies. I scanned the dock, then the marina beyond. More and more people filled the sidewalks, some looking like tourists, others like natives, and not one of them wearing a t-shirt proclaiming, *I'm a Demon!*

I turned back to Jason. "I don't know. It might."

His jaw clenched. I could almost see his temple throb. "Going to tell me why?"

"I'd rather not."

He opened his mouth. Clamped it shut. Ground out, "Fine. But I still need to refuel. There's a pump on the dock. I'll drive the boat over, and we can leave when I'm done." He pointed to a service building at the end of the marina. "There's a convenience store in there. We at least need bottled water and snacks." His gaze travelled over my body. "Get yourself some meat."

Then he turned and stomped toward the boat.

I hurried over to the store and bought over-priced supplies, including some pepperoni sticks. I told myself they were for Geordi, but even I didn't believe me. When I came back, Jason was still refueling, but I noticed Eric sitting on the end of the dock, propped against a low rail.

His back was to me, gaze focused out to sea. He still looked pretty bad, but on dry land, at least he wasn't as green. If he could float above the deck, it might solve the whole motion-of-the-ocean problem, but apparently, it didn't work that way.

Maybe Michael would know what was wrong, or at least, why Eric was still here. But if I told him, what would he do?

In the first place, he'd discover my newfound affinity for dead folks. If I knew one thing for sure it was that Michael had his own agenda. Maybe my "talent" wouldn't interest him, or maybe it would. Until I knew more, I didn't want to advertise it.

The second outcome of telling Michael was that, probably, he'd whisk Eric off to wherever he was supposed to be, and that would be the end of it. I'd never see him again, unless we crossed paths after my own death became official. Right now, I couldn't honestly say I was ready to give him up. That may sound selfish, but I'd never been half-dead before. Having a friend on the Other Side was something I clung to as I tried to carve my way through my new, freakish existence. But if Michael could help Eric— could somehow heal him and make him whole again— did I have the right to seal his fate without at least asking what *he* wanted?

With a sigh aimed at my own dratted conscience, I moved to the pier next to him and sat on the edge, dangling my feet over the side. "How are you feeling?"

He didn't seem surprised by my presence, and I wondered if he knew I was there all along. "*Bon.* The *mal de mer* is better, although it may return when we are back on the boat."

"Good. And your wound?"

His lips thinned. "The same. It is nothing. Do not concern yourself."

"Obviously, that's not going to happen."

He held his torn shirt tightly closed. "If you are thinking to check it again, do not bother. It is just as bad, and there is just as little that you can do."

"Maybe I can't help. But…I might know someone who can."

He raised an eyebrow. "Who? Your *friend* over there?" With a slight jerk of his head he indicated the refueling station, where Jason was replacing the nozzle in the pump.

I glared at Eric, momentarily forgetting my noble purpose. "There you go again! Why do you keep referring to Jason like he's some kind of criminal? He's *not*." I paused. Eric was a cop, after all. "Is he…?"

Eric glanced at Jason, then pursed his lips. *"Ne te fâche pas.* I have no knowledge, personal or professional, that your friend is guilty of wrongdoing. But that does not mean he is *not* guilty, of something." He frowned, considering. "I do not know why, but I feel as though I have seen him before."

"Maybe he looks like someone you know. Don't cops meet tons of people all over the place? They must all run together in your mind."

"Perhaps." He didn't sound convinced, but he let it drop.

I cleared my throat. "What I started to tell you was that I have a…connection, of sorts, who might know something about your wound, or why you're still here."

He studied my face, and I felt heat creeping up my throat to my cheeks. "*Eh bien*. This is not a new acquaintance. Why have you not spoken of this before?"

"I don't really know if he can help." I broke from Eric's intent gaze and looked at my shorts, fiddling with the hem. "The thing is, he might…take you away…if I tell him about you."

Eric waited, and when I didn't speak, he reached out and gently lifted my chin. His eyes searched mine for a moment. Then he lightly brushed his fingers over my jaw and down to the base of my throat. It took everything I had not to lean into his caress.

He inclined his head once, as if acknowledging some unspoken communication. "*Bon.* We will not speak of this again."

Instantly I felt like I'd said or done the wrong thing. "But your wound—what if it never gets better? What if it gets *worse*? If I can help you—"

He cupped the back of my neck, his fingers warm, his touch light. "I do not know why I am here, but I know this. There is a purpose for everything. It was not a mistake that you were there when I died, and it is not a mistake that you are with me now, like an angel, to guide me." His lips curved. "I like that. My angel—*mon ange.*"

I choked at the irony of *me* being anyone's guardian anything. "I'm hardly an angel! And as for guiding a dead guy, isn't that like the blind leading the blind?"

His fingers stilled. "Is there something you wish to share with me?"

Me and my big mouth. Luckily, the boat pulled up next to the dock and Jason called out, "Hyacinth! We're ready—let's go!"

Eric gave an aggrieved sigh and released me. "Saved by the boat, of all things."

Jason had looked away again, so I stood, wiping sweaty palms on my thighs, then held out my hand to Eric. He grimaced but accepted the help, and I hauled him up. When I would have let go, he instead pulled me to him, our forms almost touching. He gazed down at me, expression unreadable.

"Mon ange. I have been *un OPJ* for many years. As you say, I have met many people, good, bad, and all that is in-between. There is one lesson I have seen them all learn, over and over. The truth will always come out, whether we want it to or not."

He brought my hand to his lips and gently kissed my knuckles. The heat of his mouth warmed my fingers, tingled up my arm, then spread through my chest and up my throat. His gaze travelled over my face, and his eyes darkened. Then he dropped my hand and stepped back.

"Be careful what you withhold—and what you seek to learn. And…from whom."

He turned and headed up the gangplank, which Jason had set out. There was no doubt Eric meant to set my blood on fire with that light kiss. But were his words meant as a warning *to me*—or *about* Jason?

Or both?

****

Back on the open sea, Jason busied himself at the helm, while Geordi sat on the deck near the stern, coloring other sections of the newspaper. Eric sat close by, but since Geordi obviously couldn't see him, I let it pass and went to join Jason at the front.

He glanced up as I sat next to him. "So. Going to tell me what all that was about?"

I thought about maintaining my pretense of ignorance, then opted for partial-truth. "I'm not sure. When I saw that guy coming from the stones, I just felt like we had to leave."

Jason flipped on the auto-pilot, then leaned back in the captain's seat. "That's it? You had a hunch, so we ran?" He paused, searching my face. "From what, exactly? A Maltese farmer?"

I tried not to squirm, then had a sudden inspiration. "The Dioguardis." Jason's eyes narrowed, so I hurried on. "You said yourself, they have an empire. When I saw that guy, he reminded me of"—I searched my memories of Nick's family for someone plausible—"of Nick's cousin. I think his name is Paolo."

The color drained from Jason's face. "You think that guy was…this Paolo character? How—when, exactly—did you meet him?"

"At Lily's wedding. It's not important. It probably wasn't him. The point is, the Dioguardis could be anywhere, even here. And he *looked* like them—tall, dark-haired, and mean."

"Even the Dioguardis can't *all* fit that description—and there are millions of non-*mafiosi* who *do*."

"I know. I said it was just a feeling." I nodded

toward Geordi, willing Jason to understand. "I *have* to protect him. I can't pick apart every hunch I get, I just have to do what I think is right."

"Fair enough." He stared at me intently, then seemed to make up his mind about something. "Hyacinth—I felt something, too. Back there at the stones."

I got the sense he'd tossed a ball in my court and was waiting to see what I'd do with it. Had he felt the energy field after all? What if he hadn't, and I let slip too much? I said cautiously, "You did? What?"

"I don't know exactly—like maybe that guy was threatening us. I know it sounds weird, but then, there's a lot about this trip of yours I don't understand." He hesitated, shifting in his seat. "And then, just as fast, it was gone. Like it had been blocked. Did you feel anything like that...?"

Could he mean the energy field? Was he saying he knew I'd deflected it, and asking how I'd done it? Too bad for him, because *I* didn't know. I might be half-dead, able to hear screaming rocks and see dead people, but I didn't have any *other* special powers. Did I?

"Hyacinth," Jason said slowly. "It might help if you let me in. Tell me what really happened. It's okay. You can trust me."

The truth was, I *wanted* to trust him. But even more, I wanted to have imagined the energy field, and to blame my reaction to the farmer on my own made-up excuse of thinking the Dioguardis had found us. That the Dioguardis would turn out to be the lesser of my two evils wasn't something I'd expected in a million years.

I opened my mouth, but no sound came out, and I

shook my head helplessly.

His shoulders sagged. "Fine. Have it your way. But there's one thing you *did* notice, whether you realize it or not. Ask yourself, why did Geordi call that pile of rocks a church?"

The question surprised me. "I…don't know. I thought maybe you said something, about Malta or the ancient cultures or something."

He shook his head. "I told him there were caves, but I never said anything about using them for religious rites. And even if I had, he's seven. Why would he call it a church?"

I started to protest, then stopped. He was right. Why *would* Geordi make that leap? If he'd heard me talk shop before, he might call it a "burial mound," or even "standing stones," but not a church. More to convince myself than Jason, I said, "I'm sure he was using his imagination."

"Maybe."

He didn't sound convinced. He looked at Geordi, still coloring in the back, and I thought I saw worry in his expression. Jason was a good person—I was sure of it, despite Eric's suspicions.

He turned and caught me staring. As though reading my mind, he said, "It's okay, you know. I'll keep you safe. Both of you."

"Safe?" I couldn't stop the note of hysteria creeping into my voice. "I don't know if I'll ever feel safe again."

"Hyacinth, I promise you—everything will be okay."

He stood and opened his arms, and I went to him. God help me, but I needed comfort, too. Jason was here. He'd thrown his lot in with me, asking almost no questions beyond what I wanted to do next. Maybe because of whatever weird spark I'd felt with Eric, or because all the stress hormones in my body reduced me to that most elemental level of "must procreate and keep the species going"—I don't know. But Jason's arms felt good. Really…good.

Partly, it was because he was *alive*. I so needed that right now, a contact with the Living—like I needed Eric to be my contact with the Dead. I needed Jason's solid strength, to remind me of what was good and decent about the world. Between Lily being gone, and knowing I had to leave Geordi, and my worry over Eric, it seemed like Death had taken over my life.

Whatever Jason's secrets, he was a living, breathing person, whose heart beat strong under my cheek, whose hands slid up my back to cradle my head against his broad chest, and I started to relax into him, feeling so secure, so…familiar.

Except…he wasn't.

I broke away. This was too weird. I was too raw.

"Hyacinth…"

I moved away. "No. Don't ask me to talk right now, or I might ask why you're here."

"I told you. It's because—"

"You're afraid of the Dioguardis," I finished. "I know. You've said. But that isn't the whole story—I *know* it's not. You know something about them, something other than what I've told you about Lily and Geordi."

Instead of the expected denial, he stared at me for a beat. "It's not what you think."

"Isn't it? That's funny, because I have *no* idea *what*

to think."

He turned away and shoved a hand through his hair, making it stand up, thick and black, all over his head. He looked like a sleek, black-haired lion, shaking out its mane to intimidate an enemy, and I pushed down another bubble of hysteria.

He nodded pointedly toward Geordi. "We can't talk about this here."

"I know. I'm sorry. I'm just afraid—that the Dioguardis might get him. And they might hurt me. Or worse…they might hurt you."

He said nothing for a long time. Then he turned away and sat again in the captain's seat. "Well, if there are Dioguardis on Malta, I'd like to put a whole lot of ocean between us and them as fast as possible. For *your* sake—and Geordi's."

He angled the joystick down, causing the boat to lurch forward, then settled it into a faster speed. I didn't disagree that escaping the Dioguardis was high priority. I just didn't know if the ocean was big enough to stop the demons from getting me first.

But I did recognize a reprieve when I saw it, so I turned and fled to the back of the boat. Even if I wanted to question Jason more, I couldn't now. It was a wonder we hadn't scared Geordi with our raised voices. I glanced at Eric, but he sat with his eyes closed, asleep, or pretending to be. Had he seen me in Jason's arms? What if he had? If he'd heard us, what did he think of Jason's questions about the stones, or his refusal to answer my own questions?

Geordi was still coloring, so I dropped down on the deck beside him, to find he'd drawn a picture of SpongeBob on the business section. Whatever he'd meant about the "church," Geordi was still relatively sane and transparent, compared to the other men in my life. He must be feeling safer—that had been a bona fide tantrum he'd thrown at the stones. I didn't know whether to be glad, or sad, that his grief had progressed.

No thanks to me. Damn it all—I could be his parent, and his Fun Aunt, too. I chose a pink crayon and began adding a chubby starfish to the page. Geordi watched, then wordlessly scooted closer until our legs touched. I leaned down and kissed his earth-scented dark hair, and we set to work, creating a cartoon world where the biggest threat was a tiny sea organism trying to steal Mr. Krabs' secret recipe.

No mafia, no demons, no ghosts or men leading double lives.

It was heavenly. And I wanted to be here forever. Every minute my resolve grew stronger. Geordi didn't need "a good family"—he needed *me*.

And I needed him. I wouldn't leave him. Ever.

Even if it meant breaking my promise to the Angel of Death.

Chapter Twelve

*"Some men are alive simply because
it is against the law to kill them."*
					~*E.W. Howe (1853-1937)*

Next morning, I awoke early in our hotel in
Denizli, Turkey. We'd made good time on the second
leg of our voyage, arriving by early evening in
Marmaris, where we had a stroke of luck. The port was
one Vadim had frequented when schlepping his
"wares," and the harbormaster recognized the boat.
When I told him Vadim had died, he was very
sympathetic, and said we could leave the boat in
Vadim's slip, indefinitely. Jason offered to pay him, but
he said Vadim had done him enough favors, and he was
honored to help us.

He also directed us to his cousin's car lot, where
we picked up a nondescript junker whose main selling
point was its cheapness. We loaded everything into the
battered trunk, climbed in—Eric included—and headed
inland, reaching Denizli two hours later at about ten
o'clock. Geordi and I were so tired, the transition from
car to hotel is a blur. Mercifully, Jason handled
everything. Despite our spat on the boat, I was starting
to care less and less what his secrets were, so long as he
kept knowing what to do. I sure as hell didn't.

Except now that we'd arrived, I *had* to figure it out.

Unless somehow Jason could hear the rock also, which seemed too far-fetched even for my current situation. But he had found us cheap rooms—one for him, another for me and Geordi, connecting bathroom between—and ordered me to get some rest. Which helped.

It was barely light, the sun still below the barren mountains to the east. The clock said six, but already hot air wafted through the open window, the noise of traffic and industry outside somewhat reassuring. I was here, now. I didn't have to have it *all* figured out. But I did need to pee, and I hadn't showered since before I died. I got out of bed and went to brush my teeth, wondering where Eric was. He'd mumbled something about taking care of himself and stumbled away. I couldn't stop him in front of Jason, and the hard truth was, I was helpless to help him, anyway.

I bent over the sink to rinse and spit, and a deep voice behind me said, "Progress?"

I shrieked, and my head snapped up to find Michael gazing over my shoulder at me in the mirror. His massive form took up nearly the entire tiny bathroom. My heart hammered like a gong, and all I could think was, *Thank God, I slept in my tank top and shorts.*

"You scared the crap out of me!"

"Apologies." He didn't sound like he meant it, but just then Jason's voice came from outside his connecting door, and he rattled the knob.

"Hyacinth? You okay in there?"

"Fine!" I called. "I, uh, saw a bug. A big one."

Michael chuckled, and Jason said, "Want me to kill it for you?"

"Of course not!"

"Sorry. Rescue it then—I'm great with a water glass and a piece of cardboard."

"No! It's, uh, fine. Really. I'm going to shower now."

"Oh. Okay." He paused, and I waited, breath held, until he said, "I'll go get us some food. If you're sure you're okay."

"Positive."

I didn't let my breath back out until I heard him walk across the room, then open and close his outer door. Either he'd slept in his clothes, or he'd been awake longer than I had.

Meanwhile, Michael simply stood there, watching me. In his warrior getup, with his heavy, sharpened blades and *objets de guerre*, it was unnerving, to say the least.

"What are you *doing* here?"

"Checking on my investment."

"Couldn't you have picked some place larger—and more private?"

He lifted a muscled shoulder, leather straps creaking. "My schedule is tight."

I leaned over and splashed cold water on my face, then reached for a towel. "Well, you should've waited. We just got here—I don't have anything to report."

"That you arrived at all is impressive."

"Gee, thanks."

His grin flashed in the mirror. Not exactly unpleasant, but definitely the hard smile of someone who'd bested many foes. More a baring of teeth than anything else. He examined me, his gaze travelling over my body, then lifting to linger on my chest.

I folded my arms over my breasts and cleared my throat. "Seen enough?"

This time the smile was decidedly wicked, and I thought the sainthood with which he was wrongly attributed might be an actual misnomer, not just a technicality.

Michael lifted his chin in the direction of my boobs. "Your wound is healed. Not only on the outside." He frowned in a clinical way, as though puzzled by me. "Extraordinary. By all accounts, you should not look this good."

"Gee, *thanks.*"

His laugh roared out, and I shushed him, afraid he'd wake Geordi. For that matter, maybe Jason had only pretended to leave. He could be at the bathroom door listening to us, or hiding below the open window. All I needed was for him to break the door down and find me talking to Michael, with his wild hair and wilder knives and axes. Worse, maybe Jason wouldn't see Michael, and would think I was crazy after all. He'd probably decide *I* wasn't a fit parent for Geordi. At least the Dioguardis didn't converse with the dead after they killed them.

"Child," Michael said, "I meant *well*—not attractive. But I am sure you knew that."

He sat on the edge of the tub, and I relaxed. A little. He was still the Angel of Death and technically, my boss. I'd never really had a boss before. During my brief stints legitimately helping at digs or working in museums, my "bosses" were more like teachers, showing me how to identify and care for the artifacts, and determine their value. This was different. I pretty much had one task to do, and Michael'd made it clear I got one chance or I was out.

His gigantic hand reached to touch my chest, well above my breasts, but still, and I swatted him away. Unfortunately, the bathroom was so minuscule, I couldn't escape.

"Extraordinary," he muttered again. "And you are not tired? Weak? Run-down?"

"No," I snapped, then forced myself to take a breath. After all, he was the only one with *any* knowledge that might help me. "There is one thing I've noticed—I'm unbelievably hungry. Yesterday, I ate meat, and it helped. But I'm still ravenous." As though to prove the point, my stomach rumbled.

"That would make sense. I am sure you have drawn your own conclusions." He thought a moment. "Death is an end to appetite. In the next world, all earthly needs vanish, but particularly your appetites. Not only for food—all hungers. For knowledge, power, love. Whatever cravings you had in Life are gone in Death, fulfilled in ways you cannot imagine."

"Okay. What does that mean for me, right now?"

"I am not sure. Perhaps rebirth re-awakens appetites you should have lost, had you stayed dead."

"Great. So instead of normal hunger, now I'll have extra-special rebirth hunger. But will I have it *all* the time? And will I have to keep eating meat?"

"Perhaps. Or perhaps it will fade." He shrugged. "I do not know much more than you. But…I could guess that hunger for meat is not the only appetite you will find reawakened."

I recalled my sudden physical responses to both Eric and Jason. Great. Not only would I crave red meat all the time, it looked like I'd crave sex, too.

As though reading my thoughts, Michael flashed another wicked grin. "Child, do not attribute *every* feeling you have to being reborn. You are still you, after all."

Oddly, that was the one thing he could have said that reassured me. "Thanks."

Except it meant I might have the hots for a dead cop, or a live...whoever Jason was. Bartender cum Babysitting Boy Scout? Given my situation, Eric seemed the better option, but what did I know? He could vanish at any time—maybe he already had—and in any case, it was unlikely we were destined to spend eternity in the same location. As a medal-earning cop he was sure to head up, while heaven only knew—ha!—where I'd go.

"Child, is there something else?"

I hesitated. Despite Eric telling me it was okay not to bring Michael into it, I couldn't quite reconcile his suffering with my conscience. I settled on, "It's about my wound. If I hadn't come back, what would've happened to it? Would it have healed, or stayed that way forever?"

Michael's eyes narrowed, though whether in thought or suspicion, I couldn't tell. "In Death, earthly needs disappear, including the need to physically heal. For most souls, when they arrive at my door, all physical states return to their ideal form."

"Meaning...what? We all become children again? Or twenty-year-olds? Or...?"

"Whatever is ideal for each individual. A man in his nineties may feel that is the best time of his life. Another may return to a state closer to middle age or younger. It depends."

"What if there's a…delay? Before passing through."

Hopefully he thought I really was asking for myself, but in the end, it didn't matter, for he said, "I do not know. The souls who stay on Earth—I do not see them. I barely have time to sort the souls I am supposed to help. Speaking of which, I must be going."

He rose, leather and weapons creaking and clanking with the effort. "Have a care, Hyacinth. As I've said, the Rousseaux are very, very dangerous." He turned toward the open window as though planning to leave that way—the thing was at most ten inches wide—then turned back. "I almost forgot—I remembered something that may be of help to you. The Rousseaux will perform the ritual to send the rock to Satan on September the fifth."

"The *fifth?* That's two days from now!"

"And a half, yes. The ritual will occur at sunset. That is plenty of time for someone of your talents to find the rock and bring it back. Perhaps it will help to have a deadline."

A deadline? It wasn't like I'd been wasting my time. "You could've told me sooner."

"It has been many centuries since the last shard was found. I truly just remembered."

"But why the fifth? What's so special about that date?"

The warrior grin returned. "Child. You really should go to Mass more often. Satan is not without a sense of humor."

He wasn't going to tell me. Probably figured knowing the cutoff was all that mattered.

"What if I can't find it by then?"

"Then you will return with me and discover which door is yours. Perhaps you will meet Satan then. Or perhaps not."

With that, he was gone. Not through the window—at least, not that I saw. He just sort of vanished, but it did seem as though the window glowed brightly for a moment. Of course, that could have been the sun finally cresting the mountains.

I didn't know how far the market was, but I didn't think it would take Jason long to get the food. And if nothing else, Geordi would be waking up. I took the fastest shower ever—it felt *so* good to be clean—and got dressed in another tank top and shorts combo. I pulled my damp hair into a ponytail, then went into Jason's room to wait, leaving both bathroom doors ajar, in case Geordi woke and wondered where I was.

Despite being a grave-robber-turned-fence, I clearly don't have a sneaky mentality when it comes to my friends. I'd been sitting on Jason's bed for a full five minutes before it occurred to me to search his room.

Duh.

I still didn't know when he'd be back, but now I had five minutes less than if I'd been on the ball, so I hopped off the bed and set to work. He'd taken the time to unpack, which was more than I'd done. The top drawer of the small dresser contained a wad of cash, his socks, and underwear—boxer-briefs, if you're curious. Shorts and t-shirts were below that, with a couple pairs of jeans in the bottom. His sneakers sat neatly on the floor next to the dresser, so he must be wearing his sandals, and a few toiletries littered the top, next to a good-sized vase filled with flowers, provided by the hotel. My room had one, too.

Also like mine, his room had a small wooden desk, empty, with accompanying chair. Bedside table with lamp. Worn throw rug, decorative shelf, and... That was it. No journal detailing his nefarious exploits, no second—third?—passport with yet another name on it. Nothing. He'd taken his wallet, of course, so I couldn't check and see if the name on his credit cards was Jason Jones, or if he had an American driver's license.

Now that I thought about it, I didn't really know what his native citizenship was. I *assumed* he was from the States, and he'd let me believe it, but I could be wrong. He acted like an American, but then, he'd acted like a lot of things that now seemed iffy.

I sat on the bed and glanced around the room again. There had to be *something*—some clue to his identity, or why he was in my life. I'm not a big fan of coinky-dinks. Like Eric, I think stuff happens for a reason, and the simple fact that Jason had shown up *right* when I needed him—when Lily left Nick, and then Vadim died—seemed cosmically improbable.

One thing was certain. His room at least was neat and bare.

Too bare...

I might travel light, but I still drop my dirty laundry on the floor or toss stuff on a chair to be dealt with later. Jason had been careful to put things away. Or rather, careful *not* to leave anything out in plain view.

Quickly I jumped up and ran my hands under the pillows and as far under the mattress as I could reach. Jason's arms were much longer than mine, so it took some wiggling, but at last I found it, tucked between the box spring and the thin mattress.

Considerably bigger than a pea, it was a gun. And though I'm no expert, it looked like a *nice* gun. A hefty automatic, and I'd bet my last Phrygian vase it was loaded.

"What the hell are you doing?" Jason asked from behind me, and I jumped and whirled to find him in the doorway holding a bag of food, looking big and mad.

I've found, when caught doing something wrong, that a little self-righteous indignation goes a long way. *"Me?* What about *you*—what about *this?"* I waved the gun, careful not to point it at him. I'm not *that* dumb.

Jason wasn't having any. He kicked the door shut and set the food on the desk—I smelled fresh bread—*yum*—before he advanced on me. "Hyacinth—put the gun down."

"No." I scooted away, but the room wasn't very big, and I wound up with my back to the wall pretty fast.

He stopped in front of me, blue eyes flashing. He'd shaved this morning, and I could see every line of his smooth, hard jaw, including the vein pulsing just below where it clenched.

"Have you ever handled a gun before?"

"No. Have you?"

"Hyacinth."

"Don't give me that!" I snapped, my nerves and exhaustion getting the better of me. "You obviously aren't the Jason I thought I knew for the last six months! You look like him—you sound like him—*but you aren't him.* You hotwire cars, get fake passports, and know *something* about the Dioguardis. Who the hell are you? Is Jason Jones your real name? Damn it!" With my free hand, I poked him in the chest, punctuating the words. "Tell. Me. Who. You. Are."

Jason didn't say anything for several seconds, just glared down at me. He had a lot of nerve. *I* wasn't the one who'd been lying about my identity all this time.

Okay, I hadn't told Jason *everything*. But I'd given him my real name, and a close approximation of my business practices. Which made me the better person. Right?

Finally, he blew out a breath and reached for the gun. I let him take it. I mean, I really don't know how to fire one—does an automatic need to be cocked first? Or is that only revolvers? Or is there such a thing as an automatic revolver?—and he was bigger and stronger than me. At least I'd save a little dignity if I pretended to hand it over on my own.

He checked the magazine—is that what it's called?—then set it carefully on the dresser. Then he walked back to where I still leaned against the wall, my brief spurt of adrenaline gone. It's a wonder Geordi hadn't woken, with all my yelling. But then, he was one and a half rooms away, and the concealing sounds of traffic outside increased as the day got under way.

"Hyacinth," Jason said quietly, arms loose at his sides, like he was trying to look nonthreatening. "I'm not going to lie to you. God knows, I've hated lying to you all this time. But I can't answer your questions yet."

"Why?" So maybe I had a little adrenaline left. "Damn it, Jason! People are after me, trying to take Geordi, and suddenly, you know how to do all the exact stuff we need, to escape, to hide, to *survive.* Anything we need, you get it done. How is that even *possible*?"

"Why are we in Turkey?" he countered. He

reached out and ran his thumb lightly over my neck, making my pulse jump before he dropped his hand. "Why did I touch your cold, dead body in that alley, thinking I'd lost you, and then see you alive and well thirty minutes later?"

Shit. I hate it when people use my own crap against me. What could I say? That whole death-and-rebirth thing was on my *Explain to Jason Someday* list, right below the chase-demons-and-steal-talking-rock thing.

"I know it doesn't make sense," he continued. "That's what you said to me. Remember? And then you asked me to trust you. Now I'm asking you to trust me. I promise, I'll make it up to you for all the lies. And some day, I'll tell you what you want to know."

He was awfully close, and awfully earnest, and I so-so wanted to believe that the only friend—the only *living* friend—I had was trustworthy.

"At least tell me you're one of the good guys."

I'd meant it as a joke, but he didn't give me the rah-rah answer I expected. Instead, he said, "It's…complicated. I can tell you that I will do everything in my power to keep you and Geordi safe from the Dioguardis, and the Rousseaux, and anyone else who tries to hurt you. But when you learn the truth…you may not want me to."

His words made no sense, but they weren't what I focused on now. His body was close. And the emotion in his eyes—the pain, the fear when he'd talked about me being dead, and now something more, something hot and urgent and unleashed—was enough to scorch me from the inside out, until I smoldered like a peat fire, burning toward the surface. It was hopeless. I was going to believe him, even though he'd revealed absolutely nothing.

"You'll tell me everything?" I managed breathlessly, lost in the dark depths of his gaze.

He leaned in closer, his mouth hovering over mine as he breathed, "*Everything…*"

And then he kissed me.

Chapter Thirteen

*"But Satan now is wiser than of yore,
and tempts by making rich, not making poor."*
~*Alexander Pope (1688-1744)*

Jason's mouth was soft but insistent, not forcing anything but letting me know in no uncertain terms he wanted this, maybe had for a long time. He tasted like mint and something else, something hot and *him*, and I don't know if it was being reborn or what, but my senses were on overdrive. The smell of him, of fresh, clean *male,* filled my nostrils. My body thrummed, and all the reasons why getting involved with anyone—with him, especially—was a stupid idea went right out of my brain, carried away on a wave of sex hormones flooding south.

I did manage to pull back and ask the first question that popped into my head. "You're not a...cop, are you?"

"No," he said, and kissed me harder.

At least I hadn't brought *two* of them along.

I pressed into him, urging him on. Even that wasn't enough. I pushed my fingers through the dark mane of his hair, twisting, pulling, walking us back until my legs hit the bed and we fell on it, his body trapping mine. He dragged my arms over my head with one hand, then trailed hot kisses over my jaw and down the side of my throat. He pushed my top up and palmed my breast, and I arched into him. He was awfully close to the good part, when I heard the unmistakable sound of a seven-year-old boy emptying his bladder into the toilet.

Merde! I pushed at Jason's chest. His haze of lust must have been worse than mine. It took another shove before he stopped teasing my earlobe with his tongue and looked at me, his expression almost comically confused.

"Geordi," I stage-whispered.

That did the trick. He leapt off me, looked hastily around the room, and then went to sit at the desk—lap tucked safely out of sight—while I fixed my tank top and my ponytail. By the time Geordi finished washing up, Jason and I looked normal again.

I glanced over to find him staring at me, eyes dark and hungry. Well, mostly normal.

The bathroom door was ajar, and Geordi pushed it open uncertainly, then ran to me when I opened my arms. He didn't say anything, just held on tight, and I squeezed back, all my raging hormones instantly replaced by motherly ones. Geordi might not have been born of my womb, but I couldn't love him more if he was.

I cast an apologetic look over his head at Jason, then pulled back and said to Geordi, "Morning, sweetie. You hungry?"

Jason stood—nothing noticeably out of proportion—and rummaged through the food bag, coming up with apples, bread, cheese and milk. He brought them to the bed, and Geordi and I spread them out while Jason—smart man—went to the dresser and hid the gun in his underwear drawer. Then he joined us and we dived in, the act of picnicking on a bed tickling Geordi's fancy enough that by the end of the meal, he was giggling and rough-housing with Jason.

The food wasn't as satisfying as yesterday's meat, but there *had* to be another way to get the iron I needed. And if I ate dairy, eggs, and fish, I'd be good on the protein part. Still, I felt like a vampire, suppressing my unnatural cravings while my energy slowly drained, knowing at some point I'd have to satisfy my thirst for animal blood. Not yet, though.

I glanced at the travel clock and saw it was seven-thirty. Time to get moving. Only I had no idea where to start. I also wondered even more where Eric had gone, and if he would come back. At least he'd missed my almost having sex with Jason.

Now that the moment had passed, I'd remembered the number one reason I shouldn't sleep with Jason or anyone else: I was dead, here on a temporary visa. The physical attraction was bad enough, but I'd seen real emotion in Jason's eyes. While I could maybe justify the sex, I couldn't mislead him into thinking I was in it for the long haul.

Prior to this, I'd never really been accountable to anyone but myself. Now I had Geordi, Jason, and Eric, none of whom would be in danger, if not for me. Never mind that Jason and Eric had invited themselves along. It was still on me if Demons from the Last Circle of Hell tortured them into oblivion. Eric, being dead, maybe had less claim on my conscience. But Jason was a few years younger than me—at least, I *thought* he was—and I felt older by the minute.

I watched him, rolling on the bed in a tickle fight with Geordi. Whatever his secrets, they must be huge if he thought I'd ditch him for them. Even so, he deserved better than being burdened with an undead woman and her mostly dead entourage. Still, after I was gone, maybe he'd keep in touch with Geordi. The thought heartened me, inasmuch as I could be heartened, knowing I couldn't "keep in touch" with Geordi myself.

"Okay, guys," I said, hoping my cheeriness didn't sound forced. "Time to break it up."

Jason let Geordi claim the last tickle and "win" the fight, then sat up and saluted. "Aye, aye, captain. What next?"

"There's a ruin east of here—Colossae. I'd like to check it out."

"Going to tell me why?"

"Nope."

"Okey-doke."

"Did you gas up the car?" He looked offended, so I said, "Don't suppose you have a flashlight lying around."

His eyes narrowed. He knew damn well I'd searched his stuff. "No. But there's a shop not too far from here. I'm sure they'll have one."

"All righty, then. Let's go!" I said, and Geordi hopped off the bed. "But first, clothes." Geordi looked down at his jammies and giggled. I steered him toward our room. "We can't go exploring in our jammies, now can we?"

Geordi ran through the bathroom, and Jason looked at me sideways. "I can think of a number of things I'd like to explore, both in and out of our jammies."

And just like that, about half my good intentions went out the window. "Stop it," I said under my breath. He moved toward me, and I backed away into the bathroom. "Geordi," I called, escaping out the other side, "wear your sneakers. We're going to do some hiking!"

Behind me, I heard Jason blow out a breath, but he let me go.

In our room, Geordi was already dressed. "Tata Hyhy, can we get sugary slugs today?"

He sounded so hopeful, and I fought down the lump in my throat. "Of course, honey."

I should've tried harder before now, but everything had been so crazy. If apricot delight would cheer him up, then I'd damn well find some.

In ten minutes, we had our hiking shoes on, sunscreen slathered everywhere, the bag of food, a map, and the car and hotel keys. We locked our doors and headed down to the street. I checked for any sign of Eric, but there was none, and I experienced a niggling pang of loss.

Even though he was dead, completely not my responsibility, and a cop to boot, I couldn't help it—I missed him. Missed his wry asides and having someone I could discuss death with. Obviously, he had his own path to follow, and if he chose to leave me, that was none of my business. At least, that's what I told myself as I tried to focus on the task at hand.

Denizli is a large city of roughly half a million people, with a booming industrial feel to it. According to Vadim, who came here regularly, the smog in winter is terrible, but now in the summer, it wasn't too bad. Our hotel was near the heart of the city, and palm trees lined the street, looking cheerful and tropical, but providing little protection against the Aegean sun.

We walked first to the shop, which had a nice

selection of flashlights, and where we also stocked up on water bottles and a digital camera with more memory than our phones. Jason didn't ask why I wanted it, just forked over the cash, and I thought if he was trying to buy my gratitude, he was doing an excellent job. I also picked up a guide book and some stuff for Geordi to do in the car, and while I was at it, grabbed sunglasses for me and Geordi, and three matching Indiana Jones-issue hats to combat the lack of shade trees. There was a snack aisle, but it mainly consisted of candy bars and chips, so I promised Geordi we'd look for "sugary slugs" later, and he seemed satisfied.

Jason quirked an eyebrow at us. "Sugary *slugs*?"

I winked at a giggling Geordi, then said to Jason, "What can I say? He loves to eat his bugs." Jason, bless him, pretended to be horrified, which only made Geordi giggle harder.

We paid for our purchases, then retrieved the car and headed east up the mountain. Though it was barely nine o'clock, the sun was merciless, and the car didn't have AC. Luckily, we didn't have far to go. I'd decided the first thing was to check out the site where the rock came from. I didn't think the Rousseaux were there already, but I wanted to get the lay of the land, in case I couldn't find them before the fifth. Plus, it might give me a clue to their current location.

Colossae is twenty kilometers east of Denizli near the town of Honaz, on a mountain of the same name. There's also Honaz Stream—formerly the Lycus River—to the north. The guidebook didn't have much on Colossae, but it did clear up a few things. For one, in Biblical times, the site was a sanctuary, dedicated to

Michael the Archangel. For another, the text said that Satan's followers had once tried to destroy said sanctuary by diverting water from the Lycus at it. But Michael sent a lightning bolt which split the rock slab and rerouted the river, away from the church, while simultaneously sanctifying its waters.

So, one mystery solved. I still didn't know why Michael or Satan coveted the leftover rock shards, but it was a start. If only I'd focused more on Christian artifacts back in my grave robbing days, but sadly, I'd been more interested in the Egyptians. Ask me anything about King Tut's mummified cats, and I'm your gal. But who specifically annoyed Satan and why? No idea.

The drive only took fifteen minutes. Partly, this was because Jason handled the junker like a race car, and partly, it was due to an apparent lack of Turkish speed limits. I glanced at Geordi in the back, but he grinned from ear to ear, so I crossed my fingers and prayed until we pulled up at Colossae.

I don't know what I expected, but for a religious site, it seemed pretty neglected. A grassy hillside sloped up to a flat area that, from here, looked empty and unkempt. There wasn't even a parking lot, or a fence.

Jason pulled up on the side of the road, and we got out and walked up the mound. At the top, he shot me a dubious look. *"This* is why you came to Turkey?"

I could see his point. Whatever city was here in ancient times had been destroyed and buried, several times over, by a series of earthquakes. No one had excavated it, because it held nothing worth excavating. I'd never asked Vadim exactly where his last catch originated, but likely it came from somewhere nearby, not from Colossae itself.

The entire site was oblong, roughly thirty meters wide by a bit longer, covered in rocky dirt and low-lying grass. A path edged the top, affording a view of the surrounding countryside: fields and meadows, pine-dotted hills, and more mountains in the distance. It reminded me a lot of the Sierra Foothills in California, which I'd visited once before I left the States for Europe.

Geordi took off across the mound in search of bugs, and Jason said, "So, what are we looking for?"

"I'm not sure. Maybe a way inside?"

"Want to tell me why?"

"Not especially."

He considered me for a minute, chewing his lip, and I had a sudden flash of his mouth hot on mine, hand gripping my wrists, palm cupping my breast. I shivered, then looked quickly away. What the hell was wrong with me? It wasn't like I was twelve, and he was my first crush.

Finally, he said, "Tell me why you want inside this hill, and I'll answer one question."

I jerked my gaze back to his. "The truth?"

"I already told you, I'm not going to lie anymore. I hated that part—hated that the person you thought you knew wasn't me." His gaze travelled over my face, as though memorizing it. "And I hate that, when all this is done, you're going to hate me."

Seconds passed while I thought it over. Did I *want* to know his secrets? Or, to paraphrase Eric, should I be careful what I wished for? Would the truth help or hinder me in the long run?

In the end, I couldn't make myself believe that whatever Jason had done was that bad. Maybe I couldn't be with him, romantically, but I could let down my guard a little.

"Okay. I want to get inside because I'm looking for something. It might be here or else nearby." I hesitated. Screw it—he should know what we were up against. "It has to do with the Rousseaux. They might be nearby, also."

His face blanched, and his gaze darted over the mound as though expecting Claude or Jacques to pop out from behind a clump of grass. *"Shit.* Are you crazy? They're—they tried to kill you—they *did* kill Nick— and your sister! I thought you wanted to get away from them!"

"I know. I'm sorry."

"And Geordi!" He looked to where Geordi lay on his tummy several meters away, happily covered in dirt, up close and personal with a new six-legged friend. Jason turned back to me. "Why the *hell* would you drag him here—right under their noses?"

This was going well. "You asked. I answered. My turn."

We glared at each other, until Jason ground out, "Fine. One for one. Go for it."

"Why do you carry a gun?"

A bleakness flashed in his eyes, at odds with his simple answer. "For protection."

"From whom?"

"People like the Dioguardis and the Rousseaux!"

Ouch. I waited, but he said nothing more.

"That's it? That's all you're going to say?"

"I answered the question, didn't I? Two of them, in fact."

"Fine. If that's how you want to play, then see how

much *I* tell *you* next time."

"Glad to hear there'll be a next time."

His gaze drifted to my mouth, and I turned away, half wishing Eric was there to balance things out. At least then I might not be so damn *aware* of Jason all the time. Even when, a few minutes later, he was yards away on the other side of the mound.

We did a thorough examination of the site, crisscrossing the top, walking the perimeter, crawling over the sides. It took two solid hours, and when we'd finished I concluded that, as near as I could tell, it was just a giant pile of dirt. If it had a secret entrance, it was very secret.

I took out the camera, stepping as far to one side as I could, and snapped enough shots to get the whole surface. Who knew what good it would do, but at least I'd have something to examine later. Then we all trucked back down the hill and walked the half kilometer north to the river.

It looked like a small, twisty little stream, nothing more. According to the guidebook, it originated on the eastern side of Honaz Mountain and flowed west, joining the Maeander River at Tripolis. Sure, it had some bends, and the map showed a bigger swerve south of the mound. But there was no cracked slab anywhere, no sign proclaiming, *The Rock Cometh from Here.*

Of course, during the thousands of years since Michael tossed down his lightning bolt, erosion had probably changed the landscape. Plus, there were more trees down here, making it harder to get the lay of the land. I suppressed a sigh and took more pictures while Jason showed Geordi how to skip stones. Then we sat on the bank and ate lunch.

For Geordi and himself, Jason had bought lamb kebabs, and they smelled heavenly. I could almost feel the spiced meat on my tongue, taste the juices on my fingers, but I swallowed the urge. I had told Jason I needed more iron though, so for me, he'd bought lentil stew and a *borek,* a thin rolled pastry filled with spinach and potatoes. Not as good as meat, but they helped. So did the bottles of *Zafer Gazozu*—fizzy lemonade—he produced from the padded cooler he'd brought.

My energy restored, I got out the map and moved farther up the bank to a break in the trees where the light was better. Unfortunately, after a few minutes of staring at the paper, nothing came to mind. I recognized many of the sites scattered across the region, but mainly through Vadim's stories, not from personal experience. I wondered yet again why Vadim kept the rock in the first place. I was sure it hadn't spoken to him—I got the impression, from the rock itself, that I was the first person who'd heard it in a long while.

Another question was, why September fifth? Michael might think I only needed to know *of* the date but knowing *why* would help me more. Too bad Eric wasn't around. He probably knew all the Saints' days and things like that. Lily took Geordi to Mass regularly, but from conversations with him, I knew he paid about as much attention as I did. Turkey is ninety-nine percent Muslim, so unless I found an internet cafe somewhere, that left Jason. We'd never discussed religion, but then, we'd never discussed a lot of things that now seemed important.

I glanced to where he and Geordi lay stretched out on the grassy bank, hands behind their heads, watching the clouds. I could practically see them digesting, their brains shutting down while their bodies made good use of all that meat. They even looked a bit alike, with their dark hair peeping from under their matching hats, sunglasses hiding their eyes. In a few years, I could see them with beers in their hands, burping and settling in for their naps.

I suppressed a wave of sadness. Maybe I could watch Geordi's progress to adulthood from wherever I went after this. I raised my gaze to the sky. Was Lily up there, watching him? Watching me? What did she think of all this? When Michael said earthly needs vanished, did he mean *all* earthly cares were forgotten, too?

I turned back to the map. I didn't have time for melancholy, or napping, or anything else. I had to figure out the next step, so I could stay here long enough to keep Geordi safe.

The map was a local one, produced for tourists wanting to explore the region's historic ruins and geographic wonders. It was hand-drawn, the places of interest linked by straight lines representing the roads between. The Turkish name of each site was written alongside an English translation, presumably to pique the interest of those who might not know that, for example, Denizli means "a locality with a sea." Which is bizarre, since it's landlocked, but what the hey?

Naturally, I'd been focusing on Colossae, assuming the Rousseaux were nearby. Since that wasn't working, I widened my net, looking at sites farther out. There was Charax to the east, and Antiocheia to the west, neither of which set off any lightbulb moments. To the south lay nothing at all for miles, until the sea, so as a last-ditch effort, I looked north and saw Pamukkale.

About twenty kilometers from here, it forms an

equilateral triangle with Denizli. I'd heard of it from Vadim—a natural wonder, made from mineral-rich hot springs leaking chalk down a series of cliffs. Over the centuries, the chalk hardened into limestone, which appears to cascade down the mountain like a frozen waterfall. Dotted throughout are terraces forming shallow pools of warm water, which is said to have healing properties. Over it all, fresh calcium carbonate makes the site a dazzling white, giving rise to its name—*Cotton Castle.*

I reached for my bag and pulled out the "map" Geordi'd drawn in Malta, before our run-in with the man at the stones—the stones that Geordi had called a "church"—and a chill shuddered down my spine. There it was, at the top of the crossword—the north—his very own white-crayon "Cotton Castle." And below that, to the south, the mountain with the stream that the "good man" split in two to save it from the "bad men."

I looked at Geordi, heart in my throat. He lay on his tummy, dipping his fingers in the "new" fork of the former Lycus River, watching water bugs dance across its surface.

How had he known to draw this? Why had he called the stones a church? Who—or *what*—had put either idea into his head?

In my current sphere of reference, there were only two possible interested parties: Michael, who I was pretty sure Geordi'd never met, and Satan, whose demons I knew he *had*.

I gathered the map and the drawing and shoved them in my bag, then ran back to my nephew, looking so peaceful and innocent in the bright-hot sun.

At least now I knew where to go next.

Chapter Fourteen

"Whoever rewards evil for good,
evil will not depart from their house."
~The Bible, Proverbs 17:13

What surprised me most about Pamukkale was the noise. When I'd thought *healing waters,* I'd subconsciously imagined *still waters.* Or at least, quiet ones. But the whole thing is formed by springs bubbling up, rushing over, roaring down the mountain—a seriously loud process. It's also huge, over fifty stories high, and about two and a half kilometers wide. The scale didn't compute until we got there, though of course we could see it from far away. It's supposed to be visible from Denizli, which is way on the other side of the valley.

All the pools are on the top third, in crescent-shaped terraces that are one of the two primary formations made by the limestone and travertine. The other formation consists of stalactites, which prop up and connect the terraces. At the base lies the actual city of Pamukkale, but since Geordi'd drawn the springs themselves, that's where we went.

When I asked about it, he said in typical seven-year-old fashion, "I just wanted to draw that."

"Did anyone...suggest something like this? Or describe it to you?"

He shook his head, and Jason looked at me curiously, but of course I couldn't explain why it mattered. At least, not without getting into details about demons and Satan and such, which would inevitably lead to *and by the way, I'm dead.* So, I dropped it, and we headed for the car.

By the time we parked and paid admission—this place was better run than Colossae—the sun was high, blinding against the white cliffs. According to my handy-dandy guidebook, until a few years ago, the site had been damaged by hotels built directly over the pools, the guests allowed to bathe—with soap and everything—in the water. Now, it's better protected. The hotels are gone, and visitors can only walk with bare feet on the terraces or in the pools.

From an archaeological perspective, it's near the ancient city of Hierapolis, built a few kilometers away by the Phrygian Greeks. They were the ones who ascribed healing properties to the waters, believing them bestowed by the god of medicine, Asklepios, and his daughter, Hygieia, goddess of health, cleanliness and sanitation. None of which explained why the Rousseaux or Satan would like it here. In fact, the opposite seemed logical—wouldn't they avoid anything to do with health, goodness, and gods? And so utterly *white?*

But something made Geordi include Pamukkale on his map, so up we trekked.

The terraces acted like stairs, ranging in height from about one to six meters. By the time we got to the top, we were a little winded, maybe partly from combing Colossae before coming here. Lunch evaporated midway up, and once again, I was starving.

I almost asked Jason if there was any lamb left, but I managed not to. Still, I *had* to figure out this whole post-death nourishment thing. I couldn't very well defeat demons on an empty stomach.

Geordi sat and dangled his bare feet in the nearest pool, while Jason caught his breath and awaited instructions.

"Just walk around," I said. "Look for any sign of the Rousseaux or anything strange."

"Care to go for round two? I'll let you go first."

Another question? I thought about it, then gave in. "Sure. Why not?"

"That was quick. Shoot."

Now that I'd taken the offer, I didn't know what to ask. I watched him watching me, his gaze steady and sure, and it hit me—forget arriving in my life. The idea that Jason, Playboy Extraordinaire, *hadn't* come on to me once, in all the time I'd known him suddenly seemed "cosmically improbable." And his abrupt reversal, now of all times—was *that* part of the randomness of the cosmos? Or like the neatness of his room, was it carefully planned?

Either way, did I want to know?

For that matter, was he really a playboy? I thought back over the last six months. He'd been gone overnight a lot, and frequently staggered home from the bar long hours after his shift ended. But…he'd never once brought a girl home with him. Single guy, living alone, never takes a girl to his own bed? Now *that* was improbable.

I took a deep breath. "All those times you went away for the weekend—were you really having one-night stands?"

His eyebrows shot up. He glanced at Geordi, who didn't seem to have heard, then back at me. "Okay, you have a right to know. I haven't been with another woman since I met you."

"Oh." As declarations went, it was a pretty good one. The hitch being, I supposedly didn't *want* declarations from him. And I didn't know if I should be relieved at his words, or mad that he'd lied. Worse, I couldn't be totally sure he was telling the truth now.

From the regret in his eyes, he must have sensed my doubts. "Hyacinth, I—"

"No, I'm good. We're good. I asked, you answered. Your turn."

He watched me for a long moment, like there was more he wanted to say, but he didn't know how to say it. That made two of us.

Finally, he asked, "What are you looking for out here that might be 'strange?'"

"I don't know," I said, then put my hands up, palms out. "I'm not dodging the question. I really don't know. Just walk through the crowds, see if anyone looks weird, or suspicious, or is doing something…odd."

"Odd like an old guy wearing socks with sandals? Or something more sinister?"

"Sinister," I said, then wished I'd hedged a bit more. Jason's jaw twitched, and I could see him weighing the satisfaction of chewing me out again for leading us all into danger, against the likelihood that, during the day, in such a crowd, we wouldn't find anything anyway.

"Fine. At least it shouldn't take long." Before I could ask what he meant—the place was crawling with tourists—he turned to Geordi. "Dude, want to hang with me? Or Hyacinth?"

Geordi squinted up at Jason, then me, his choice obvious. I tried not to feel hurt. After all, it'd been a while since he'd had a positive male influence in his life, if ever. Nick started abusing Lily soon after Geordi was born, and barely treated his son and heir any better.

By contrast, Jason played with Geordi, talked with him, treated him like a person. And he had the same body parts. For a boy who'd only had his mother and auntie around most of his life, Geordi must be in hog heaven.

"It's okay, sweetie," I said, "you can go with Jason."

His face lit up, then he glanced apprehensively at his hero, clearly wondering if this was the correct manly response. Jason grinned and raised his hand for a high-five. "Awesome!"

Geordi jumped up and thwacked Jason's hand— that had to hurt—then they turned and headed toward the right half of the hill. Jason jumped down to the next terrace, reaching up to swing Geordi over, and in five seconds, I lost sight of them.

"I'll do this half, then," I said, but no one paid any attention.

This terrace alone had a dozen tourists on it, dressed in a variety of styles. I saw typical Americans—shorts and T-shirts—next to Muslims in long robes, and even folks who looked like they came from Africa or India, dressed in wrapped cloths and turbans. Multiply that by dozens, if not hundreds, of other terraces, similarly crowded, and how the hell we were supposed to spot anything "unusual" was beyond me.

Part of the problem was I didn't *know* what I thought I'd find. I only knew Geordi'd drawn a picture of this place, after spending time with two of Satan's baddest minions.

I tried to be systematic about it, but the terraces weren't regularly spaced, being clustered in some places, isolated in others. The differences in height made climbing difficult, and though I had a water bottle, it didn't take long for me to feel overheated, over-tired, and out of sorts.

After an hour, I'd seen no sign of the Rousseaux, their minions, or anything that might interest them. Who knows? Maybe demons *liked* being baked alive in the murderous sun, smelling the stench of sweaty bodies, while going deaf from the incessantly roaring waters.

I paused to catch my breath. Maybe the map was a fluke. Maybe it didn't mean anything, and I was on a wild goose chase. I should probably sit tight until the fifth, then wait for the Rousseaux to show up at sunset. I knew they'd be at Colossae, and I knew when. Why not?

Except I didn't like leaving things to the last minute. I'd much prefer sneaking into the Rousseaux's lair, stealing the rock, then getting the hell out of Turkey before they missed it.

For lack of a better idea, I took out the camera. I ought to do some shots from the bottom, to get the big picture, but in the meantime, I snapped photos of this ledge, and the ones nearby. Maybe when I downloaded them, something would stand out.

"Bon," said a hoarse voice behind me. *"C'est*

vraiment tu."

I jumped and whirled to find Eric inches away, watching me. "Jeez—why does everyone keep doing that? Where have you been? How did you get here?"

He looked exhausted, but his mouth quirked up. "Miss me?"

"Yes. No. What are you *doing* here?"

"The locals. Said the water might help."

He sounded more tired than he looked, and I frowned. "Did it?"

"You tell me. Am I better?"

I examined him critically, then admitted, "No. I'm sorry."

In fact, he looked worse. He'd been in bad shape before, his wound raw and red in parts, putrid and black in others. Too much activity had tired him, and the color of his skin fluctuated from gray to green to yellow. But despite all that, he'd seemed upbeat. Or at least, as upbeat as a dead cop with a heavily ironic personality could be. Now, he faded more and more. Not literally—he still *looked* solid. But he swayed on his feet, and I could tell he had trouble focusing on my face.

I touched his forehead, then yanked my hand away. "You're burning up!"

I glanced around, looking for a way to cool him off, but the sun burned the white limestone, and the water in the springs was warm. He didn't have real flesh anyway. How was I supposed to bring down the body temperature of someone who didn't have a body?

"How did you even get here?" I asked.

"Car. Hitched a ride." He gave a weak smile. "Dematerialized, I think you called it."

I remembered what he'd said about doing that to get in his car. He must have been desperate, to try it again. Was that what weakened him so much? Did it require a big expenditure of ghostly energy? Was *dematerialize* even the right term, given he wasn't made of "matter" in the normal sense of the word?

Maybe the heat *was* his energy. If so, then it was draining, fast. I had to do something, but what? There was nothing here but the hot springs and the tourists.

The tourists.

Though the crowded terrace was small, a few meters long by another couple deep, and I'd been conversing with Eric in a normal-to-loud voice, *nobody* paid us any attention, as though the crazy lady talking to no one was…normal.

An older man wearing what amounted to a loin cloth and a turban came toward us, and as an experiment, right when he was at Eric's elbow, I said, "Hey! Watch where you're going!"

The man's gaze jerked up and flicked to Eric, and he said something apologetic in a language I didn't recognize.

"De rien," Eric replied, and I tried to pick my jaw up as the man went on his way.

"He can *see* you? He's…dead?"

"Of course. I told you the locals directed me here."

So he had. I glanced at the crowds. Holy crap— they all looked the same to me. Except for their dress. I realized now that those wearing loin cloths were probably the Dead, from times before khaki and cotton-spandex blends. No wonder Jason thought our search would be fast, as only a third of the visitors wore modern clothes. And it didn't follow that all of *them* were alive, either—look at Eric.

But if the Dead looked like the Living to me, how would I ever tell them apart? Would I spend the rest of my time here wondering if Geordi could see the people I met? There *had* to be a way. At least with Eric, his wound made it obvious. Which brought me back to, why didn't the rest of the Dead show evidence of whatever killed them?

I turned to Eric just as a truly ancient woman sidled up. Her dark eyes and thin-lipped mouth almost vanished in the crags of her face, and from its center, her bulbous nose stood out like a sunburnt beacon. She couldn't have been above five feet tall and almost as wide, with a bosom that took up the entire space between her neck and her waist. A dirty scarf covered her head, giving off an Eastern European peasant vibe, and when her skirts moved, knobby, dirty feet peeped out. They seemed strangely petite, given her bulk, as did her calloused hands.

Ignoring me, she touched Eric's arm, speaking to him in heavily accented French, supporting my theory that she'd lived in Russia or one of its former states. "*Allons y!* I haf made a place vhere you vill rest until is time."

"Time for what?" I asked. "Eric, what's going on?"

The woman glanced at me sharply, her grip tightening on Eric's arm. "Who she is? Vhy she speak viz you?"

"It's okay…Nadezhda," Eric wheezed. "This is…the one…who helped me."

Her eyes narrowed, nearly vanishing above her jowly cheeks, and her gaze traveled over my face. All at once, she jerked back. "Is you—I haf heard of you!"

Then she cackled. I'd never heard anyone cackle before, and it was about as witch-like as you'd expect. Not exactly evil—not like the Rousseaux, or the Dioguardis. Just unpleasant or disquieting or…something. Plus, I didn't like the possessive way she clutched Eric's arm.

"Eric," I said, "who is this, and where does she want you to go?"

Eric tried to speak, but he was now almost too weak even for that. He sagged, and I reached for his free arm, supporting the side Nadezhda wasn't already holding.

"You come now," she said urgently, pulling at him. "Now, or you no make it."

I planted my feet, pitting my legs against her bulk. "Make it 'til what?"

The heat rolled off Eric in waves, worse even than Claude's had been. "S'okay," he said, barely audible over the constant roar of the pools. "Want…to go…with her. 'Til tonight."

"You can't go—you don't even know her!"

One corner of his mouth quirked up. "Didn't…know…you. Worked out."

His eyes were sad before he looked away, and I thought, *I'm losing him—he's giving up.*

Nadezhda urged him toward the edge of the terrace, but I held on tighter. "Wait! What are you going to do to him? What's happening tonight?"

She shot me the evil-eye. "I safe him. You no safe him." She spat on the ground. "You Destroyer. You no velcome here."

What the hell? I looked at Eric, but he no longer seemed aware of me. The others on the terrace, however, suddenly *were.* All around us, the Dead gathered, as though Nadezhda had summoned them. They advanced, crowding us, herding us forward, the strength of their numbers sweeping us along the narrow terrace like dust before a hot wind.

"Get back!" I cried pushing at them with one arm while trying to keep a grip on Eric with the other. "Leave us alone!"

Eric's eyes rolled back, his head lolled, his lungs made a sound like a death rattle. He was literally a deadweight under my straining muscles. I tried to heft him up, to get a better grip, but he was heavy and unresponsive, and desperately I tried to keep him from slipping further away.

Nadezhda cackled again, and the Dead murmured, most in tongues I didn't understand. But I caught a few words here and there—*thief*, and *her*, and *Destroyer* again. Dead fingers clawed at me—I clung harder to Eric, the grossness of his wound, its fierce smell of decay, nothing compared to the lifeless vortex surrounding us, suffocating in its emptiness.

Hands tore Eric's arm from my shoulder, yanked him away. Other hands dug into my arms, legs, shoulders, dragging me backward.

"Stop!" I shrieked, searching the faces around me for Eric. Bright eyes regarded me curiously, like they didn't know what to make of me. Old, dried fingers with dirty nails and the toughness of worn leather clawed at me, like a thousand spiders crawling over my skin. They were in my hair, pulling at my clothes—I shoved them away, but they only came right back.

I saw a flash of blue and tan to my left. *"Eric!"*

It was useless. The Dead outnumbered me, and he

couldn't fight them, or didn't want to, or both. Hot fingers slid around my throat, tightening, crushing my windpipe. I clawed at them, digging, frantic, but even in death, they were stronger—*I couldn't breathe*—my heart thudded, trying to force oxygen up to my brain. My vision silvered, my skull pounded, my legs buckled.

Then Nadezhda said, *"Nyet,"* and the hands were gone.

They were all gone. The whole mass of inhumanity slipped away, crowding down the slope. I fell to my knees on the terrace, choking, gasping for air, with one thought playing over and over in my mind: *I can't let them take Eric!* I crawled forward, but someone kicked me in the chest and I fell back, over the far side of the terrace. The drop was only a few feet, but I landed hard, what breath I had left knocked out of me.

I forced myself to stand, coughing in the dust raised by my fall, then scrambled in the direction I'd seen them go, down and to the right. I searched frantically in all directions, screaming to be heard over the roar of the waters, *"Eric!"*

Nothing. They'd been swallowed by the crowds—by the Living and the Dead that swarmed over the springs. I sagged against the cliff, chilled to the bone despite the hot limestone. Tears burned my eyes; my heart was cracking. I hadn't known Eric long, but I liked him—needed him—needed that bridge to the afterlife, that one connection I still had to Lily. More, selfishly, I needed him for me. There were things he might know that Jason didn't, and I couldn't lose that.

"Eric," I moaned. "Don't leave me. Please—I need you to come back!"

"Hyacinth?"

My head snapped up. Jason stood on the terrace across from me, hand on Geordi's shoulder. Geordi, who looked at me with frightened blue eyes. The expression in Jason's own eyes indicated I'd finally crossed any reasonable boundary of sanity. The corded muscles of his neck stood out, and his jaw was so tense, I could see the blood pulsing through his veins. He kept his voice down, but the effort for control only emphasized his fury.

"Who the *hell* is Eric? And why do you keep talking to people who aren't there?"

Chapter Fifteen

*"Life is pleasant. Death is peaceful.
It's the transition that's troublesome."*
                                        ~Isaac Asimov (1920-1992)

The drive back to the hotel was silent and uncomfortable. Jason was even madder than when he'd caught me with his gun. Was that only this morning? My days were so packed, I'd lost all sense of time. It was late—almost dinner. I had a mere two days until sunset on the fifth, and I was no closer to finding the Rousseaux. It would help if I had *any* idea where to look, not based on a child's crayon drawing.

In the backseat, Geordi was quiet as ever. If the Rousseaux had said or done anything to traumatize him—beyond killing his mother and father—he didn't show it. By now, *I* probably worried him more than they had. Jason was right to be pissed. Whatever else he'd done, his concern for Geordi was indisputable. Plus, he'd pretty much dropped everything to help me, and here I was, paying him back by acting crazy at every turn.

More and more, I *felt* crazy. Not just out of my depth—seriously wondering if Michael and Eric, and giant force field bubbles, were all figments of my imagination, and I lived in an alternate reality from everyone else.

Which technically, I did.

I forced myself to take a breath. I wasn't insane. I just knew things about Death and Life that most people didn't. It would be okay—I would make it okay.

Jason pulled into a parking space near the hotel and killed the engine, then didn't move, just sat there, holding the steering wheel, staring out the windshield. I glanced back at Geordi, who'd fallen asleep, his head lolling at an angle that made my neck hurt just watching him. I looked away to find Jason's steady gaze boring into me.

I tried to remember the old Jason, the one I'd thought of as unflappable. Though actually, he still didn't seem agitated. The anger he directed at me was sure and strong, and I shrugged helplessly. "What do you want me to say?"

"How about telling me what the hell is going on?"

"You first." Ha. Let him weasel out of that one.

Jason gave a short fast shake of his head. "No. My secrets are in the past. Over. Done with. Yours are here, right now, affecting us every day. You brought Geordi to Turkey, *right to* the bastards who killed his mother—who I *thought* killed you." He paused, eyes dark. "Ever since that night, you've been acting strange, jumping at shadows, talking to people who aren't there. I've *seen* you—heard you. You asked me to trust you, and I've done everything I can to help. But trust goes both ways. Tell me—what the *hell* is going on?"

Part of me wanted to tell him so badly—to share my burdens and have him comfort me—someone *alive*—who'd tell me I wasn't insane and that I could do this. But therein lay the problem. He *would* think I was insane. Until a few days ago, *I* would have thought so.

"I can't," I said at last.

"Bullshit. Who's Eric?"

I shook my head. "No one. Just someone I thought I recognized."

Being reborn must have impaired my ability to lie, because clearly Jason didn't buy it. His jaw twitched, and he ground out, "At least tell me what's wrong. You're tired and pale all the time—except when you eat meat. What is it? What happened to you? And don't give me that crap about stress over your sister. This is physical, and it's eating you up. Tell me what the *fuck* it is, so I can fix it."

Apparently, he was even more observant—or I was worse off—than I'd thought. Maybe both. I'd been chugging along, but the truth was, I *didn't* feel as well as I had after eating massive quantities of bacon. But telling Jason I was the Walking Undead, who needed to devour animal carcasses to keep going, was even lower on my list than the Demons from Hell scenario.

"I—I can't," I said again, and watched him shut me out. It was truly remarkable—I could see his face close off, pushing me away, leaving me utterly alone. I didn't even have Eric now. Death was a huge scary unknown. But I wasn't really a part of Life anymore, either.

"I'm sorry." I looked down to hide my tears. "I appreciate everything you've done, for me and for Geordi. I hope—" A lump rose in my throat and I swallowed hard. "I hope you'll stick around a little longer. You're good for Geordi. I know he means something to you—for his sake, please don't go yet, even if you don't care what happens to me."

Jason was silent so long, I thought he might be

planning to leave then and there. Finally, he blew out a breath. "Jesus, Hyacinth. I didn't think I was *that* good an actor."

My head jerked up. His gaze flicked over the tears running down my cheeks and he said, "Shit," and reached for me, hauling me across the parking brake and settling me on his lap, curled against his chest. I knew I shouldn't, but I couldn't help it—I let him hold me, let him cradle me in his arms while I cried harder.

"It's okay," he murmured, sliding his hands over my shoulders and back. "Everything will be okay. We'll figure it out. I'm not going anywhere."

I couldn't remember the last time I'd felt this safe, this protected, this…turned on. *Crap.* I started to pull away, but Jason's arms tightened, the erratic thump of his heart next to my cheek and the swelling in his shorts telling me he was as aware of me as I was of him.

He shifted me slightly, tilting my head back so he could look into my eyes. The steering wheel at my back kept us close, and though I knew it was wrong, I was still glad.

"Hyacinth. I—" He shook his head. "It's not Geordi. He's a great kid, but I'm not doing this only for him."

His expression was serious. Intent. He was going to kiss me again, and God help me, I wanted him to, more than anything. I couldn't. I had to stop him, stop this, before it went too far and I fell for him—if I hadn't already. So I searched for something to say to push him away.

"Who *are* you?" He froze, and I pressed my advantage. "Why did you come here with me? Why are you in my life in the first place? Why won't you tell me who you really are?"

My success was momentary. He tangled his fingers in my hair and pulled me closer. "Because when you know, you'll never let me do this again."

And then he covered my mouth with his, nudging my lips apart, urgent and demanding, until I opened to him. I think I moaned. Or he groaned. Or both.

Thank God Geordi was a sound sleeper, because everything was suddenly hot and hard and...*Jason*. I felt him putting himself into the kiss, showing me what he hadn't been able to say for the past six months. Whatever role he'd been playing, whatever the reason for it, *this* was the underlying Jason. The friendship—the emotion—the reasons I'd liked him and enjoyed being with him—they were real and true, regardless of anything else.

He broke the kiss, breathing hard, eyes so dark I lost myself for a minute.

"Um," I said.

"Yeah." He brought my head back to his shoulder, smoothing my hair while our pulses slowed. At last he said, "You need to eat."

I nodded. Between the crying and the making out, I didn't have the energy to argue. Behind us, Geordi stirred, lifting his head to look around blearily.

"Hungry, kiddo?" Jason asked, and Geordi nodded, then stretched, giving no indication he thought it odd I was on Jason's lap.

Jason said to me, "There's a place around the corner. I think they make hamburgers. We can leave the car here."

Geordi got out without prompting, and I started to open Jason's door, but he stopped me.

"I might be doing this for you—and believe me, sometimes I wonder why—but if anything you do hurts Geordi…"

His voice trailed off, but I got his meaning. Warning received.

Then he added, "And if, after everything I've done, you do go and get yourself killed, I'll never forgive you."

If he only knew.

****

Dinner revived me. There were grape leaves stuffed with lentils, raisins and rice for me, and something resembling American hamburgers for the guys. Jason tried to order me a burger, but I refused. Lentils have lots of iron, more per calorie than beef. Of course, meat was hard to beat for protein, but I'd have to try. And, God forbid, if I needed cholesterol—well, I'd eat more eggs. Which, come to think of it, would help with the protein, too. But I had a suspicion it was the "red" in red meat I needed. Some sort of blood out, blood in ratio, which sounded as far-fetched as anything else, but I couldn't shake the conviction.

By the time we finished, the sun was long gone. I'd already decided the next thing was to visit the library at Pamukkale University, where I could print out all the photos I'd been taking. Plus, I could finally find out the significance of September fifth, and do more in-depth research about the region, in case anything led me to the Rousseaux. It was too late to go tonight, though, so I told Jason we'd go in the morning.

As always, he said, "Sure," and paid our bill, and we headed for the hotel.

Not only that, but he invited Geordi for a

"sleepover" in his room. Maybe to give me time alone. Or maybe he thought I might freak out and frighten Geordi more. Whatever the reason, Geordi was over the moon, and the idea worked for me. I had my own plans.

I couldn't just abandon Eric. He might not belong on Earth, and he certainly needed help, but whatever Nadezhda had planned, it couldn't be good. Plus, if I could learn what kept him here, and why he was so sick, it might help me figure out my own long-term possibilities.

I turned out my light and waited an hour, until I was sure the guys were asleep, then crept through the bathroom to Jason's room. Sure enough, they sprawled on the bed, snoring in unison, Jason's arm flung out with Geordi's head on it. I moved to the dresser and carefully lifted the car key, then froze when Jason stirred. But all he did was roll onto his side, his arm curved protectively over Geordi.

And just like that it hit me. My own personal lightning bolt. What if Jason didn't just "keep in touch" with Geordi? What if he *adopted* Geordi?

I backed away, closing both bathroom doors. I left my room and tiptoed downstairs, thinking hard. Leaving Geordi at all was horrifying. But Jason had put his life on the line to keep us safe. Who better to *keep* keeping Geordi safe? It was obvious they'd bonded. And no matter what Jason said about coming to Turkey for me, he clearly had Geordi's best interests at heart.

Of course, that didn't necessarily translate to, *I want to be a single dad.* But I had a while yet to work out the details.

The night was warm, and in a city this size, there was still plenty of traffic and activity. Too late, it occurred to me I was a woman alone, out after dark, in a Muslim country. At least I'd foregone my usual shorts and tank top, instead choosing capris and a more modest blouse. But I should've brought a scarf to cover my head.

I couldn't go back, though. I'd made my escape, and my sense of urgency about Eric grew. The night deepened, and I had no idea what Nadezhda planned, or when she'd do it.

I did have an idea about where, though. One of the things Hierapolis is famed for is its necropolis—a City of the Dead. Apparently, a very diverse one. Christians, Jews, Muslims, and members of virtually every other religion, came there to die, over many centuries. Sarcophagi are next to burial mounds are next to house-shaped tombs. If Nadezhda had marshaled the Dead to "help" Eric, then what better place to harness their energy?

The drive across the valley only took ten minutes. Less traffic than during the day, and I can be a lead-foot myself on occasion. I parked near the North entrance and got out, grabbing the flashlight from the trunk. So far, the moon illuminated the path, but it was good to be prepared. I passed the unmanned gate—no surrounding fence to keep late visitors such as myself out—and aimed for the outskirts of "town," about one and a half kilometers southeast, up the colonnaded main street. Easy enough in the day, somewhat creepier at night, and it was a relief to leave the wide-but-deserted areas and enter the more protected necropolis.

However, as soon as I did, I realized the flaw in my plan. While it made sense that Nadezhda would bring Eric here, "here" was a maze of graves and tombs—

around twelve hundred of them—spread out over roughly two square kilometers. It would take hours to wander all the way through, but I had to try, so I took a deep breath and picked a direction.

The bulk of the Dead, as with the Living, are commoners, buried in individual or family graves. Tombstones and markers, when present, were eroded and hard to read, but I saw a truly fascinating mix of faiths, nationalities, occupations and ages. No wonder the Dead didn't want to leave—this had to be one of the most cosmopolitan cities for their kind, anywhere.

Adding a socio-economic upgrade to the mix were sarcophagi, sunk into the earth, or roofed and raised on substructures, many with decorative marble fronts. Some were so large and elaborate, they put my apartment to shame, and I wondered at the wealth and status of their inhabitants. If you've got an eternity stretching in front of you, why not spend it in style?

Less ostentatious—but not necessarily lower in class—were the tumuli, dirt mounds nearly invisible in the dark, whose small, earthen entrances would open onto passages leading to vaulted underground chambers. Who knew what treasures lay within—the most modest exteriors often hid the richest finds.

Of course, these tombs had been pillaged—or, if you prefer, "excavated"—many times over. But it was a long time since I'd been around this many graves. I hadn't realized how much I missed it—the hunt, the exploration, not knowing what lay inside, but knowing I'd find *something*.

With a pang of regret, I pushed on. This wasn't the time, but maybe I'd come back once Michael had the rock back. One thing at a time.

Besides graves and tombs, the necropolis also contains other points of interest. There's the nymphaeum, a huge fourth century fountain that sent water from the springs down to Hierapolis, and also the Sacred Pool, in which visitors can still swim among submerged Roman era marble columns. Near this was an actual ruined church, and I crossed myself as I passed. Old habits. Or maybe it was the atmosphere, the dark and the stars above, the ancient bones below. Everywhere I walked was quiet, and peace, and…nothing else.

No Dead, no Nadezhda, and patently, no Eric.

So much for my hunch.

After an hour, I found myself near the ruined Temple of Apollo, supposed founder of the City. I'd been so sure I'd find Eric here—briefly I considered packing up and heading back to Denizli. After all, as I kept telling myself, he wasn't my responsibility.

Right. He'd saved our lives by leading me to his car. I at least owed him for that.

I'd been standing there lost in thought for several minutes, when I noticed it—a whisper-soft vibration, familiar, but not as strong as when the rock was close by.

Shit.

I spun around, trying to sense its location. The moon was far overhead, the sky lit with stars. In some areas, the necropolis was bright as day, in others, the mounds and structures cast sharp-edged shadows, dark as pitch, blacking out whole sections. By my best guess, it was close to midnight. I could've used the flashlight, but in this place, it felt disrespectful.

So did the racket I was making. I forced myself to

stop, to stand still and focus, until I attuned myself to the air and the water and the earth. *There.* To the left—south, I thought—a low hum, like a faint, elemental tuning fork.

Turning toward it, I picked my way over the uneven ground, around graves and crypts and rocky outcrops, tracking by feel as much as sound. Sometimes I lost the vibration and had to backtrack, but eventually it grew, getting stronger as I stumbled along.

I was past the Temple now, on a hill that seemed to have sprung full-blown in front of me. The mountains blocked the moon, making it hard to see more than a few feet ahead. The vibration was less intense than when I held the rock in my hand, but I felt it nearby, possibly right in front of me. I slowed, feeling my way even more.

I was in some sort of building or stone walkway. I use the term "in" loosely as, like everything here, this was a ruin, walls and ceiling crumbled, floor uneven. I hurried along as best I could, heart thudding, the vibrations increasing by the moment.

It's here—I'm going to get it back.

I turned a corner in what must have once been a passageway through the structure. The hum was louder now, although still not strong. I turned another corner—*so close*—

And came smack into a dead end, a walled-off stone arch.

Damn.

I stepped back, looking on either side, and discovered the arch butted up against the hill itself. Perhaps there was a cave—I was *sure* the vibration came from the other side. The walled part looked newer

189

than the rest, the stones rougher and less worn, the joins between them tighter. Much tighter. Whoever sealed it *really* didn't want anyone getting through.

No. I didn't come this far to be thwarted again. Frantically, I scraped at the bricks, trying to get purchase in the cracks, or find a hidden lever to open the wall. Which sounded pretty Hollywood when I thought about it, but I had to give it a shot.

Nothing.

There had to be another way inside. I reversed direction, until I was outside the structure, then scrabbled onto the hill, looking for an entrance behind where the arch should be.

Sharp grasses cut my fingers until they bled, but I couldn't find it—not even a mole hole. I wanted to weep with desperation, but I couldn't stop, couldn't let myself give up, and I scraped harder. I could barely feel the vibrations now. I sank to my knees, fingernails black with dirt.

It's here. I know it is—let me find it. Please let me find it.

So intent was I on finding the rock, I forgot all about my original reason for coming tonight. Which made it doubly heart-stopping when a sharp cackle came from beside me.

I shrieked and fell back onto my rear, looking up to find Nadezhda grinning at me, her teeth oddly white in the pitch-black. "Ah, you haf come for him." She moved aside.

Whether it was a trick of the moon, or a gap in the mountains, I don't know, but this area was lighter than where I'd been searching. There, in a hollow on the nearest hillside, a small circle had been cleared of rocks and grasses. Around this milled many of the Dead I'd seen before, or at least, many dressed the same, in turbans and loin cloths or peasant rags. They danced in seemingly random fashion, forming an irregular mass within the circle.

In the center, a man was tied, spread-eagle, completely naked. A man with light hair and eyes I knew would be filled with cynicism, though at the moment, they were closed. A man whose gaping chest wound looked blacker and more rotten than the last time I saw it.

I might not have found the rock. But apparently, I'd found Eric.

Chapter Sixteen

"The last enemy that shall be destroyed is death."
~The Bible, 1 Corinthians 15:26

"What are you doing to him?"

Fear made my voice sharp in the hollow night, and I lurched forward, only to have Nadezhda's hands clamp like vises onto my arms.

"I help him. You see."

"Help him what? Die more?"

"Da."

"What?" I twisted to escape, using my whole body for leverage, but her bulk was about as movable as a tank, and she simply ignored me.

"Is time. Vatch."

Helpless, I did.

The mass of spirits began to dance faster, whirling, arms and legs waving frenetically. There was no clear pattern, but soon groups of two or three began to break off from the pack, approaching Eric, then dancing away at the last moment. Occasionally, one of them bent over him, but I couldn't see what they did. Each time, Eric jerked convulsively, straining against his bonds, only to loll back weakly seconds later.

"Stop them!" I cried, struggling harder. "They're hurting him! Let me go!"

"Nyet." Her voice was calm, authoritative, her grip

unrelenting. "He dead, *da*. But he no *complete* dead. Zey complete it for him. You vatch—zey help."

Horrified, I stilled, trapped as much by her hands as by what I saw. Even if she'd let me go, I couldn't look away. *Eric—please—I'm here, I'm with you. You're not alone. I won't leave you.*

The dancers' ghost-clothing whipped to a frenzy as they gyrated on the hillside. The women's hair whirled around their heads, long braids slapping their partners, or loose locks vibrating in clouds that obscured their faces. The men's hips thrust back and forth, the sexuality of their dance older than the oldest ancient rite. Arms and legs pinwheeled everywhere, obscuring Eric. All at once, a dozen of the dancers descended on him, crowding close. They bent forward, *en masse,* and then—

He *screamed*.

I'd never heard a dead man scream. It was…*awful.* More painful than fingernails on a chalkboard, more anguished than a mother losing her child. And it went on and on and on, until I thought my head would split, then my heart.

"No!"

I finally wrenched myself free. But I was too late— the spirits straightened and stepped away, the dancing stopped, and Eric's screams died to a low moan.

"Let me through!"

The mass of spirits blocking my path turned as one, and I got a good look at them. Their grinning teeth were black with ghost-blood, and bits of putrefied ghost-flesh smeared their faces, like children who'd got into the jelly jar, their grotesque smiles a mad caricature. The bile rose from my gut, sick and sour—my hands and feet went cold and useless, my head swam. I swayed, pulling back, I had to get away—they were reaching for me—

No. They were…helping me. The mass parted, gentle hands pushed me forward. I staggered, then fell on my knees and touched Eric's pale, damp face.

It was cooler. *Much* cooler. I looked at his bare chest, expecting at best to find the wound as rotten as before, and at worst, to see it newly ravaged by ghost teeth, leaking fresh, red blood.

Instead, it was almost gone.

Before my eyes, the skin knit itself together, covering what appeared to be healthy flesh and organs. Dead, but healthy. The healed areas showed a faint network of scars, but his skin was pink and clean, the blue of his ghost-veins making him look even more alive.

He was also still naked. I glanced around. The Dead dispersed, occasionally glancing my way, but otherwise seeming respectful. Nadezhda waddled up and cut Eric's bonds with a knife produced from her skirt, then handed me a blanket. I spread it over him, then moved to his head.

"Eric," I said softly, and his eyes fluttered open.

He stared as though not recognizing me. Then he smiled. *"Mon ange."*

I laughed through my tears. "I keep telling you— I'm not anyone's angel." I searched his face. "How do you feel? What did they do to you?"

He frowned. "Don't know." He focused on Nadezhda.

"Zey eat your vound," she said matter-of-factly. Her calm glance met my no doubt sickened one. "Zey

194

dead—proper dead. Him, no. Vhen he die, he should pass from zis vorld, but he trapped. His vound, it lives. Grows—feeds on his soul. Ze Dead take vound into zemselves, a little bit each. So small, it no hurt zem. It vill die, and he vill heal. He proper dead now."

She seemed quite proud of the whole thing, and I had to admit, it made sense. I mean, was it any different than a mother sucking poison out of the snake bite on her child's arm?

"But what kept him here in the first place?"

She peered at me for a long moment, then shrugged. "He Christian—he should go vhere zey go."

"Are you all pagan, then?"

She spat. "Pagan—is *Christian* vord, for vhat zey no understand." She gestured at the departing Dead. "Zey no vish to leave. Some no believe in your God, in your Heaven. Ozers, *da*—but choose to stay."

She obviously knew more about this than I did. I wanted to question her more, but Eric stirred, shivering violently, so I asked, "Is there another blanket?"

Her face creased in a frown. *"Da.* I get it." She waddled away, leaving us alone.

He regarded me solemnly. "You came back."

I nodded. I couldn't explain to myself why I had, let alone to him. His whole body shook, and it occurred to me he'd be warmer indoors. But surely Nadezhda would have suggested moving him if it were possible. I reached for his hand under the blanket. Far from the earlier heat, his skin was now ice cold. He gripped my fingers convulsively, and somehow, I found myself lying next to him, trying to warm him with my body. He brought his arm out from under the blanket and held onto me, eyes drifting shut while he shook.

Nadezhda found us there a few minutes later. She'd brought several blankets, which she piled over us, then she lay down on his other side. We made an odd little trio, but then, none of this was any weirder than the rest of my situation.

Gradually, Eric's tremors slowed, then stopped. His pseudo-breathing became more regular, and he relaxed. Nadezhda closed her eyes, clearly settling in for the night. I hadn't planned on staying, but after all this, I sure as hell couldn't leave. My own lids were heavy. I yawned once. Then I fell asleep.

****

When I awoke much later, I was sprawled with Eric under the mound of blankets. Nadezhda was gone, and so was the moon. It was pitch black, and we were alone. At least, I hoped we were. I wasn't exactly afraid of the Dead now, but I didn't think they liked me much. There were those hands choking me at Pamukkale, and the foot that kicked me off the ledge.

Nadezhda had called me the *Destroyer,* and not in reference to Eric. Her ghostly lair had to be close, since it only took a few minutes for her to bring the blankets—maybe in one of the crypts nearby. If I could find her, I'd ask her what the hell she'd meant. I'd also just remembered the rock. Hearing it had driven Eric from my mind and finding *him* made me forget *it.* So much for multi-tasking. If I planned to parent a seven-year-old, I'd need to work on that.

I sat up, trying not to wake Eric, and looked around. Based on my jumbled memories, I was only a few yards from the last place I'd felt the vibration. Probably too much to hope it was still detectable, but I had to try. Starting from where I thought I was standing when Nadezhda found me, I spent fifteen minutes walking outward in concentric circles, staying quiet and moving slowly. Unfortunately, whatever I'd sensed was now gone, or I wasn't in the right area after all. I returned to Eric feeling depressed and out of sorts.

Nadezhda sat on a grave marker a few feet away, waiting for me. "I bring him clothes," she announced, indicating a neatly folded pile near his head.

"Thanks."

She pointed to a stone next to hers. "Sit."

Well, why not? I'd wanted to question her, and I was at loose ends. Having found Eric, I didn't know what to do with him. I'd lost the rock again, and I still had Geordi and Jason to worry about. Sitting with a ghost-witch amidst thousands of dead people seemed like the perfect way to while away the night. Which, I noticed, waned fast, it being much lighter now than when I woke. I'd have to head back soon, or my only two living friends would find me gone—assuming they hadn't already—and freak out.

As soon as I was settled, Nadezhda demanded, "Vhat you do viz him?"

"I don't know. Is he…okay?"

In the deep gray of the early dawn, her eyes were reflectionless pools. *"Da.* And, *nyet.* He full Dead now—but he maybe no belong here still."

"What do you mean? There are lots of Dead here—why shouldn't he be one of them?"

She shrugged. "He no like zem. He Catholic—he *believe.*"

She said it like this explained everything, and in a way, it should have. Michael should have been at Eric's death, should have guided him where he needed to go.

So why hadn't he?

I hated this, hated not knowing *why*, or what to do. "Then why didn't he pass on?"

"Vhy you are here?" Her gaze was sharp, and I looked away fast. She didn't know—*couldn't* know. Could she? Did the Dead have special powers of perception?

I countered, "Why do the Dead hate me?"

She laughed. Not a cackle for once—a deep wheeze of amusement, her eyes crinkling and her whole body shaking with mirth. *"Da*, zey hate you. You no treat zem viz respect. You and your partner—you vell-known to ze Dead."

Partner? Shit. Of course the Dead hated me. I stole from them—Vadim and I both had. Especially Vadim, who'd "rescued" artifacts from graves all over this region. But being the Life-centric beings, we were, it'd never occurred to us the possessions still *meant* something to their owners. If I were a hardworking stiff, coming back to the crypt after a long day doing whatever the Dead do, and I found all my creature comforts gone—well, I'd hate me, too.

Nadezhda, ever observant, watched all this process in my expressions, then nodded toward a still-sleeping Eric. "Zey like zat you help him. You still help, maybe zey no kill you."

Great. I already wondered what to do with him. Now, if I made a mistake, an Army of the Dead would be out to get me. On top of the Mob and the Demons, it seemed a bit much.

Eric stirred, and Nadezhda pushed her bulk off the gravestone. She was so short that with me sitting, our eyes were nearly level.

"Where are you going?" I asked.

"Home. He yours now." She turned to leave, and I scrambled off my own stone.

"Wait—"

But she moved surprisingly fast, weaving through the crypts and tombs before vanishing into the shade of the hillside. I would have followed her, but I could hear Eric stirring behind me. Besides, the sky was seriously lightening. *Merde*—I had to get back to Denizli.

I turned in time to see Eric zipping the pants Nadezhda had brought him. He was still shirtless, though. I'd seen rather a lot of his nakedness last night. At the time, I'd been too terrified of the Dancing Dead to focus on anything else. Now, his muscles—smooth, *healthy*—rippled invitingly in the pre-dawn light. His ordeal had left him a little gaunt, or maybe he was just lean, not an ounce of excess flab anywhere. I felt a rush of something both inappropriate and disloyal to Jason, and quickly averted my gaze. Not that I was *with* Jason. But everything was so complicated, and lusting after Eric would make it worse.

After a moment, he said, "You can turn around now."

I started at the sound of his quiet voice, then wiped all improper thoughts from my mind and faced him. He'd pulled the shirt on and was finishing up the buttons. The clothes suited him—khaki slacks that hugged his narrow hips, and a loosely tailored white shirt, which he left open at the neck, the sleeves rolled up. His old clothes, torn and bloody, had been beyond repair, but his socks and casual dress shoes were fine, and Nadezhda'd left them nearby.

"How do you feel?" I asked as he laced them up.

"Bon. Never better."

His tone held the habitual note of irony, and I thought, some things never change. He finished with his shoes and stood, fully meeting my gaze for the first time. His expression was…intense. But at the same time, unreadable. I didn't know what to do with it— what to do with him. And he clearly expected me to know.

"What next?" he asked quietly, as though wishing to respect the peace of this place.

"I have to get back. To Denizli. You can come with me…if you want."

Why was this so awkward? After what we'd shared, we should have an easy bond. Instead, perhaps because I felt responsible for him, and he felt obligated to me, we were tied together whether we wanted to be or not. Plus, I couldn't help feeling that what he knew about me was way too personal for such a short acquaintance.

He took a step forward. *"Mon ange…"* His voice was low and hoarse, but from emotion, not pain. The last thing I wanted was his gratitude, especially when all I'd done was take him up on his offer of a car.

I said on a rush, "I've got to get back. I can't wait any more."

The sky was light enough that I had no trouble seeing the terrain. We were a good fifteen minutes from where I'd parked the car, and there was still the drive across the valley after that. Jason and Geordi would be awake for sure by the time we got back, and I'd have to pretend I'd gotten up early and gone out, to cover my all-night absence.

Eric's eyes darkened, but after a moment he

nodded. "Of course. I will come with you."

We folded the ghost blankets and left them beside one of the tombs for Nadezhda to find—it still freaked me out how *real* they felt—then Eric followed me through the necropolis onto the museum path, which led to the North exit. In my hurry, I stumbled on the uneven trail, and he reached out a hand to steady me. I was increasingly aware of him, of his "body" as I persisted in thinking of it, close behind me. Before, he'd needed my help. Now he was strong and whole, and helping me. Our dynamic had changed, and I didn't know how to deal with it.

We passed through the gate to the bus parking lot in the rear, where I'd left the car. I opened the passenger door for Eric, then got in the driver's seat and we took off.

I have to say, if the Turkish police had been around, I would've been stopped, ticketed, and probably arrested on the spot, considering the number of traffic violations I committed in my race back to Denizli. Of course, it being Turkey, maybe I wasn't doing anything wrong.

Eric grabbed the safety handle when I first floored the accelerator, then shrugged and relaxed into the seat. I suppose being "kind of" dead, then having your putrid parts chomped off by ancient spirits, to make you "full Dead," might account for a *laissez-faire* attitude toward haring down the highway at top speed.

By the time we reached Denizli, the day had fully begun. The city was awake, markets and stores opening, the business of Life in full swing. I parked in the spot the car had been in before, ran around to get Eric's door—I didn't have time to wait while he dematerialized, even supposing he'd want to—then hurried into the hotel with him right behind. Now that he'd been "healed" he kept pace better, and we made record time up the stairs.

As we passed Jason's door, I checked the bottom, hoping to see if the light was on, but the seal was too tight. I inserted my key into the lock on my own door and turned the knob, pushing inward a crack. Thank God—my room was dark, the heavy curtains drawn, and the bathroom doorway showed that it and Jason's room beyond were also unlit.

I tiptoed inside, waiting for Eric to follow, then closed the door quietly and fumbled in the dark to set my purse on the dresser.

"*Mon ange…*" Eric began.

"Shh," I whispered needlessly, since no one but me could hear him. "I need to change—go somewhere else or turn around or something."

"*Ta gueule!*" he said at the same time the bedside lamp clicked on, revealing Jason sitting upright on the bed, legs out, fully dressed and—yet again—mad as hell.

"Tell me where the *fuck* you've been all night, and who in God's name you're talking to, or Geordi and I walk."

Shit.

"I tried to warn you," Eric murmured, and I couldn't even tell him off, because Jason stared me down, just waiting for me to take another ride on the Crazy Train.

His gaze took in my slept-on-the-ground, hair-messed-up, dirt-covered appearance, and hardened. He pushed off the bed, advancing on me, and I backed up, bumping into the dresser.

"Jason," I began, but stopped. I had nothing—no way to explain this that wouldn't make him madder. So I tried a change of subject. "Where's Geordi?"

"Still asleep." The look in his eyes was terrible. "I came in here at midnight, after he conked out, figuring we could finally talk. Imagine my surprise at finding you gone, without even a note to keep me from going insane with worry." His hands fisted at his sides, but I don't think he was even aware of them. Everything he had was focused on me, his long, lean body tensed, hair standing out like hackles on an angry cat. "I mean it. I want answers—*now*."

Beside me, Eric was pretty tense himself. "Ask him who he is. Make him tell you *that,* before you tell him anything."

While I agreed with Eric on principle—Jason had a lot of nerve demanding answers from me, when he'd revealed so little—still, I didn't want to alienate him more than I already had. The down side to him being so adept at getting us here was that I was now thoroughly dependent on him. And he'd been patient overall—I didn't really blame him for being mad now.

"I'm sorry. I didn't mean to worry you. I had to do something, and it couldn't wait."

"What could be so damn important you risked your *life*—jeopardized Geordi's safety—to go God knows where, doing God knows what, at night, *alone?*"

Put like that, it did sound like a bad idea, but the logic was wasted on Eric. He *thrummed* with so much energy, my hair crackled. He stepped toward Jason, hand twitching to his side where I assumed his gun holster should have been.

"It's okay—I'm okay," I said carefully, hoping Eric would know I spoke to him, while Jason would think the same.

"No, it is not," Eric said tersely. "He should not speak to you this way. *Nom d'un chien*—I have seen him somewhere, I am sure of it!"

A muscle in Jason's jaw twitched. "You're lucky you weren't raped or murdered. I promised to keep you safe—I can't do that if you don't tell me what the hell is going on."

"*Safe.*" The viciousness of Eric's tone made me jump, and Jason's eyes narrowed. Eric glowered at him. "He does not keep you safe. Ask him—ask why he is here. *Ask him who he is.*"

Cold fear shuddered down my spine. Even though Jason was right there, watching me, I turned to Eric. "You know. Don't you?"

Eric met my gaze steadily. *"Non.* But—" he began, at the same moment that Jason yanked my arm and spun me around so hard I stumbled, only to have him haul me back up and pin me against the dresser.

"Ouch!" I yelped as it jabbed me in the spine. "Let go of me!"

His grip tightened even more. "Answer me—*what in God's name is going on?"*

In a heartbeat, Eric was at my side. *"Cochon!"* he spat, as though Jason could hear him. "Release her!"

I'd never seen him this worked up, except the first night we met. *That* was terrifying. I had to calm him down. For one thing, he was barely recovered from his ordeal, and all this anger couldn't be good for him. For another, he popped with so much force, anything he did might affect *me,* whether he meant it to or not.

I didn't think Jason would hurt me on purpose, either, but how could I tell Eric that, without making Jason madder? Jason's eyes flashed, almost black with fury, but I saw fear in them also. I'd scared him—was scaring him more right now.

I blew out a breath and said deliberately, "Jason. I know you aren't trying to hurt me."

"Fils de salope!" Eric snapped. "I know his type— if you do not tell him what he wants, he will hit you next."

The statement was so outrageous, I turned to Eric. "He *won't!* Jason would *never* hit me."

Big mistake. Making my words seem like a total lie, Jason gave me a shake so hard, my teeth smacked together. *"Who the fuck are you talking to?"*

I shook my head, but before I could speak there was a loud *crack!* like a fast, sharp lightning bolt. The air sizzled and popped, and my hair stood on end. And then the vase of flowers on the dresser flew up and smashed Jason on the head.

He stared at me for half a second, stunned, before his grip loosened and he toppled over.

"Bâtard," Eric muttered.

"Tata Hyhy?" said Geordi from the bathroom. "Did Jason die?"

Merde.

Chapter Seventeen

*"It may be that we have all lived before and died,
and this is Hell."*
~*A.L. Prusick (1941-2008)*

"Jason's fine, sweetie," I said quickly, dropping
down beside him and hoping I wasn't lying. Eric
sizzled behind me, but I couldn't demand explanations
in front of Geordi, so I said, "He just had
an…accident."

Geordi's somber gaze took in the smashed vase
and nasty red welt blooming on Jason's forehead. "Oh."

Jason would have a doozy of a headache when he
woke up. But would he remember how he got it? Either
way, I was screwed. If he remembered what really
happened, he'd want to know why a vase conked him
on the head of its own accord. And if he *didn't*
remember, he'd think I threw it. Geordi'd apparently
chosen scenario number two. He hesitated in the
doorway, watching me uncertainly.

"It's okay," I said as reassuringly as I could. "Jason
tripped and bumped the dresser, and the vase fell."

Geordi still seemed doubtful, but he came and sat
on his knees by Jason's head. I cast a quick glare at
Eric, whose sizzle had slowed to a simmer, and
mouthed, *What the hell was that?*

"I do not know." I glared harder, and he raised his

hands. "Truly, I do not. I was…upset. Your *friend*"—he made it sound like a dirty word—"hurt you. I stopped him."

Geordi was absorbed in watching Jason for signs of recovery, so I shook my head and mouthed, *He wouldn't.*

Eric's eyes flashed, his temper spiking again. "Believe what you will. I know different."

You think *different.* Damn, it was hard having a conversation like this.

His expression darkened, and beside him, the remaining items on the dresser twitched.

Stop it!

Eric fisted his hands at his sides, his tension palpable. My purse actually lifted a quarter inch off the dresser, when Geordi said excitedly, "Tata! He's waking up!"

I turned in time to see Jason's eyes flutter then re-close. *Damn.* Not that I wanted him to stay unconscious. I just didn't want him to wake up *now,* while a bunch of inanimate objects danced around the room. Behind my back, I made a *get out* motion with my hand at Eric.

"Non. I will not leave you with him."

I twisted around. *Go!*

The dresser itself shook, and for one intense moment Eric and I stared each other down. Then he turned and flung himself at the door. There was a crackling *pop!* and he vanished through the solid wood.

I faced Jason in time to see him drag his eyes fully open. He looked at me for a moment, then at Geordi. "Hey, kiddo. What're you doing up?"

"I heard when you fell on the vase."

Jason's gaze slid back to mine. "Oh, really?"

"About that—"

He shook his head. "Ow. Don't. I know what I saw."

Crap.

Geordi watched us with interest. He'd gone to bed pretty late last night and slept in his clothes. His very grubby clothes. I said, "When was the last time you had a bath?"

"I don't know."

Jason caught on and gave him a little push toward the bathroom. "Why don't you take one now, and then we'll go find breakfast?"

Geordi wasn't stupid. He knew we wanted to get rid of him. "I'll take one later."

Jason sat up, wincing and touching his forehead. "Now, kiddo—or no sugary slugs."

"Did you find some?" I asked, surprised, since I still hadn't told Jason what they were.

"No, but I said we'd look for a market today after the university. *If* he takes a bath now."

Geordi glared at us. "I don't need one."

I reached over and lifted his arm, making a show of examining the large blotches of dirt and old sunscreen coating it. "Hmm. Nice and clean."

He rolled his eyes, in a perfect imitation of Lily. "Okay. Fine." He even sounded like her, and I fought down the sudden lump in my throat.

"Do you need me to start the water for you?"

"No!" He jumped up. "I can do it!"

With that he was off. A minute later, the tub was filling loudly, and Jason and I were as alone as we could be. "So," I began, but Jason cut me off.

"I'm sorry." I stared at him blankly, and he grinned then winced. "Your expression is priceless."

"I just don't get why you're apologizing. I mean, not to remind you or anything, but you were kind of mad."

"I know. You scared the hell out of me. When I came in here and found you gone, I thought—" He paused, scrubbing a hand over his face. The dark circles under his eyes attested to how little sleep he'd had, and the red welt was becoming an ugly purple bruise. "I thought the Rousseaux took you. I couldn't leave Geordi, and I didn't know what to do—what to think. So I sat and waited, all night. And then you came back, safe." He stopped again, searching my face.

"Safe, but…not necessarily sound?" His silence said it all, and I hurried on. "Look, it's not what you think. Probably. What *do* you think?"

He shrugged. "It really isn't any of my business. You didn't ask me to come with you—I offered. You don't owe me any explanations."

Which was maybe our biggest problem. If we didn't owe each other the truth, then where was this going? Whatever *this* was, and not that it could go very far before Michael whisked me away. Still, Jason's calmness was almost more painful than his anger, because it felt so…distant.

He watched me, ever observant, and I wanted to crawl into his arms and be comforted. Which was a bad sign. "Damn it. Why do you always have to be so *nice?*"

"It's a curse. If it makes you feel better, I can yell some more."

What I had in mind had nothing to do with yelling,

and a lot to do with kissing him, and unfortunately, my thoughts must have shown on my face. He didn't reach for me—I so wanted him to—but I could see the tension in his frame, different than his anger, but just as powerful.

"Why do *you* have to look at me like that? Like you want me as much as I want you, but something's in the way. What is it? What's stopping you, us, from getting what we both want?"

My breath caught, and I shook my head helplessly. We were only a few feet apart, but it felt like miles. I might have reached for him, despite everything, except that just then, Geordi shut the water off, leaving us in silence.

"That's one reason right there," I said, nodding toward the bathroom. "I have to find the thing I'm looking for—return it—and get Geordi settled."

Jason's eyes narrowed. "What do you mean, get him settled? Where will you be?"

Crap. "I—"

"Fuck. You're going to leave him, aren't you? Find him a family and go back to your single life." I tried to respond, but he shoved himself off the floor. "Forget it. I said you didn't have to explain. And if you won't stick around for him, why the hell would you do it for me?"

"Jason—"

But he was gone, stalking to the bathroom and shutting the door behind him. I gave him credit for not slamming it, which would have scared Geordi again. Everything was so messed up. If Jason only knew how much I wanted to stay. Maybe I should tell him—come clean about everything. But would he believe me? Or think I was making up crazy lies, to put him off?

Since he clearly didn't want to talk now, and I had other things to worry about, I stood and knocked on the bathroom door. "I forgot something in the car. I'll be right back—I didn't want you to worry."

Silence.

Finally, Jason said, "Thanks."

Eric might have stormed off, but I had a feeling he hadn't gone far. I just couldn't see him leaving so soon after choosing to stay. And besides, where would he go?

Sure enough, I found him right outside the hotel, leaning against the wall. I joined him and we stood in silence, watching the people passing by. Natives on their way to work or school, tourists either blending in or not. A myriad of humanity, of Life, but I felt no more connected to it than I had to the Dead of last night.

"They do not know I exist," Eric said at last.

"None of them?" He shot me a curious glance, and I clarified, "They're all alive?"

"You cannot tell?"

"No," I admitted. "Not by sight, anyway."

"Eh bien. And…why is that?"

I hadn't meant to tell him, but suddenly it all came pouring out. Vadim, the rock, the Rousseaux, Lily, Geordi, and Nick—and then Michael, the landing pad, and being sent back—so jumbled and rushed, I was surprised Eric understood half of it.

When all the words had left me, he said, "That must have been very hard for you."

Which struck me as funny, in a more-than-slightly hysterical way. "Yeah. About as hard as what you've been through. What right do I have to complain?"

He reached for my hand. His skin was cooler than before, but still warm, his grip firm. "You have every right to be upset. Being dead, yes, that is stressful." His expression hardened. "But to see your sister killed before your eyes—no one should see this, no matter their sins."

My blood chilled. "Is that—did you—"

His face was devoid of emotion. "When I was sixteen. She was a police officer."

"Who…?" But I already knew.

"The Dioguardis."

I didn't know what to say, but it didn't matter. He looked through me, remembering. "She was to testify against them, so they raped and shot her. They made me watch, then let me go, as a warning to anyone else who might think to challenge them."

"I'm sorry," I said, the words horrifically inadequate. "I can see why you hate them."

"Not only them. All like them—anyone who commits such vile, evil acts against the innocent. Murderers, rapists, thieves—each in their own way is despicable."

I swallowed. What would he think, if he knew what I'd been in life, and what I might be in death? A thief, a fence, a liar, and someone who hoped to cheat the Angel of Death out of a morally binding contract? Did it matter that I'd be stealing from Satan? That the lies I told and the promises I broke were to protect Geordi, and keep him from the very family Eric despised?

As if sensing my gaze, Eric turned. "Leave him—leave your *friend*. He is not who he claims to be. He will hurt you—I am sure of it."

I shook my head. "You're wrong. Maybe he hasn't

told me everything, but he would never harm me." I couldn't keep the doubt from my voice, and self-consciously crossed my arms.

Eric glanced pointedly at my hands, covering the bruises Jason had made. "He already has. Leave now, before he does worse." I opened my mouth, and he lifted a hand. *"Chiant!* I can see you will stay. *Eh bien,* perhaps he will not hit you. But emotionally—he will destroy you."

"You don't know him like I do," I said lamely. In truth, I didn't know Jason at all.

Eric's gaze softened, and he reached out, lifting my hands off my arms and replacing them with his own. His fingers were strong, and he smoothed them gently over the bruises. "Perhaps. But I know *you*, and you deserve better."

I shook my head again, caught in a fierce need to set him straight. "You have no idea who I am. You think because I can see you, it makes me special and good. I'm not—I'm really not!"

He smiled, and the irony was back. "I know more than you think." He took my hand and kissed it, his lips lingering on my skin. He straightened, holding both the hand and my gaze. "When I died, I lost my way. You helped me find it. That is who you are—who you have always been. Now, I will help you. I will not desert you."

It seemed I'd acquired another minion, which was touching and surreal and not necessarily a bad thing. "Thank you," I said at last. "You don't have to do this."

He gave my fingers a final squeeze and released my hand, then added softly, "I also do not poach. But if your *friend* hurts you again, ever, I will kill him."

I believed him. Now that I knew about his sister, I understood why Jason's actions upset him. "What happened upstairs, anyway?"

His eyes darkened, and he gave off a frisson of electricity, like a power line ready to arc. "I was afraid for you. I thought if I was alive, I would smash his face in. Then I saw the vase. I did not think, *I will use this*. It simply…moved…the way I wanted it to."

"You didn't pick it up? With your hands?"

"Non. It was more that the vase became an extension of me. I thought of it, and it rose to the occasion, so to speak. But objects—I cannot move them with my hands."

"And the door?"

His mouth quirked up. "Now that I am 'full Dead,' *comme l'on dit,* that at least is easier." The smile vanished. "And I *am* Dead—I can touch them, feel them, in the same way I felt the Living when I was alive. The Living, whom I can no longer touch. But you…I can touch."

"I told you– I'm not really alive."

He gave a fast, hard shake of his head. "That is where you are wrong. You are not *less* alive than these people around us. You are *more* so." He moved closer and, placing one hand on the wall next to my ear, he used the other to gently brush my cheek. "Being reborn—it is a gift. The choice is yours what you do with it."

His gaze dropped to my mouth, and he ran his thumb lightly over my lips. They parted, and my breath caught as I wondered if I was about to be kissed by a dead guy.

"Mon ange…" He leaned in, and without conscious

thought, I angled my head to meet him.

Then abruptly he pushed away from the wall, and I fought to hold myself up on suddenly weak knees.

"I do not poach," he repeated, eyes hot and hard. "But that does not mean I will not remind you of your other options from time to time."

Hoo-*boy*.

****

Two hours later, Jason, Geordi and I parked at the University of Pamukkale, *sans* Eric. After beaning Jason on the head, swearing fealty to me, and nearly sizzling my clothes off, he'd refused to come back upstairs. Instead, he said he had "something to do," and he'd tell me about it later if it panned out. Once a detective, always a detective—which could be bad for me in the long run, but for now, I let it pass. I did remember to ask if he knew anything special about September fifth, which he didn't, so I was still at square zero on that one.

Jason was still pissed, but he relented halfway through breakfast, which we'd had at an American-style café near the hotel. He watched me take an unenthusiastic bite of my veggie omelet, then took the sausage from his plate and dropped it onto mine, ordering, "Eat."

It smelled so good, and I felt so low, I didn't put up much of a fight. He signaled the waiter, and somehow, I downed six more links.

After which Geordi said solemnly, "You look better, Tata."

Ouch. I must've been in bad shape. "Thanks, sweetie. If only sugary slugs did the trick."

He giggled, then took one of his own links and put

it on my plate. "It's a salty slug!"

I smiled through an overwhelming urge to cry. He'd watched, seen what Jason did, and tried to help. This had to stop—I had to get myself together, so *I* could care for *him*. With that in mind, I picked up the link and ate it, trying not to moan with pleasure, then evaded Jason's penetrating gaze and finished my eggs. It was now Meat—two, Vegetarian—nada.

Feeling frustrated—but physically much better—I waited while Jason paid the bill, and then we made our way to the university. Despite its name, it's located across from Pamukkale, on this side of the valley, in Denizli, so parking took longer than our travel time. Once we found the library, Jason conned the girl at the entrance into letting us in by claiming we were foreign exchange students who'd forgotten our ID badges. She caved so fast, I didn't feel so bad about being deceived by him.

Once safely inside, I looked at him sideways. "You speak Turkish? Really?"

"Only the tourist version."

"Enough to say please let us in, and how about a date?"

He nodded at Geordi, standing nearby. "You want to get into this now?"

"Not really."

"Okay, then. What's the plan?"

I got the camera out of my bag. "Can you find a computer and print out the photos I took? I'm going to look for books about the nearby ruins."

"Sure," Jason said and took the camera.

Geordi immediately concluded that playing with computers would be more fun than searching through boring old history books. "Can I go with Jason, Tata? Please?"

"Of course," I said, and they headed off.

Thirty minutes later, I sat at a table littered with books, feeling more confused than when I'd started. Thanks to the library's multilingual online catalog, I'd located several English-language tomes, and many more in Turkish, which had pictures at least to help me get a better sense of the locale. Along with geographic wonders and gorgeous scenery, the area is rife with sites of religious and archaeological significance, none of which screamed *Demon Lair* at me. Quite the opposite, in fact, as most are dedicated to various ancient gods, to the Christian God, or to innumerable saints. Plus, I'd felt the rock in Hierapolis, and nothing I read changed my conviction that it was there. The question being, how to get to it?

But of course, the only book about the site at Pamukkale was in Turkish. It even contained a photo taken inside the necropolis, that looked to be of the place where I'd felt the rock. I couldn't be sure, though. It had been very dark, and one bricked up archway looks much like another. I tried asking a librarian to translate the text, but his English, while better than my Turkish, was still limited. He said something about "the place of the Dead," but when I explained I already knew the arch was in the necropolis, he shook his head and pointed at the photo again.

"Door—*kapi*. For the Dead. *Ölü*."

Disappointed, I took the book back. "Thanks."

"*Tuğla*. Brick." He tapped the wall inside the arch, searching for the words to make me understand. "Ah…*Kalsiyum silikat*."

217

Now *that* I recognized. Calcium silicate is a very strong, heat resistant type of brick, achieved when quartz and lime are added to the clay from which the brick is being made. The process wasn't common in ancient times, but then, I'd noticed that the wall inside the arch seemed newer than the arch itself. Why was its composition important, though?

"I know those bricks are newer," I said, and he nodded vigorously, beaming.

"*Evet*—yes—*tuzak.* Trap. Ah, heat." He motioned with his hands, like heat rolling in waves. Did he mean the bricks trapped heat inside the passage? I shook my head in confusion, and he tried once more, saying something I swear sounded like "plutonium."

What the hell? Was he implying that the necropolis was a source of nuclear energy?

"Er, okay," I said, and he smiled and nodded again, pleased he'd been able to help.

I returned to the table. Along with the historical and geographical tomes, I'd also grabbed some books on Christianity, and I now switched to these.

About one percent of Turkey is Roman Catholic, so one of the books was in Latin, of which I knew enough to get by, while the other was in English. Both listed a litany of Saints' Feasts for September fifth, but I didn't recognize the names, and on cross-referencing, none of them seemed to have any bearing on the situation at hand. No glaring connection to Michael, or the episode at Colossae, or anything else. To be thorough, I also looked up Michael himself, but his feast day was listed as September twenty-ninth. I shoved the book away just as the guys walked up.

"Find anything?" Jason asked while Geordi pulled

up a chair and started flipping randomly through the volumes.

"No," I said. "Unless you can also *read* Turkish?"

I half expected a "sure," but Jason said, "Sorry. Like I said, I speak tourist, but that's it."

"Never mind. Can I see the photos?"

He plopped them on the table, then sat by Geordi, who'd already given up on the books and was scribbling on a piece of scratch paper with one of those short, eraser-less library pencils. Jason picked up another one, and soon they were engaged in what looked like a highly competitive tic-tac-toe tournament.

The photos were sorted by location, so I started with Colossae. Unsurprisingly, nothing new leapt out at me. It was still a barren, flat hill, near an unexceptional wandering stream. Without much hope, I switched to the Pamukkale set. As expected, the site was far less crowded than I'd first thought when taking the photos. Barely a third of the people I'd seen then showed up in the pictures, and more and more I realized how "real" the Dead looked to me.

I glanced around the library. Were some of *these* people dead? How would I ever tell them apart? Of course, if I didn't get the rock back for Michael, it'd be a moot point.

I examined each photo carefully, not seeing anything of interest, and finally came to the last one, which I'd taken right before Eric found me. Again, nothing but the ledge, the hot springs, and assorted live tourists. I threw it down on the pile and blew out an aggravated breath.

Jason glanced up sympathetically. "Maybe if you told me what you're looking for?"

"I wish I knew."

Geordi abandoned the game. "Can I help?"

"Sure. Why not?"

He leaned across the table, looking at the top shot, and immediately asked, "Who's that?"

I picked the photo up, heart pounding. Could he somehow have seen Eric, even though *I* couldn't see him in the picture? And what did it mean—what would I do—if he had?

But no. It wasn't Eric he pointed at. It was a woman, dressed like a Russian peasant. Solid and real as any of the tourists around her.

Nadezhda.

She was so close to the photo's edge that I hadn't registered her until now. I turned to Jason. "Can you see her? That woman there—*can you see her?*"

He shot me one of his concerned-for-my-sanity looks, but obediently checked the photo. "Short woman, wearing a dress and scarf?" I nodded, and he said, "Of course I see her."

Which meant…she wasn't one of the Dead.

Which *also* meant…I wasn't the only living person who could communicate with them.

I pushed back from the table, gathering up the photos. "Let's go—we need to get back to Hierapolis. Now."

Chapter Eighteen

"You have to learn to do everything, even to die."
~Gertrude Stein (1874-1946)

Pamukkale was about as crowded as yesterday, but at least now I knew Jason and Geordi weren't aware of *all* the folks milling around. I didn't think Nadezhda would be on the terraces, so we went straight to Apollo's Temple in the necropolis. From there, I made educated guesses and retraced my steps of last night, winding through the graves with Jason and Geordi in tow.

Once again, the sun shone directly overhead, but wherever the Living and the Dead were, it wasn't here. I supposed the terraces with their healing waters, and the museum at Hierapolis with its air conditioning, were a bigger draw for live tourists in this heat. But I expected to see at least a few of the Dead, since this was their "city." Maybe they all had day jobs or were still asleep and would come out later.

At last I recognized the ruin where I'd lost the trail of the rock. For form's sake—I didn't really think it would be so easy—I put my hand on the closed arch. Nothing. Not even a tremor or a hum to tell me the rock was there. Jason eyed me curiously, but I shook my head and moved outside the passage, clambering onto the hill. From there, it was a simple matter to find the place where Eric had been healed. None of the Dead were here, either, but evidently, I'm predictable.

"There she is, Tata!" Geordi squealed excitedly. "The lady from the picture!"

Nadezhda sat cross-legged on a low tomb, elbows on her knees, watching us. "I vaiting." Her gaze flicked from me to Jason, then landed on Geordi, and her brow furrowed. "Come."

Wonder of wonders, he obeyed. Not that he was ordinarily shy. But she was a strange woman, on a ruin in Turkey, and I would've expected a little caution. Instead, he walked right up and looked her in the eye. She didn't say anything, but clearly some sort of exchange passed between them. At the end of it, she nodded decisively.

"You okay." She reached in her pocket and took something out, handing it to him. "You like bugs. Zey like you. Keep zis. It belong viz you."

"Thank you," Geordi said solemnly, and put the small object in his own pocket.

She pointed to a hillock a few yards away. "Go. Is bugs."

Geordi grinned happily and skipped off to investigate.

Jason's face was oddly tense, and he whispered, "Who the hell is she?"

"I don't know," I whispered back. "But I think she can help me."

His eyes narrowed. "With what?"

Nadezhda's head snapped up, and she said sharply to me, "Speak. You haf questions. I no can answer, if you no ask."

I looked at Jason. He looked back. Finally, he

ground out, "Fine. I'll help Geordi." He started to turn away, but I reached for his hand.

"Thank you. For this—for everything."

I expected recriminations, or even a wisecrack. Instead, he blew out a breath and shook his head. "I don't know what the hell you're doing, and it scares the crap out of me. But you trusted me, even after I lied to you. I don't deserve a second chance—but I'm going to take it."

He laced his fingers through mine and pulled me to him. The kiss was fast, over almost before I registered it. He released me and stepped back, and I wobbled a little.

"You need meat," he said, "but think you shouldn't. I want you—and *know* I shouldn't."

He went to Geordi, and Nadezhda cackled.

"You gotta problem viz zat one. Or maybe viz…ze dead one?"

As openings went, it wasn't bad. I pulled myself up beside her. "Why didn't you tell me you were alive?"

"Vhy you no ask?"

"You walked and talked with the Dead. It never occurred to me another living person could do that."

"Ve are alike, zen, you and me? Both of us…living?" Her expression was canny, but I wasn't ready to have *that* conversation. I was here for other reasons.

"I can talk to them, hear them, feel them. But you—you physically *tied* Eric to the hillside. How is that even possible, when he has no body?"

She contemplated me for a moment, then said, "I use ghost cloth."

"You mean you can control spirit objects?"

She didn't answer, just lifted a shoulder. Or tried to. She was so rotund, the only change in her stance was that one side of her bosom lifted a fraction of an inch higher than the other.

I tried a different tack. "Eric moved a vase. Is it something like that—if the Dead can influence objects in our world, does the same hold true for us, with stuff in theirs?"

She shrugged again, and I tamped down my frustration. On to the next subject. "You're Eastern Orthodox, right?"

About eighty percent of Russians are, so I was hardly surprised when she nodded. *"Da.* I vaz." She gave me a sly, sideways look. "I Old Believer. You know vhat is zat?"

Actually, I did. "You follow the old ways of the church, from before the reforms in the seventeenth century. Well, the old ways of the *Russian* church." I gave her a sly look of my own. "Which, itself, split from the Roman Catholics six hundred years before that."

She beamed, and I felt oddly proud of myself.

"You good student."

"Not good enough. I haven't been to church regularly since I was a kid."

She waved a hand dismissively. "In Russia, ve Christian, *da.* Does not mean ve go to church. Vhat ist you vant to know?"

"What happens on September fifth?"

She thought a moment. "Is feast of Holy Prophet Zechariah and Righteous Elizabeth."

It took some searching through my spotty Catholic memories before I came up with a match. "The parents

224

of John the Baptist?" How on earth were they connected to all this?

"Da," Nadezhda said. Then, evidently feeling chatty, she added, "September the six, now—is much bigger day. Is feast of Saint Michael."

I stared at her. "I thought his feast was at the end of September."

"In *Roman* Catholic Church, *da,* but is minor feast. Pah. In our church, is very important. September the *sixth."*

Well, hell. But if Michael's feast was on the sixth, then why would the Rousseaux perform the ritual on the fifth?

And then a big ole *well-duh* lightning bolt hit me in the head. Stupid, stupid, stupid. My mentors would be ashamed. Vadim would turn over in his grave, if he hadn't been cremated.

Of *course* the ritual would happen on the fifth. Virtually every ancient religion, including early Christianity, began their holy observances *at sunset on the day before.* Sheesh. It was a wonder Michael thought me resourceful at all. Clearly, I'd gotten *way* too soft in recent years.

I sat back, thinking over the facts as I now knew them. Satan tried to destroy Michael's sanctuary at Colossae, but Michael stopped him by splitting the river slab and rerouting the newly-sanctified water. Since then, Satan and Michael both had hunted down the resulting rock shards. I still didn't know why, but I could guess. Most likely, the pieces either held some of Michael's powers, or acted as their source, or something along those lines. Obviously, Satan wanted to destroy the rocks to weaken Michael, and by doing it on the very day when Michael's importance was celebrated by the Russian Church, he really thumbed his nose at Heaven.

Saturday at sunset. Barely thirty hours from now.

I turned to Nadezhda. "When I was here last night, I found a…cave, or something." I hesitated. She might have helped Eric, but for all I knew, she worked for Satan. He'd have good reasons to want the Dead walking the Earth—maybe she was his shepherd or something. Still, she knew more of this area than anyone else I was likely to meet, so I pushed ahead.

"Maybe on the other side of that archway?"

I pointed to the one in question, and she promptly said, "*Da.* Is Plutonium."

What the…? The same thing the Turkish librarian had told me. But what in the world could nuclear bombs have to do with Michael and the rock?

And then it kicked in. For the second time in under five minutes, I allowed myself the briefest of self-flagellations. It's a good thing my education was self-taught, largely free, and I had no parents, because if I did, they'd rail at me for wasting their money. My only excuse was that the librarian's mention of calcium silicate had got me thinking of minerals and elements.

Not *plutonium,* as in the isotope used in nuclear reactors. *Plutonium* with a capital "P," as in, the realm of the god Pluto—an entrance to the Underworld. The absolute perfect place for Satan's minions to hang out, store rocks, and generally make a nuisance of themselves.

I jumped off the tomb. "How—where—? I need to get inside!"

"Nyet."

The absolute refusal in her tone was more than I could take. "God damn it!"

It came out as a shout, and Jason and Geordi looked up, startled. I forced myself to calm down, waiting until they returned their attention to the dirt and its creepy crawlies.

"I have to get inside," I repeated. "It's a matter of life and death."

"No one get inside. Is closed."

"I know *that* entrance is closed—there must be another one."

Nadezhda nodded. *"Da.* Is lots of gates to Plutonium. Is one at Temple of Apollo, viz iron grate. Zey tell you all about it at museum."

I started to snap at her again, then made myself stop. She wasn't arguing with me, but instead appeared to be stating well-known facts. "If there are lots of gates, and everyone knows about them, why can't I get inside?"

"Poison."

That was the last thing I expected. Death by Demons—sure. Turkish laws forbidding entry into historic sites—absolutely. But…poison?

She gave a toothy grin. "You hold temper. Is good. You not know everyzing. Is poison in caves—gas. Ancients use for sacrifice. Birds, animals. Gas rise from below and zey die. You go in all ze vay, you die." She shot me a sideways glance. "If you no already dead."

I glanced at Jason and Geordi, but they didn't appear to have heard, so I asked cautiously, "Are you saying the Dead can enter the Plutonium safely?"

She let my deliberate misunderstanding pass. "Maybe. Maybe not."

227

"Meaning…?"

"Gas no affect zem—*da,* is true. But safe to enter?" She shook her head. "Is gate to Undervorld. Zey go in, maybe zey no get out."

Poison gas and a doorway to Hell. No wonder the arch was walled off. "Please—at least show me the other entrance. The one at the Temple."

She thought a moment. *"Da*—I show you." She hopped off the tomb, calling loudly to Jason and Geordi, "You come, too."

They stood and joined us, wiping their hands on their grubby shorts.

"Come where?" Jason asked.

"Plutonium," she said, and his face blanched.

"What's wrong?" I asked, and Jason's gaze snapped to mine. Far from the fear I'd expected, his expression was furious.

"What the f—" At the last second, he remembered Geordi, and toned it down. A bit. "What in the name of *Christ* is going on? Why do you need to go there?"

"I can't tell you."

Jason looked like he wanted to shake me. Good thing Eric wasn't around, or we might all have learned just how well he could harness his new "dead energy."

"I've been patient." There was a hardness to Jason's voice that, despite everything, I hadn't heard before. "But this is too much. You will *not* take Geordi near the Plutonium."

"How the hell do you even know what that is?" I demanded, forgetting Geordi myself.

"I can read a damn guidebook, too!" Jason was so angry, his blue eyes darkened until they were almost black. Nadezhda grinned at him and cackled, and he rounded on her. "How can you even *think* of taking a child near a cave filled with poison gas? Of taking *anyone* there?"

She shrugged, unperturbed by the fact that he towered over her, exuding more outrage by the second. "Is safe at Temple. Apollo vill protect. Your friend— she go. Boy, he go viz her. *Da?*" I nodded emphatically, and she looked at Jason again. "Is up to you. Stay or go."

She turned and waddled toward the Temple, and I grabbed Geordi's hand and followed. After a moment, the crunch of sneakers on the path behind let me know Jason had relented. Which was a not-so-secret relief. I'd gotten used to having him at my back, so to speak, and though he might be mad as hell, I really didn't want to face this alone.

It took a few minutes to wend our way through the necropolis. Last night and earlier today, I hadn't paid much attention to the Temple itself, regarding it primarily as a landmark from which to branch out my search for Eric, and then for Nadezhda. Now as we approached it, I looked more carefully, memorizing details of the terrain, in case I needed them later.

I'd left the camera in the car, but even if I'd brought it, I wouldn't have used it. The truth is, after making such amateur mistakes, and missing so many details, I wanted to flex my muscles, see if I still had the skills that got Vadim to partner me in the first place. He'd always said cameras make you lazy. Photographing a site meant you never really looked at it or experienced its nuances, subtleties of time and place that might not show up in the pictures. Plus, downloading and printing takes time, and if you forget the photos later, you're screwed. Better, he said, to use your mind's eye. Presumably, you'd always have *that* with you.

Mine was rusty, that much was certain. I should have used it more at Colossae and Pamukkale. Who knew what I'd missed, peering through that narrow lens instead of absorbing the bigger picture. Today, by contrast, it felt good to be unencumbered, just me and the site.

Well, me, the site, and various of my minions.

Not much remains of the Temple, it having collapsed several times over the years, during successive earthquakes—the same ones that flattened Colossae. The Temple wasn't a total pancake, but it was close, a jumble of broken tan stones and columns resting on slightly sloped ground. The earth and dead grass were similar in color to the ruin, and its relative flatness left us exposed to the elements, and to anyone who might be watching. I did a quick check, but saw no one, which was only mildly reassuring. I had a hunch demons and their ilk would either have powers of invisibility, or else be really good at hiding.

The Temple was about fifteen or twenty meters square, with steps on all sides leading up to a formerly-columned dais. As noted, the columns now lay scattered across the surface, but an annex below and to one side of the dais was in halfway decent shape.

It was to this that Nadezhda led us. There, below the Temple proper, a portion of the wall extended out into the low hillside, maybe one meter wide and around one and a half meters high. Atop this, a small arch added another meter or so. As Nadezhda had said, there was a padlocked iron grate over it, and I eagerly approached it, hoping to see beyond, into the Plutonium.

Unfortunately, Nadezhda either hadn't known, or didn't see fit to mention, that behind the grate's rusty bars, less than a meter in, this arch was also walled off. Not only that, but the lower portion of the opening was filled with dirt.

I tried the grate, anyway. Maybe I could poke around in the dirt and learn something useful. But though it rattled, the padlock was secure, the casing sound, and there was no way I could open it, unless I came back later with a bolt cutter or a saw. Since the stones inside looked to be as tightly joined as the ones at the other entrance, there didn't seem to be much point.

Except…

While Nadezhda eyed me knowingly, Jason glared angrily, and Geordi watched curiously, I wriggled and squirmed until I got my arm between two of the bars. By dint of also wedging my shoulder through, I was able to barely touch the back wall with my fingertips.

There. A faint, vibrating hum.

Like a tuning fork, below the Earth's surface, calling me, begging me to come get it.

Crap. It looked like I'd have to try after all.

****

By the time we got back to the hotel, it was late afternoon, and we were all more than a little cranky. After I'd felt the rock, I pulled my arm out from the grate, then felt the stones all around the arch for any further vibrations. Unfortunately, today it felt much more…distant…than last night. I could barely sense it inside the grate; outside, I couldn't detect it at all.

Nadezhda, deciding she'd done her duty, or simply losing interest, waddled off to wherever she spent her days, and Geordi ran around the nearby hillocks, examining clumps of grass for new species of bugs. When I asked what Nadezhda had given him, he handed me a shiny black scarab, possibly from one of the nearby tombs. Or it could have been from the gift shop. Now that I knew she wasn't dead, she seemed a lot less mysterious. Either way, it was the perfect trinket for Geordi, so I gave it back, and he went on his way.

Meanwhile, Jason was still pissed, but he grudgingly agreed to be my lookout, standing guard while I made my way around the perimeter. I wasn't sure how the Turks felt about their national historic sites being fondled by lapsed-American tourists, and I didn't want to find out.

Of course, Jason could only see the Living, not the occasional Dead who wandered by, but this was okay for two reasons. First, I doubted the Dead could "tell on me," even should they want to. And second, if I could detect a pattern in who Jason saw versus who he didn't, it might help me learn to distinguish the two myself. Fortunately, neither paid us any attention. Still, it took a long time to work my way around, touching every stone I could reach, checking for the rock and an alternate entrance.

After a couple of hours, I came up empty-handed on both counts, but I did gain a thorough knowledge of the Temple's nooks and crannies, which made me feel a little better. More confident—more *me.* Like putting on a sweater I hadn't worn in a while, I tried on my Grave Robber skin. It turned out to be comfortable and familiar, and I was pleased to learn I hadn't forgotten everything I knew.

Jason held his tongue while I searched, merely giving a low whistle any time someone approached. He was also silent in the car on the drive back. We'd missed lunch, but I was too tired to care, so when he and Geordi decided to go back to the café for more burgers, I declined.

"You need food," he said stiffly—the first full sentence he'd managed since we'd fought about the Plutonium.

"I know. But I really don't want to go anywhere. Bring me back something." I hesitated. Oh, what the hell. I could live on my principles, or I could *live.* "A burger, maybe…?"

I could tell I'd surprised him. "If you're sure." I nodded, and he unbent further. "Good. You need it. C'mon, kiddo—let's go get your Tata Hyhy some meat."

They went off with renewed purpose, and I headed upstairs to peel off my dirt-encrusted clothes and take the world's longest bath, while downing the world's biggest glass of water. If only ice were readily available here. It was the one thing I truly missed about the States.

By the time I finished, the sun had almost set, but the guys weren't back. I toweled off, then flopped on my stomach on the bed, naked, enjoying the breeze from the window on my skin. After toiling and sweating in the hot, dry dust all day, it felt heavenly to be clean and cool and saturated with water, inside and out.

Of course, now I had only twenty-four hours to find the rock, but at least I was more relaxed. That had to help, right? The low rays from the sun turned the walls of my room to copper, and I shut my eyes, feeling warmth like molten gold flowing through my veins, my muscles, tissues, bones, until minutes later, I'd practically melted into the bed.

I had about a second's warning, a sudden frisson of white-hot heat from the hall outside my door. There was a crackle, like a match bursting into flame, and then a familiar voice said, "*Mon ange*, I have found—*Mon Dieu.*"

I shrieked and grabbed the quilt, twisting and yanking it with me as I rolled onto my back and covered myself as best I could. "Eric! Don't you know how to knock?"

"*Non,*" he said, and I felt bad for forgetting he couldn't touch things like doors anymore. I don't think he noticed the *faux pas,* though. He stared at the place where the quilt barely covered my breasts, a dazed expression on his face.

"Up here," I said, pointing to my face. "*Hey*—up here.*"

He shook his head to clear it and met my gaze briefly. The look in his eyes sent a steaming-hot blush all over my skin, which only got worse when he dropped his gaze to my toes and did an excruciatingly slow and thorough perusal of every inch of me not covered by the quilt. Which was quite a bit.

"Are you done yet?"

"*Non,*" he said again, and moved to stand by the bed. He reached a hand out and lightly brushed my bare neck where it joined my shoulder, then dropped his fingers to the skin above my breast. An entirely pleasurable shudder passed through me, and his eyes darkened. "I may be dead. But apparently, it is still possible for me to feel…certain things. Particularly when there is a beautiful woman—a *naked* beautiful woman—spread delectably on a bed before me."

"I thought you didn't poach," I managed weakly, and pulled the quilt tighter.

"I do not." He dropped his hand to his side and sat on the bed, which was only marginally better than when he touched me. I could still feel his presence, like an electrical current arcing between us, carrying waves of desire so strong and hot, I needed another shower to cool off.

"I am sorry I did not alert you to my presence before entering your room."

"It's okay. We just have to figure out a new way for you to knock." I thought for a minute. "Before you came through the door, I felt you. Your…heat."

He seemed surprised. "Truly?"

"Yes. For a second. Maybe next time, you could pause outside the door, and when I feel you there, I can let you know it's safe to enter."

"Mon ange—it will never be safe for me to enter a room in which you reside." He watched me, and his eyes widened. "You feel it now. Do you not?"

There was no point in denial, so with flaming face, I nodded.

He held my gaze. And then—he *pulsed* at me. I don't know how else to describe it. I felt him deliberately send a wave of his desire to me, felt my body receive and accept it as though he'd physically touched me. And boy, did he know how to touch me.

In about half a second, I was going to throw the quilt and caution to the wind, but abruptly he withdrew.

Standing quickly, he moved to the window, his back to me. If he was half as turned on as I was, I could see why he'd want things to, er, settle down before facing me.

After a moment he said softly, "I will not do that again." He turned and while his lower half looked under control, his eyes burned bright. "Unless you ask me to. And then, it will not be poaching."

I managed to nod acceptance of his terms, for that's clearly what they were, and he added, more calmly, "But I will try to 'knock' in future, so as not to catch you unawares."

"Thanks. That would be good." I paused. The moment had passed, but I was still naked, and Jason and Geordi were overdue. "Er, when you came in, you mentioned finding something…?"

"Of course. In all the excitement I had forgotten. I did not find something—I found someone. Your friends, the Rousseaux. They own a villa in Denizli."

Chapter Nineteen

"I do not fear Satan half so much as I fear those who fear him."
~St. Teresa of Avila (1515-1582)

This time, I left Jason a note. He'd still be pissed, but I couldn't help that. I also felt guilty for dumping him with babysitting duty again, but I had to get back to the Temple, and I didn't want Geordi there at night. Luckily, I'd taken the car keys with me when Jason and Geordi headed for the café, or I would've been screwed.

After Eric dropped his bombshell about finding the Rousseaux, I'd shooed him into the bathroom while I dressed and pulled my hair into a ponytail. With my "deadline" less than a day away, I'd already planned to return to the Temple tonight, armed with better grave-robbing implements. But now that Eric assured me the Rousseaux would be otherwise occupied, it was even more urgent.

I couldn't believe it never occurred to me they'd own a luxury villa instead of hiding out in a hot, dusty ruin. Considering their massively expensive car and clothes, it should have been a no-brainer. I couldn't even blame my lapse on having left the grave robbing business, since I'd "retired" in order to fence ridiculously expensive artifacts for the über-rich.

Duh with a capital D.

"You're *sure* the Rousseaux are staying home tonight?" I asked Eric.

We were in the car, en route to a supply shop *l'hôtelier* had recommended. If he thought it strange that I needed a bolt cutter, rope, and a rock pick, he'd held his tongue, and when I asked him not to mention any of it to Jason, he'd merely nodded and gone back to his own business. Very discreet—or totally uninterested. Either worked for me.

Eric said, "They have hired caterers and decorators. It appears they are hosting a party."

I let out a breath. "That's perfect. We can break into the Plutonium and get the rock back, then call Michael down before they know it's missing." I glanced at him. "Are you sure about this? You don't have to do it. I can find another way."

He lifted a shoulder. "I am already dead. What more can I lose?"

"But Nadezhda said—"

"Ouais. You told me. I will not allow myself to be dragged down to Hell."

I pulled into a parking space outside the supply shop, turned the car off, and faced him. "How can you be sure? No offense, but neither of us really knows what we're doing."

"Your faith is touching."

"Eric!"

He reached for my hand, his careful, light touch reminding me more, not less, of his earlier fierce desire. "I will be fine. This was my idea, *non?* There is no other way."

"But—"

"You must get the rock. You must remain on Earth and find a home for your nephew. I can help. It is settled." I opened my mouth, but he cut me off. "Please. I am not entirely selfless. The longer you remain, the longer I have to do this."

He lifted my hand almost to his lips, the heat from his mouth caressing my skin as though it were living breath. He raised his gaze to mine. Then, still watching me, he lowered his mouth, giving my hand the lightest, most sensual of kisses.

Damn, he was good at this whole seduction thing.

A slow smile lit his eyes, and he dropped my hand. "I repeat—it is settled."

If he considered this "settled," I'd hate to see what his idea of *un*-settled was.

I got out and went into the shop, leaving him in the car. This place clearly catered to the archaeological crowd—my own little slice of heaven. Good thing I'd only taken a little cash from Jason's stash, or I would've stocked up on all sorts of tools I didn't technically need for this job. With a small sigh, I picked out the essentials, paid the bill, and returned to the car. Then we drove across the valley to Pamukkale.

Jason and I probably should have moved our base of operations over there by now, to save time and gas, but oh well. I wondered briefly why the Rousseaux didn't keep the rock in their villa. Maybe they thought it would be safer at the Plutonium. Between the poison gas and the gate-to-Hell thing, it was basically Satan's wall safe.

The Rousseaux must know Michael wanted the rock. But at the same time, they must not know about me, or they would have obliterated me long ago. My thoughts drifted to the farmer on Malta, and I felt a twinge of anxiety. *Was* he a demon? Did he know about the rock? Could he have alerted the Rousseaux to my presence, and warned them I might come here?

I suppressed a shiver. Probably best to keep ignoring the parts of this related to Satan, Demons, and Hell. Same way I ignored the "Lily's dead" part. Any time I focused too much on either of those, I frightened myself to death or got horribly depressed. Better to keep pushing all that down for examination later. Much later.

Except I couldn't totally ignore the Hell thing because Eric was about to risk getting sucked down there—*voluntarily*. Which made no difference to my conscience, whatsoever. If he got trapped, it would haunt me to the end of my days. However long that turned out to be.

"You're still sure?" I asked after we'd parked, gotten out of the car, and started to pick our way through Hierapolis toward the Temple.

He didn't even grace me with a reply, probably realizing I was just nervous. Maybe he was, too. Being a cop, odds were he'd had to deal with some pretty awful stuff, but that didn't mean he liked it. Still, he'd made it clear that his strict moral code took precedence over everything else. No doubt he'd buckle down to even the most unpleasant activity, if he thought it was the Right Thing To Do.

I gave a mental head shake. Me—turned on by a *cop*. A dead one, but still. I could hear Vadim now, telling me how stupid I was being. And yet, I couldn't help it. I thought of Eric's lips on my hand, his fingers laced through mine—pictured his arms around me, his mouth tracing light kisses over my face, my teeth teasing that firm lower lip, my tongue tasting his.

I bit back a moan, and ahead of me, Eric stopped on the trail and turned around. His eyes glinted in the lingering light from the just-set sun.

"What?" I said, also stopping. "What's wrong?"

"I felt you. Just now."

"You *felt* me?" *Merde.* "You mean…"

"Ouais. Your lips—they were soft. Your mouth, generous. *Et puis,* you did something…"

His voice trailed off, and I was glad of the low light at my back, hiding my hot blush. "Oh. Sorry."

"Do not apologize. It is good I am not in this alone."

He resumed leading the way, and I followed, embarrassment putting an end to my more inappropriate thoughts. On the other hand…

The path widened as we reached the colonnaded walk, and I hurried to catch up. "About what you said back there—I didn't know it worked both ways. The sensing each other, I mean."

"I suppose I did not, either. It just…happened." He looked at me searchingly. "When I was on the hill with the Dead, I could swear I felt you then as well. It is in part why I fought to heal myself." A slow smile curved his mouth. *"Bien sûr*, that was less…*pleasurable*…than this."

What could I say? On the one hand, I was glad to help. On the other, it made everything more complicated.

"This could be a good thing," I said, and Eric's smile widened, making my face flame. "No! For tonight—for what we're about to do."

At the hotel, I'd told him what I'd learned from Nadezhda, and it turned out he'd gleaned a little knowledge of his own, from the Dead at Pamukkale. While the gasses kept the Living away from the Plutonium, the Dead had at various times forayed inside. Many returned, some did not. The ones who did told of twisty little passages, of needing to go down in order to get back up, of false entrances and exits, and always—*always*—of the incessant heat and the urge to follow it, to give in, to allow oneself to be sucked into oblivion.

"If you can sense me," I continued, "maybe it will help you find your way back out."

"Perhaps," Eric agreed, and I started to say again that he didn't have to do this, then stopped. It wouldn't do any good, and his ironic smile only proved the point.

I threw up my hands. "Okay. All right. But please—you have to come back. If you can't find the rock, or it's too far in, just leave. Promise me."

"Very well. I promise."

I only half believed him, but at least he'd made the effort. Besides, I really didn't have another option, unless I chose to wait for the Rousseaux to bring the rock out for me. Somehow, ambushing Demons of the Last Circle of Hell still didn't seem like something I was qualified for.

We reached the Temple, walked around to the side with the iron grate, and I got out my tools. Eric lounged against a chunk of broken stone, watching me. We both knew he couldn't help with this part, and as soon as I picked up the bolt cutter and popped the padlock off the grate, a rush of memories and familiar sensations washed through me.

God, I'd missed this.

"Impressive," Eric said, and it occurred to me that maybe I should've pretended I'd never broken into a building before. One of Eric's eyebrows quirked up as though inviting an explanation—or a confession—but I ignored him and set to work.

It took some doing, but I managed to remove the grate without damaging it. The lock couldn't be salvaged, but at least it could be replaced. Once the grate was off, the opening was large enough that I should be able to wedge myself in under the arch. Originally, before Eric hatched his plan to help me, my idea was to take off the grate and use the rock pick to hack at the stones inside, until I made an opening large enough to fit myself through. I didn't know what I'd do about the poison, but I thought I could at least learn if the rock was still within.

Instead, Eric assured me that, with practice, he was getting more comfortable passing through barriers. I got the sense it wasn't something he wanted to do *all* the time—for instance, he still let me open and close doors for him, when possible—but he swore it took very little out of him. And in this case, it would save a ton of time and damage to the Temple.

Of course, I'd have to remove at least one brick in order to get the rock out. But damaging the wall was pointless if Eric came up empty-handed, so I'd worry about that later.

"Ready?" I asked, and he nodded. I stepped away from the alcove, and he moved to the spot where I'd stood. Then he turned and without warning dragged me into his arms.

He didn't kiss me, just held on, sharing his heat.

There was desire, yes, but something else as well, something elemental, which he gave out and took back from me. It flowed between us, energy in, energy out, warmth and heat and a soft light I saw in my mind's eye.

"To strengthen our bond," he whispered, and then he released me and faced the alcove.

Before I could marshal my thoughts, the now familiar crackling sound popped around him, and he was gone.

Sudden irrational panic whipped through me. "Eric!" I tossed the pick into the alcove, then hauled myself up and placed my palms on the stones at the back. "Eric—can you hear me?"

From the other side came a faint chuckle. "*Mon ange.* You will literally wake the Dead if you do not lower your voice."

I sighed with relief. "You're okay? You made it through?"

"Yes. Again, a little faith." There was a short pause. "I am in a tunnel. It descends rapidly. You will not be able to hear me for long. Can you feel my presence through the stones?"

We hadn't had time to practice any of this, so I wasn't sure what to do, but in the end, I didn't have to *do* anything. As soon as I wondered if I could still sense him, I did. It was that easy. Even through the bricks, I could tell exactly where he stood.

"You're close to the wall, perhaps a meter to the"—I oriented myself—"to the south."

"Bon. I can sense you as well." There was another short pause, and then I heard the disappointment in his tone. "But the rock—I do not sense it at all. *Et toi…?"*

It was as we'd suspected then. It wasn't my death that made me aware of the rock. Of course not—I'd first sensed it when wholly alive. But a tiny part of me had hoped that Eric, being dead, would have the same ability.

I took a deep breath. We'd discussed this, and had come up with Plan B. If I could sense the location of the rock in the Plutonium, and I could also sense Eric, I might be able to direct him to it. Now that we knew he could sense me, it helped, but the chance was still slim.

Then there was the not-so-small matter of him "carrying" the rock out. Beaning Jason with the vase was the first and only time he'd done anything like it. But that was a short, fast action, whereas this would be longer and more involved. He seemed to think he'd figure it out, though, so I pressed my palms against the stones and concentrated on the one thing I could do.

At first, Eric's presence in my mind was so strong, I felt nothing else. Panic rose again, and I forced myself to focus.

There—I detected something behind Eric. The sensations coalesced, then separated into two distinct threads, and, somehow, I knew *this* one was Eric, and *that* one was the rock.

"Yes!" I said. "I feel it—just barely. It must be a long way in."

"Then I had better get started."

He moved away, and I called out, "Eric! Wait—"

But he was already too far. I drew another shaky breath. I had to stay calm, or this would never work. I left my palms against the stones and closed my eyes, attuning myself to the night as I had when I felt the rock here before.

It worked. As my breathing slowed, the two threads became more vivid in my mind. The rock's was still thinner and dimmer, but Eric's was strong and bright, and I let out a sigh of relief. Then I tried to figure out how the hell to show Eric's thread the way to the rock's.

Neither changed position in my mind, and I knew they were still far apart. I shifted my concentration to the rock's thread, so faint, I kept almost losing it, but at last I pinned it down. Its energy felt…different…than in Marseille. Smaller, and less…sure? Had the Rousseaux already altered it, in preparation for the main ritual? Or was it simply too far inside the Plutonium for me to accurately sense it?

More than that, though, it felt as if the rock didn't recognize me. The whole thing sounded crazier by the second, but I couldn't shake the sensation that the rock wasn't sure it wanted to go to me. Surely, I was better than Demons from Hell?

I took a deep breath. Then I "grabbed" the rock's thread and held on, while simultaneously reaching for Eric. To my surprise, Eric's thread pulsed in my mind, brighter and stronger than before. Had he felt my "touch"?

At the thought, it happened again, warm, solid, *good* energy, and I knew he had. Not only that, I knew he was pretty far in, at a crossroads. All at once, the two threads in my mind shifted and switched and I instantly saw he needed to take the left-hand passage to get to the rock.

But how to tell him? It was one thing to feel a connection, and know he felt it, too. But how could I actually direct him anywhere?

I tried thinking *left-left-left,* but nothing happened. The two threads stayed put in my mind.

Think. What was it about the rock, that I could feel it? Or Eric?

What was it about *me*, that made any of this insanity a reality?

The rock. Eric. Me.

Vibrations, like a tuning fork, thrumming out from the center of the Earth. An elemental connection, like molten iron, snaking through solid stone.

And…a vessel, to receive them both, hold them for a while, and release them when necessary.

I didn't need to *push* Eric and the rock together. I couldn't. I needed to open myself up and let them both in—allow their energy to fill me and, well, use me.

As soon as I had the thought, the rock's thread glowed brighter, and it stopped fighting me. I opened myself to it, let its energy slide into me, through my veins, filling my organs, then did the same with Eric's. When I felt them both deep inside me, I pulled the rock's thread closer to Eric's, and suddenly felt him move down the left passage.

I barely had time to process my sheer relief when I sensed him coming to another junction, this one with three tunnels branching out. But it was easier this time—as though the rock trusted me now and was eager to be found. Without me consciously doing anything, its thread pulled closer to Eric's again, and he chose a passage and moved on.

This happened over and over, countless times. Eric drew closer by the second, until abruptly, he was there. I felt his excitement—felt the rock's—the two threads merged into a spark so bright, it was almost too much.

247

And then, just as quick, Eric's thread pulled away, back outside of me. It thinned, grew dimmer, and I felt the rock's terror at losing him, almost as great as my own.

Eric! My mind screamed it, though I knew he couldn't hear me. *God—no!*

He was so far in—Hell must be sucking him down. *That* must be what the librarian meant when he said the stones trapped the heat. And he'd mentioned the calcium silicate in the bricks. Could the quartz, which was so common around here, protect Eric? Even if it did, I had no way to tell him about it now. Stupid of me not to think of it sooner, when we were still together.

Cold panic wracked my chest. I'd almost lost him once—I couldn't face that again. I forced oxygen into my lungs, dug my nails into my palms, anything to cut through the fear. I felt in my mind for Eric's thread, desperate, seeking any sign of him. *There*—but it was faint, a shadow behind my eyelids instead of the bright, warm cord it had been moments before. I pulled at it, but it lay limp and unresponsive, drifting relentlessly farther away with every passing second.

Don't give in—you are not *allowed to leave me!*

Suddenly, I remembered what had happened on Malta. I stopped my frantic mental scrabbling and sat perfectly still, picturing a clear bubble of sorts, like the one I'd felt or seen or whatever it was, at the standing stones. Somehow, I knew to picture the way it formed, pulling quartz and lime, and other elements I didn't recognize, from the surrounding stones, the passage floors, even the dirt and grass. I thought of all the elements in the earth and wove them together.

I held the bubble for a moment, picturing its

strength, then I took it, and like a cart on a pulley, I hurled it down a thread of my own, sending everything I had to Eric.

Then I waited and prayed, harder than I ever had in my life.

At first, nothing happened. Then like a hand grabbing a rope, I felt him latch onto my thread. I sat bolt upright, eyes tightly shut, and pictured the bubble enclosing him, protecting him from the heat. There was a moment of confused grasping, my thread, the rock's, his, all merging, twisting and tangling together, before each thread sorted itself out.

His grip tightened, he gave a tug—the universal signal for *pull me out!*—and I did. I pulled as hard as I could. I felt him move forward, but slowly, as though he were being sucked backward after all.

The bubble.

It seemed I could protect him or pull him free—not both.

Which left me only one alternative.

With a sob of anguish for the risk I was about to take, I took a deep breath, then gave a fast, hard tug on my thread. With an energetic *pop!* the side of the bubble closest to me burst into a million particles of glittering light as Eric and the rock tore through and rushed toward me at breakneck speed up the passages. I felt the dark heat clawing at him, but the half of the bubble that was left behind slowed it down, absorbed some of it. And the closer Eric got, the stronger his thread, the more sure I was he wouldn't be sucked back in.

I jumped down from the alcove and grabbed the pick. Despite the wall's tightly-joined appearance, it wasn't hard to loosen one of the stones. I found a place in the mortar that had already started to crumble, took careful aim, and gave it a sharp tap. The mortar gave way, and I wedged the point of the pick between two bricks, wiggling and forcing it inward until with a scraping, cracking noise one of them broke free and tumbled to the ground.

Just in time. I no longer needed to picture the threads in my mind—both Eric and the rock raced closer, so close, I simply felt them like "normal." Whatever the hell normal was.

I released them, felt them shimmer out of my body just as something small shot through the opening in the stone wall. A moment later, I heard the familiar crackle and Eric appeared, pale, shaken, looking worse than when his wound ate at him. He stumbled forward and wrapped his arms convulsively around me, and I dropped the pick and clung to him.

"You made it. You're here you're safe."

"Ouais." His voice was hoarse, his face gray in the moonlight.

"What happened?"

"Don't know. Found the rock—tried to touch it. Couldn't. Thought of the vase."

"You made the rock an extension of yourself?" He nodded, and I said, "Then what?"

"I moved it…the heat…too much. Wanted to let go. Of everything. You."

As though to deny the power Hell had tried to exert over him, he clutched me tighter. I didn't say anything. I didn't need to. He was here. He'd made it out. I buried my face in his shoulder, and he cupped the back of my head. He murmured in French, words of endearment I shouldn't have let him say, but in the aftermath of crisis I couldn't stop him. I didn't want to.

Finally, though, I remembered the reason we'd come here—why he'd almost been sucked down to Hell. I sensed it on the ground nearby, stronger than when it was in the Plutonium, but still fainter than in Marseille. Reluctantly, I pulled away, but Eric understood.

"Go—take it. That is why I brought it to you."

He leaned against the Temple while I turned and hunted in the dark. It took several passes, stooping over the uneven ground, before I pinpointed it. I reached out and picked it up. And immediately realized the problem.

The rock felt unfamiliar—because it *was* unfamiliar.

I turned to Eric, so shocked I could barely get the words out. "It's the wrong one. This isn't the rock I've been looking for."

Chapter Twenty

*"And the house, when it was in building, was built
of stone made ready before it was brought thither."*
~The Bible, 1 Kings 6:7

I was so stunned by the enormity of what we'd
done I couldn't think.

Apparently, we'd broken into Satan's "safe" and
stolen a rock I didn't know existed, that Michael might
not know had been found. This could be good—
Michael wanted all the pieces of the broken slab, didn't
he? Or it could be bad—this wasn't the piece I'd agreed
to find, and might not fulfill my obligation. Worse, it
was close to midnight—almost Saturday. If this rock
didn't do the trick, I had less than twenty hours to find
the other one.

I looked at the piece in my hand. Similar color and
composition—it could easily have come from the same
source as the first shard. Plus, there was that whole "hot
and humming at Hyacinth" thing. But instead of being
half the size of a football, this piece was smaller than a
tennis ball. One side curved outward, rough and pocked
with indentations, the other was sheared flat. If I had to
guess, I'd say this was an outside piece, where the other
rock's all-flat sides and jagged edges indicated it came
from the interior.

Of course, now that I'd reached this lovely

conclusion, it didn't help. I was so worn out I could hardly stand. I'd barely slept in the last two days, on top of not eating since breakfast. Whatever Eric had gone through to get this rock had taken a lot out of him. Maybe too much—he still stood, propped against the Temple, looking about ten seconds away from total collapse.

"Let's get out of here," I said, slipping the shard into my pocket. I needed food and sleep and time to think. I didn't have much of the latter, but I sure as hell didn't want to face Michael or demons or anyone else in my current state. Including Jason, but that was unavoidable.

I took the brick I'd removed from the wall and slid it back into place. With the mortar scraped off, the fit was loose, but to the casual observer it might pass muster. The bars on the grate were relatively straight, and I got it back into place, but the lock was toast. I left it next to the grate, gathered up my tools, and led the way to the car, where we tossed everything in the trunk and drove back to Denizli.

At the hotel, Eric split. While asking after the Rousseaux today, he'd also found a place to stay, a sort of hospice for the Dead, and truth be told, I was relieved to not have to worry about him and Jason at the same time. I waited until he rounded the street corner, then headed upstairs.

I figured Jason would be waiting up for me, angry, and I wasn't disappointed. When I opened the door to my room, he sat on the bed just as he'd done this morning, arms crossed, legs out. He'd left the lights on this time but put Geordi to sleep in his room again.

I closed the door, fished the rock out of my pocket

and dropped it on the dresser, then faced him. He took one look at me and slid off the bed, coming to me and pulling me close.

It was so different from Eric, but God, I needed this too. Wordlessly he walked me back to the bed and sat me on it, then picked up a bag from the side table and spread the contents before me. Cold cheeseburger and fries, warm soda.

"Eat," he said.

Somewhere in my brain, I knew it wasn't a very good burger. And yet, my taste buds nearly melted when the meat hit them. I'm pretty sure I moaned. I ate it and the fries so fast, I honestly don't remember chewing. I downed the soda, then looked hopefully at the bag.

"More?" Jason asked.

I nodded, and he disappeared through the bathroom, coming back a few moments later with half a wrapped burger in one hand and meat sticks in the other. "Here's the rest of Geordi's that he didn't finish, and I picked these up at the store."

He sat on the bed while I polished off the burger and tore into the meat sticks. They turned out to be spiced lamb, and my only regret was that I couldn't chew them fast enough.

"Hey—slow down a little," Jason said. "There's more where that came from. It's actually a pretty good grocery store. They even sell apricot delight. I got Geordi two boxes, and I think he finished the first one already. I told him we'd go back tomorrow."

I nodded, still incapable of speech. Between the burgers and the lamb, my stomach was now actively engaged in digestion, which meant the rest of me *really* wanted to zonk out. Jason cleared away the garbage, and I leaned back against the pillow. Just an hour or two, that's all I needed, and I'd be raring to go.

I was vaguely aware of him turning off the light and climbing into bed next to me. He wrapped me in his arms, and I think he might have kissed the top of my head. Then I passed out.

****

When I woke hours later, Jason still spooned me, his arm across my chest, his breath warm on my ear. It felt good—safe and secure. Which paradoxically made me feel bad.

Whatever had happened with Eric had also felt good. And right. So either enjoying Jason was disloyal to Eric, or wanting Eric was disloyal to Jason. And the real problem was that I shouldn't want *either* of them. As I've said, the few relationships I've had were on the casual side. No serious attachments—no "one that got away," or even "one that got close." But I'm no good at one-night stands, either.

Vadim, on the other hand, knew how to string women along. It's a good thing he was like a brother to me, because if he'd tried to get me into bed, I'm sure I would've believed every lie he told me along the way. On the day he died, he had *two* women on the boat with him. They wore life vests, he did not. I'd never thought to ask *les flics* for their names. I was in such shock, there were lots of questions I didn't ask then—and many more I should have asked Vadim, before he died.

Like, *did you happen to pick up any screaming rocks on your last trip to Turkey?*

I felt the low hum of the new rock, which I'd left loose on the dresser last night, too tired even to drop it in a drawer. Hiding it wouldn't do any good, anyway. I mean, Demons from the Last Circle of Hell probably wouldn't be stumped by pine boards and cherry veneer.

I counted back in my head. It was at least six months since Vadim's accident. No, wait—it was exactly six months. He'd died on March fifth.

The fifth.

I shot up in bed, startling Jason awake. He squinted at me. "Wha—?"

The clock—I had to crane my neck around him to see it. *Merde.* It was nearly eight. I jumped off the bed, noting I still wore my grubby tank and shorts from last night. I needed to change—no time for a shower—and call Michael down, both of which required I be alone.

"Get up!" I said to Jason. "Go back to your room—I need to change."

He yawned and stretched. "What's the rush?" He paused, coming more fully awake. "Never mind. You aren't going to tell me, just like you won't tell me where you went last night or who you were with."

"Please—I don't have time for this." I hesitated. "It's today—the thing I have to find—I have to get it back by sunset. If it all works out, I'll tell you about it then. I promise."

His gaze flicked to the rock on the dresser. "That's not it?"

I shook my head.

"But…you thought it might be. That's what you were doing last night—picking up a rock." His tone implied what his words left out, that I was a looney-tunes for risking my life, and his and Geordi's, hunting down boring little bits of stone. "And…these rocks have something to do with you and the Rousseaux."

I nodded.

"Fuck, Hyacinth!" He got out of bed, towering over me. "Are you working for them? God damn it—tell me! Are you one of them?"

The attack was so far out of left field, I staggered. "Why on earth would you think that? They killed my sister!"

"How the fuck should I know? Maybe they got their teeth into you—sucked you into their world—you got in too deep." He grabbed my shoulders, digging into my skin, his eyes almost black with fear-fueled rage. "Get out—it's not worth it. Whatever hold they have on you, *it's not worth it.*"

"No—it's not what you think!"

"Then why are you looking for these damn rocks for them?"

So that's what this was about. I should have told him sooner. If not everything, then I should have been clearer about what I did say. No wonder he was freaking out, if he thought I'd hooked up with the demons who killed Lily. Not that he knew they were demons, but still.

"I promise," I said, "I am *not* working for the Rousseaux."

"Then you're working with them."

"*What?* Are you insane?"

"No, but I'm finally starting to think you are."

I forced myself to take a breath. If he already thought I was crazy, I might as well tell him the truth. His reaction to *that* would have to be better than this. Or maybe I'd just had it with lying. Telling Eric worked out. Of course, he was dead, and already part and parcel of the Crazy New World of Hyacinth Finch, while

Jason still had no idea what he'd gotten himself into.

"Look," I began, *"I am not working for or with the Rousseaux.* Okay? I'm—"

There was a sharp tap on the door, so startling, I jumped. Jason's gaze snapped to the door and he placed a finger over my lips. I suppose, since I was the one both the Rousseaux and the Dioguardis had an interest in, it made sense to let him do the talking.

"Quoi?" he called out.

A muffled male voice said, "Message for Ms. Finch."

So much for our cover as the Leclercs. Not only had the man used my real name, he'd spoken in English, not French—not even Turkish. I glanced at Jason, who looked as worried as I was. Of course, he probably thought it was the Rousseaux.

"Expecting someone?" he asked in a low voice.

"No. Nobody knows I'm here—I swear!"

He searched my face, then squeezed my shoulders in a clear order to stay put. He went to the door, the lack of a peephole forcing him to open it a crack to see out.

"Je regrette," he said, *"qu'il n'y a pas de Finch ici."*

"Are you certain? I had thought this was the correct room."

Merde.

Okay, *one* person knew I was here, and with the door open, that deep, booming voice was unmistakable. I moved quickly around Jason, ignoring his attempt to keep me hidden.

Sure enough, Michael stood in the hall, dressed in long robes and a very Turkish turban. Unfortunately, the costume only emphasized his lack of resemblance to the Turks. He was too pale, too bulky—he filled the hall, his beard flowing down his robe, his brown eyes twinkling. Great. Like Satan, the Angel of Death also had a sense of humor.

At least I wouldn't have to call him down.

"It's all right," I said to Jason. "This is…" I looked at Michael, whose grin widened. I'd get no help from that quarter. "A…friend. I need to talk with him."

Jason glared at me. "Alone? No dice."

"Please—just…please…" Damn Michael anyway, for putting me in this position. Not only did Jason think I was nuts, he thought I'd gone over to the Dark Side. And here Michael was, popping up out of nowhere, dressed like some giant, hairy Biblical figure—which technically, he was—making me a liar for saying no one knew I was here.

"I assure you," Michael interjected, "Hyacinth will be perfectly safe with me."

Even I wasn't sure of that. Jason's eyes narrowed, and he said, "Who the hell are you?"

"A friend. Of her partner, Vadim. I helped him with his, er, final journey."

Luckily Jason still stared suspiciously at Michael and missed the shock no doubt spreading across my face. Michael had sent Vadim on his way? But Vadim was an atheist. Now I had even more questions. For one thing, it occurred to me after all this time that if Vadim *was* an atheist, he should still be on Earth somewhere. Maybe I could find him—ask him about the rock, the accident, everything.

But did Michael mean Vadim had actually gone to Heaven, or, quite possibly, to Hell, and was lost to me forever? That had to be it—Michael had said repeatedly that he didn't interact with souls who chose to stay here. Damn, damn, damn.

I looked at Jason. "It's okay. Really."

Jason stared down at me, several emotions warring in his eyes. Anger, fear, and…hurt. Like I'd betrayed him. Maybe I had. But—why did he think it now? What in the last few minutes drove him over the edge? He turned wordlessly and went through the bathroom to his room, closing both doors as he went.

I felt his leaving like a physical blow and took an unconscious step after him before remembering my giant, oddly-dressed visitor standing in the hall. Jason would have to wait. But I made a promise to myself then and there. I'd started to tell him the truth, and I'd finish, at the first opportunity. I'd earn back his trust if it killed me. Again.

Feeling the first real hope I'd had in a while, I motioned Michael in and shut the door.

"Well?" he said promptly.

With everything else, I'd nearly forgotten the rock shard. Might as well get the hard part over. "I didn't find the rock yet. Not the one I had in Marseille, anyway. But I did find this."

I picked the shard up off the dresser. Its hum was stronger now, and it practically glowed with happy energy. When Michael saw it, his eyes widened, and he looked as surprised as when I'd told him I sensed the first rock. He took it from me, turning it in his hands.

"Child—how in God's name did you retrieve this? It is so small—even I can barely sense it. Where was it? How did you get it back?"

"Does it matter?" If he could withhold information,

why shouldn't I? It was a gamble, given his power over me. But something in me still wanted to keep Eric a secret, and I couldn't see how to tell Michael about the Plutonium without revealing Eric's part in it.

Michael studied me. "Very well," he said at last. "It does not matter. But I am impressed—such a small piece."

"Then…we're good? This fulfills my obligation to you?"

"No."

Merde. Not exactly unexpected, but still. "Please—it's a piece of your sanctuary. I got it back, from Satan himself. Surely that's good enough?"

"You stole this…*from Satan?*"

Oops. So much for evading the truth. "From the Plutonium at Hierapolis," I admitted. "That's basically Satan's foyer, right? Or one of them. He had to know it was there—maybe the Rousseaux were going to send it through to him, with the other shard."

"Child, you never fail to amaze me." He saw the hope in my eyes and shook his head. "But no, this does not satisfy our bargain. You were to find the rock the Rousseaux took from you. While it is beyond incredible that you are able to sense shards so small, this one won't do."

"Why? For pity's sake—tell me why you need the rocks, so I can do my damn job!"

He seemed surprised. Maybe he wasn't deliberately withholding information after all. I suppose the more knowledge someone has, the less it occurs to them that others might *not* have that knowledge, or that it could be useful.

"It is less that I need them, and more that Satan

wants them. You mentioned my sanctuaries. I assume you know the story of Colossae?" I nodded, and he continued. "After I split the rock, the waters of the Lycus became forever holy. Satan hates that—hates that I stopped him and brought something better to the world in place of what he tried to destroy. He wishes to find the shards of rock, so that he can piece them back together."

"I thought he wanted to destroy them—to finish what he started."

Michael shook his head. "The ritual the Rousseaux will perform—it is to seal the rock's energy, before they send it to Satan."

"So it won't affect him—harm him in some way?"

"Precisely."

"But if that's the case, wouldn't destroying the rocks make more sense? They really couldn't hurt him then."

"Think, child. What would happen if, instead of destroying the rock shards forever, Satan found enough pieces to rebuild the slab?"

It took a moment, working backward through the legend, for me to hazard a guess. "I suppose he could force the river back to its original course. But, would that be enough to un-sanctify it?"

"Perhaps. Perhaps not. But that is not the only consideration—as I'm sure you've guessed, the rocks hold some of my power. While the pieces remain separate and on Earth, they are harmless. What do you suppose would happen, should they be reconnected?"

He waited expectantly. I think he wanted to see how I worked it through, and I tried to remember any knowledge I'd gleaned over the years, that might be relevant.

"Logically, piecing the slab together with your powers in it would recreate your sanctuary, and increase your strength on Earth."

"True. That is *one* logical conclusion."

I blew out a breath. Not that, then. What would be the flip side?

"Okay. If putting the rocks together doesn't increase your strength, it must…" *That's it.* I turned to him excitedly. "The ritual—it *cloaks* your energy in the shards, in small chunks. If Satan finds enough pieces and links them together, he can seal off that much of your power." I felt a sudden sick understanding. "Not seal it off—he can use it for himself. The power will become his, not yours, destroying the balance you've maintained since the dawn of time."

"Exactly."

Unfortunately, now I understood why finding this shard didn't help. "This piece is so small, it won't make a difference, will it?"

"That is correct." He turned the shard over, rubbing his thumb tenderly over the rough side. "This is a beautiful piece. To me, they all are. But it is an edge piece, and not critical to the structure." He placed the shard in a pouch on his belt, then raised his gaze to mine. "I do not make bargains lightly. I am sure you can understand that what I have done, allowing you this time on Earth, puts me at great risk. If I let one soul return, all may want to. That is neither possible, nor right. I could be banished forever, even as I banished Satan so long ago." His tone was sad, but firm. "You have until tonight, to retrieve the original rock."

What could I say? I might help my clients steal and

backstab their way to extraordinary art collections, but I had a code of honor. I couldn't blame him for holding me to my word.

"Can you at least tell me where at Colossae the ritual will be performed?"

Michael shook his head. "Truly, I do not know. Believe what you will, but I am still neither omnipotent nor omniscient." He thought for a moment. "I would say near the river, but as that is the site of Satan's failure, he may find it too humiliating. My best guess would be at my church."

"And where on the site is *that?*"

"Child. It is thousands of years since these events occurred. Much has changed the land—not to mention my memory. But I believe there is a bend in the river where, if you face the mound at sunset, then look to the west, it will appear as though the river pours directly into the sun. I am fairly certain the church would be due south from there."

"Great. Thanks a bunch."

He gave me a sympathetic look. "I am truly sorry. I know how impossible this seems. However, I am beginning to think you are even more resourceful than I first thought." He shook his head in wonder. "How ever did you survive the poison gas?"

Damn, I'd hoped he'd forgotten that part. I hedged. "Maybe being reborn helped. I didn't have to go far, and I wasn't in there long."

Michael examined me for a long moment. "Perhaps. As I've said, there is much I do not know of your situation. Still—stealing from Satan himself. Incredible." He paused, and when he spoke again, there was genuine concern in his tone. "Have a care,

Hyacinth. Satan does not like to be cheated."

And with that, he vanished.

Disappointment washed through me. Despite my better judgment, I'd allowed myself to hope this shard would be enough. On top of that, I'd forgotten to ask about Vadim. Not that I could focus on him now anyway. I only had a few hours to get the original rock back, and unfortunately, the most likely place left to look was the Rousseaux's villa.

But thanks to Michael, they weren't even the worst I had to worry about. Call me crazy, but it really hadn't occurred to me just *how pissed* the Prince of Darkness might get at being robbed. Even if I'd only taken the first rock, Satan probably wouldn't have been too happy with me. Stealing from him twice—I shuddered to think what would happen if I were caught.

If *we* were caught. Because now I'd dragged Eric into this with me. I hadn't asked exactly what happened to him in the Plutonium, but if he was almost sucked into Hell, it couldn't be good. I wondered how close he'd gotten. Close enough for Satan to sense him, maybe even recognize him if he came near enough again?

Best not to think about any of it. Best to focus on the immediate task: finding Eric, so he could take me to the Rousseaux. I needed his help with that, at least. But first, I needed to make sure Jason would stay with Geordi.

I changed into fresh clothes, then headed through the bathroom, pausing at his door to gear up for another fight. He'd be pissed that I wanted to run off alone, *again*. But I couldn't risk Geordi's life, or his. Me, I didn't *have* a life, unless I got the rock back. Of course,

Jason didn't know that, and I was sure we'd end up in another shouting match before I got away. I took a deep breath, heart pounding, palms sweaty. I had no time—I prayed that however unpleasant this was, it would be over fast.

I knocked once and pushed the door open—only to find when I got through that Jason was gone.

And so was Geordi.

Chapter Twenty-One

"Man's enemies are not demons, but human beings like himself."

~Lao Tzu, ca. 6th century BCE

"Bâtard. Espèce d'salaud—fils d'cochon—j'vais l'niquer la guele. Je—"

Eric continued in this vein for a solid minute, creatively insulting Jason and describing in great detail what he'd do to him when we found him. *If* we found him.

Panic rose and I shoved it down. I did *not* strike a bargain with the Angel of Death, and agree to rob demons and Satan, only to have the reason for it snatched from under my nose.

After discovering Jason and Geordi gone, I'd raced down to the street, hoping I'd catch them or find some clue to their whereabouts. The car was still here, so they couldn't have gone far, but there was no sign of them on the crowded block. Right about then, Eric had rounded the corner and found me on the curb, head in my hands, trying not to throw up. He, on the other hand, looked none the worse after almost being sucked into Hell eight hours ago.

"They went to the store," I said. "The car's here. I'm sure they just walked to the store."

"Without leaving a note?"

"If they did, I deserved it. I did it to Jason first."

Maybe that's what this was—Jason had finally decided I deserved some payback for all I'd put him through. If that was his plan, it was working fine, thank you. I was pissed and scared and—I hated to admit it—hurt. All of which Jason had felt toward me at one time or another. Maybe most of the time since we'd left Marseille.

Problem was, at no point in our relationship had he ever been petty. Mad as hell, yes. But he'd stuck around, been there for me, no matter what. Why leave now? And why take Geordi, when he knew it would kill me?

"The store—it is within walking distance, *non?*"

Eric was right. I jumped up. "Jason said it's near the place where he got the burgers." I turned in that direction, and Eric followed.

It wasn't hard to find. I asked the manager of the restaurant, since I assumed that's what Jason had done, and he told me where to go. Unfortunately, it was a dead end.

"I remember them from last night," the store owner said when I asked. "Tall man and a small boy, dark-haired, yes? But I have not seen them this morning. I am the only one here. I would know."

I swallowed my disappointment. "Thanks. Can you at least show me where the apricot delight is?" If nothing else, I'd get Geordi more sugary slugs. An affirmation of sorts that I *would* see him again, and soon.

"Certainly." The man led the way down an aisle. "Your tall friend—he asked for apricot delight as well. It is a favorite treat of your son, yes?"

I started to correct him about Geordi being my son—and then my blood froze and I stopped in my tracks, Eric bumping into me. *"What did you say?"*

The man turned to look at me in confusion. "Your friend—he asked for apricot delight."

"By name? He asked for it *by name?"*

"Of course."

He obviously thought I was off my rocker, but I had to be sure. "He didn't call it sugary slugs, or ask Geordi—the little boy—to describe it to you?"

The man shook his head decisively. "Not at all. It was the first thing your friend said when they came in—*Please tell me you sell apricot delight.* Just like that."

I was going to be sick. Or collapse. Or both.

Oh God. Ohgodohgodohgod.

The owner walked a few more paces down the aisle, and showed me the place on the shelf where Geordi's favorite treat was stocked. Somehow, I got through picking up a box, paying for it, and returning to the street, but I don't remember any of it.

"Quoi?" Eric demanded as soon as we were outside. "What is it? What has your *friend* done now?"

I said numbly, "He knows what sugary slugs are. And I didn't tell him."

"Perhaps your nephew described them to him?"

Oh God—I really was going to be sick. "No. Geordi doesn't know what they are—if anything, he might say they're orange slices. I don't think he knows what an apricot is."

Eric pursed his lips. "I do not like your friend. This is true. But, I am still not certain I understand…?"

I had to breathe. Had to force air into my lungs.

Last night, Jason said he bought Geordi *apricot delight,* and I was too tired to notice. Now, wave after wave of nausea rolled through me. I'd been so grateful for the comfort he offered, so relieved to know he was my friend.

"It's a family joke." My tongue felt like lead and I had to work to get the words out. "No one knows about sugary slugs—there's *no way* Jason could know they're apricot delight—unless he's been spying on me."

Shit.

Right after Lily filed for divorce, that's when Jason showed up. Worked his way in, made me trust him and...*like* him. Even after I knew he wasn't who he pretended to be, he strung me along, providing everything I needed, right when I needed it. He'd said I would hate him, but, oh God, I'd refused to believe him. Possibly the only time he'd told me the truth, and I wouldn't listen.

The question was, *why?* Why spy on me? Why come to Turkey? Why take care of me, of Geordi, only to snatch him now?

But there was something else, something far, far worse. Spying on me *wasn't* the only way Jason could know about apricot delight—and there was one other person who knew the joke. I recoiled from the thought, then made myself examine it anyway.

What if Jason found out what sugary slugs were...*from Nick?*

Was Jason working for the Dioguardis?

My brain refused to accept it—*not Jason*—not the person I'd trusted most, next to Lily and Vadim. God, I'd *kissed* him—considered doing much more—he made me feel so *safe.*

The words he'd said in Marseille came back to haunt me: *From what I've seen of the Dioguardi empire…*

Shit. I'd even thought he'd make a good guardian for Geordi.

Which brought me up short. If he was working for the Dioguardis, why not take Geordi the night Lily died? She'd pushed him into Jason's arms—why not run straight to Nick's family and hand him over?

Oh, God. I couldn't breathe, couldn't feel my hands or feet.

Eric pushed me to the curb. "Bend over. Put your head between your knees. It will help."

I did what he said. It didn't help.

Eric. He'd said all along that Jason looked familiar.

And then I knew—should have seen it before. Not that black hair and blue eyes are that unusual. But Geordi had them—and Nick, and Nick's father—they all did—the signature look of the Dioguardis. I'd seen Jason's blue eyes dark with passion, run my fingers through the soft black mane of his hair.

And the height.

At just over six feet, Nick was on the short side for his family. Unlike his son, who was shaping up to be taller, like Nick's father, or his cousins.

Like…Jason.

The resemblance was there the whole damn time, and I'd never even noticed.

Ohgodohgodohgod.

Jason was a Dioguardi. And I *gave* him my nephew.

When I found them, I'd kill him before Eric got the chance.

****

In some bizarre way, I only felt worse when Eric and I trucked back upstairs at the hotel and found that not only had Jason left me the car keys, he'd also left a wad of cash. He'd betrayed me, destroyed any trust I'd ever had in him—did he have to be so goddamned *nice* about it?

He had cleaned everything else out of the room, though, including his belongings, Geordi's backpack, and their fake passports. He even took their toiletries from the bathroom.

"So it is certain he left on purpose," Eric said, as though I might still have doubts.

"Looks that way."

At least he hadn't said *I told you so,* though he had every right. He *had* told me—so had Jason. I had to stop going in circles.

"*Alors—on y va?* Where next?"

Every fiber in me screamed that I needed to get Geordi back. But sunset was only a few hours away. If I didn't get the rock by then, I'd lose him to the Dioguardis forever.

"Rock first, then Geordi," I said, pocketing the money and snatching the keys. "Let's go."

Eric grabbed my arm as I headed for the door. He vibrated with suppressed anger, but he drew a deep ghost-breath and blew it out. "I do not like Jason. *Et puis,* you know *comme j'déteste les* Dioguardis. But…I do not believe he will hurt your nephew. Truly."

I nodded, unable to speak. Since I'd figured the awful truth out, I'd been a little worried that Eric would abandon me, too. Either to hare off after Jason himself, or because of my severely questionable judgment. Eric must have guessed some of my past by now. Once he saw me break into the Rousseaux's villa, how long would it be before his morals killed his desire? For now, he was sticking by me, though, and I knew he meant what he said.

The Rousseaux were holed up half a mile from Pamukkale University in Çamlik, one of the more chi-chi parts of Denizli. I couldn't believe they'd been so close this whole time. The villa was partway up a hill, with breathtaking views of Denizli, the river valley, and the far mountains. Pamukkale was a brilliant white slash near the base of those mountains, and I thought maybe the Rousseaux liked that they could see Satan's doorstep from their living room. Like moving across the street from your parents, so you could run over for help when needed. I pictured the kind of "help" Satan could give his demons, and suddenly felt naked and exposed, as if he could look out from his hellish prison at any moment and see straight into my soul.

Eric saw me shiver and frowned. "*Qu'est-ce qui se passe?*"

"Nothing," I lied. "Just want to get this over with."

I drove past the villa once before parking around the corner a block away. We got out, and I grabbed the rope and a selection of the chisels I'd bought yesterday. I didn't have a lock pick, but back in the day, I'd been pretty handy at an old-fashioned jimmy. Of course, the Rousseaux probably had a high-tech security system, but I didn't know what else to try.

Eric led the way to a service road behind the block of villas. We were halfway down the alley, but I tried again to make him go back to the car. "It's not too late—you can still turn around." I hesitated, then thought, what the hell? It had to come out sometime. "You know…I've broken into bigger villas than this, all on my own."

"Perhaps. But you *should* not attempt this one by yourself."

"Then you don't…mind? About my, er, career?"

He made a noise in the back of his throat that could have been a snort. "*Mon ange.* I am a detective. Did you not think I knew?"

"But do you *mind*?"

He stopped and took my hand, holding it lightly. To give him credit, along with no I-told-you-so's, he'd also refrained from cashing in his Poaching Chips. I got the sense this was less about my feelings, and more about waiting for the right moment, but I appreciated it nonetheless.

"I removed the rock from the Plutonium," he said, "I am in this, whether you like it or not."

"But that's exactly it. Satan's power almost dragged you into Hell. Aren't you afraid he or his demons will recognize you—your scent or your essence or something?"

"The only thing that frightens me more, is you confronting those same demons alone."

"I did it before."

"*Ouais.* And it got you killed."

"I still survived."

He smiled then, one of his rare full-watt, no-irony ones, that transformed his whole aspect. "Nevertheless. It is just as likely they will recognize you as me. I am coming with you. It is settled."

He squeezed my fingers and let go, then started walking again. Damn his arrogance. Being "full Dead" didn't make him immune to danger. I should know. Plus, he hadn't answered the question of how he felt about my background. Which could mean anything, or nothing.

On the other hand, I *really* didn't want to face this alone. Even if Jason hadn't betrayed the hell out of me and absconded with my nephew, I hadn't planned on bringing him along for this. Maybe Eric couldn't do more than stand by my side, but at least I'd have that.

As alleys went, this one was nicer than the one behind La Boutique des Antiquités. Hell, it was nicer than the actual street my shop fronted. Decorative shrubs lined the backs of the properties it served, and it was wide enough to accommodate several landscape trucks parked on either side, and still allow for a full-size delivery truck to drive through, should the need arise.

The villas themselves gave off a definite air of Wealth and Superiority, similar to the homes of my clients in Marseille. Of course, chi-chi outer appearances often hide sad, petty lives. I'd seen how the other half lived and frankly, I was happier in my small apartment.

"Ah," Eric said, stopping midway down the alley. *"C'est celle-ci."*

In front of us was a heavy wooden gate, reinforced with iron bands across the top and bottom, flanked on either side by a tall cream-colored stucco wall. The gate sported a raised coat-of-arms in the center featuring a roaring black lion, standing on its hind legs and surrounded by three ornate green frogs, all on a blood-red background bisected by a wide gold band.

I looked up at what I could see of the villa beyond.

The building was three stories high and essentially square, though the top floor stuck out past the ones below on two sides. Brown shutters framed the windows, and dark beams crisscrossed the stucco of the house itself. That combined with the coat-of-arms gave it a vaguely Tudor-esque look—which was immediately destroyed by the iron balconies jutting out in random fashion from the upper floors. Finally, a flat brown roof sat on top, making the whole look chunky and overbalanced, like a child's blocks stacked lopsidedly and called a house.

"For a luxury villa, this isn't very exciting," I said.

"Perhaps not on the outside. But from what I have heard, your demon friends did not skimp on the interior."

Apparently, they had skimped on security. The intercom lock on the gate seemed kind of paltry for Demons from the Last Circle of Hell. Then again, they had all the Dark Arts at their disposal, so probably the keypad was just to keep out casual burglars.

Wishing I *was* a casual burglar, I dropped the rope and chisels and placed a hand on the gate. There—the now familiar tuning-fork vibration rippled through my fingers and up my arm.

Thank God.

"It's here," I said in answer to Eric's inquisitive look. "Muffled. But definitely here."

"You are sure? It is the correct one?"

"Positive."

And I was. Now that I'd felt another piece of the rock, I immediately recognized this one. The differences were subtle—I couldn't pinpoint them. I only knew this was the same vibration I'd felt in

Marseille. I took my hand away, and the sensation faded.

What I didn't tell Eric was that even when not touching the gate, I felt the heat coming in waves from the villa. I'd felt it as we walked down the alley, and now it nearly singed my skin. Eric didn't seem affected, but then he'd never been involved with demons. Still, I would've thought if he felt Satan's energy from Hell, he'd feel the Rousseaux's. I didn't want to worry him, though, so I shut my mouth and went to work.

For the heck of it, I tried the keypad first. Six-six-six? Nope.

Eric quirked an eyebrow at me.

"Worth a shot."

"Thirteen?"

That didn't work either, and neither did other combinations in that vein, so, not having time to waste, I picked up one of the chisels. A screwdriver would've been better. From what I could tell, the keypad was rigged only to the gate's lock, not the gate itself, meaning if I loosened the screws, we might get in without setting off the alarm. We might have tried scaling the wall, but I hadn't brought a grappling hook, and there was nothing nearby to use as a ladder.

"Or," Eric pointed out for the third time, "I could pass through the gate and retrieve the rock, as I did at the Plutonium."

"No," I said and went back to chiseling the screws.

"*Mon ange*—"

"No." Sometimes, he was as bad as Jason. I felt a pang of nausea—*Geordi*—and shoved it away again. I had to focus. "You can't pass through the gate. They'll notice. They'll notice me sooner or later, but maybe not

until I've gotten the rock." He opened his mouth, and I cut him off. "Besides, I told you—this piece is larger. No offense, but I don't think you can move it by yourself."

He made a frustrated sound, but what could I say? He might want to be Officer Ghost and save the day, but this time, I had to do it myself.

"Still talking to yourself?" said an achingly familiar voice behind us, and I dropped the chisel and whirled to find Jason lounging against a truck parked across the alley.

"Putain!" Eric said and took a step toward him. *"J'vais l'tuer—"* He raised his hands, and one of the larger chisels on the ground started to shake.

"No!" I told him, then picked up the tool myself and pointed it at Jason. "Where's Geordi?"

"Safe."

"Bullshit. You took him to the Dioguardis—*to your family."*

He gave a hollow laugh. "Figured it out, did you?"

"Who sent you? Nick's parents? Did they think Lily'd run to me with Geordi, and you could snatch him?"

"Only half right. I was there to protect Geordi. I just didn't know it would be *from you."*

"What on earth are you talking about?"

"Christ, Hyacinth. Get the fuck off your high horse—I *know* what you are."

Eric put a hand on my shoulder. "Let me take care of him—I will make him say where your nephew is first, I swear it."

It wasn't an idle offer, and believe me, I considered it. But something in Jason's tone bothered me. He genuinely believed I was more evil than he was.

He shoved off the truck and crossed the alley. Anger rolled off him in hot waves, and his eyes smoldered almost black. It struck me, after all this time, that his weren't the only eyes I'd seen do that. But I couldn't pull the memory out while he loomed over me, breathing fury, his chest rising and falling with the effort at control. Jason, the most laidback guy I'd ever known, looked about ready to explode.

"How the fuck did you hide it from me?" His gaze flicked over my face. "You must have one hell of a shield. No wonder you wanted Geordi for yourself."

"Jason—you aren't making any sense!" I took a step back, and he advanced. Even with everything else, I'd clung to my belief that he'd never hurt me. Now, I wasn't so sure. Eric seemed to agree and moved as though to restrain him.

Jason lifted a hand and I cringed, but instead of hitting me, he used his thumb to pull my eyelid up, searching for I don't know what. Eric vibrated so violently, all the chisels rattled on the ground and the rope moved like a snake. But Jason didn't notice. He dropped my eyelid and shoved me on the shoulder so that I stumbled back into the Rousseaux's gate. It clanged like a gong, the security pad jiggling with it, which only seemed to piss him off more.

"God damn it, Hyacinth! Why the fuck are you breaking in?" He was shouting now, beyond caring if the neighbors—or the Rousseaux—heard us.

"I can't just knock on the damn door!"

"Why? Are you double-crossing them? How could you be so stupid? How could you do this to Geordi?"

"Do what? For God's sake, Jason, what the *hell* do

you think I've done?"

"Mon ange," Eric broke in. "You must lower your voices. They will hear us."

Too late. The gate gave a loud groan and creaked inward, and I lost my balance. Jason's arm shot out as I tried to right myself, tried to turn and run, but there was no time. The gate was already wide enough for a man to step through. An oily man, wearing an expensive suit, gold watch, and pricey shoes: Claude Rousseau, followed by his soulless chauffeur and the truck driver who'd killed Nick, Lily and me. Behind them came two more empty-eyed thugs, and in a matter of seconds, we were surrounded.

"Ah," Claude said, looking at Jason, whose face was ashen with shock. "I thought so. You really should be more careful." He made a tsking sound. "Letting your shield down. I would expect that of someone much younger. But it was good of you to announce your presence."

Jason looked at me in horrified anguish.

"Dear God," I managed. "Jason—*what is going on?* Who—*what*—are you?"

Claude turned to me, startled recognition flashing in his blue-black eyes before they went back to their emotionless void. "Mademoiselle Finch. I am *very* surprised to see you. As for him…" Claude looked at Jason and shrugged apologetically, before spearing me with his gaze again. "Your friend is a demon. And he thinks you are, too."

Chapter Twenty-Two

"Death is not the worst that can happen to men."
~Plato (ca. 428-347 BCE)

Eric grabbed me as I swayed—my vision silvered—this couldn't be happening.

"Sit," Eric ordered and, surprisingly, Claude seconded him.

"Your dead friend is right. You should rest a moment."

That answered one question, anyway. Claude could see Eric. Jason still couldn't, though. His gaze searched roughly the space where Eric stood.

Jesus. Jason was a *demon*—shouldn't he be able to see the Dead?

I couldn't breathe—the Dioguardis had Geordi—and he'd been delivered to them *by a demon.* My head cleared, and I launched myself at Jason.

"You *bastard!* Where the *hell* is my nephew?"

He staggered when I hit him, surprise turning to rage as his hands clamped on my arms, pinning them while I flailed. I needed to punch him—gouge his eyes out—do *something* to ease the ache of knowing I couldn't help Geordi. But Jason was still a helluva lot taller and stronger than me—he lifted me off the ground, and I was helpless.

"Geordi is somewhere safe," he snarled, *"from*

you."

"I am *not* a demon!" I shouted.

"Neither am I!" he shouted back, his eyes going dark again.

"There," Claude said conversationally. "You see? The true hallmark of a demon. The eyes go black when the shield goes down."

As though to prove the point, Jason shot Claude a murderous look, and his eyes blackened further. Eric took a step forward, but Claude waved a negligent hand, and Eric stayed rooted to the spot, struggling against some unseen force.

"Bâtard—release me!"

"He will not harm her. I will bring her to Jacques."

Claude's utter calm chilled me more than Jason's fury. Apparently, it got through to Jason, too. His face cleared, his eyes going blue again, and he set me on the ground, gripping my arms tight.

"If you aren't a demon," he said slowly, "then what are you? And why are you here?"

"Why are *you*?"

He held my gaze a moment, then leaned close and inhaled deeply, exactly as though sniffing my scent. Then just as fast, he released me. "Thank God—I believe you."

"Gee, thanks. I don't believe you. How the *hell* do you explain your eyes?"

But Claude had decided the show was over. "Enough," he said and clapped his hands once. And that's the last thing I remember for a long time.

****

"Hyacinth…?"

I came to groggily, head pounding, tongue thick. I

felt worse than I had on being reborn. Hungover and sick to my stomach, red fire behind my eyelids.

"Hyacinth—thank God. It will wear off. Listen to me—you'll be fine when it wears off."

Jason. It was Jason's voice. I heard the underlying fear, and for a moment, I forgot what he was. Then it all came rushing back and I sat up, forcing my eyes open.

Too fast. I swayed, and he reached out to steady me.

"No." The word came out a dry croak, and I scooted away. My vision was blurry. I kept seeing double, but when I shook my head to clear it, I wished I hadn't and shut my eyes again.

"Try to stay still," Jason said, but he didn't come near me.

After a sickening, woozy minute, I tried my eyes again. They decided to cooperate, and I looked around. A room. We were in a room. A pretty nice one. Oriental carpets, rich wood furnishings, expensive art throughout. The Rousseaux's villa.

I twisted until I saw the door. Forcing myself up on shaky legs, I rushed toward it.

"Hyacinth! Don't!" Jason scrambled up after me, but he was too late.

About a meter from the door, I smacked into something hard yet invisible, my forehead ricocheting off it, and I fell back, Jason catching me before I hit the ground. I shook off his arms and dodged away again, my temple throbbing.

"Don't touch me! Don't *ever* touch me again!"

He lifted his hands, palms out. "Hyacinth—I'm sorry."

"For what? Being a Dioguardi—or a *demon?"*

"Jesus Christ. For the last time—I'm *not* a goddamn demon!" He paused. "Shit. Damn. *Fuck.*" He dropped his head to his hands. "I said I wouldn't lie to you. Maybe you're right—in your eyes, I am a demon."

Hearing him say it was a shock all over again. I expected denial, lies, attempts to persuade me. My stomach roiled and my skin crawled and I couldn't give in to any of it. Incredibly, finding out my neighbor, friend, and almost-lover was a creature from Hell was *not* my biggest problem.

"I have to get out of here." I looked around for a clock and, not finding one, made my way to a set of French doors that opened onto an iron balcony.

"The windows are protected, too."

"I know that!"

I skirted around him, ignoring the hurt in his eyes, then put out my hands and felt through the air until I found the barrier. Not even a shimmer gave it away, and it made no sound when I smacked it with my palm. But it was hard as diamonds and just as impenetrable, curving toward the wall on either side of the doors. I looked through to the outside. *Merde.* I couldn't see the sun, but the light was warm, the shadows slanted. Late afternoon, then.

Oh, God—Geordi.

Icy-hot sweat beaded my face and hands. I rounded on Jason. "Are the Rousseaux here?"

"No. They left after sealing us in. Took their pets with them."

It took a moment to figure out he meant their thugs. Another creepy reminder that this was Jason's world, not mine. "How long?"

"Four hours."

"I was out for *four hours?"* Ohgodohgodohgod—I had no time—less than three hours, and I still had to get to Colossae.

Jason looked at me curiously. "You should have been out until Claude released you. You aren't a demon. I believe you on that. But…what *are* you?"

Ha. Wouldn't he like to know?

"I don't have time for this. Tell me how to get out." He started to shake his head, and I lost what little control I had. "God damn it! I know you know—tell me how to get past your little demon friends' invisible walls!"

A muscle in Jason's neck corded, and I could practically feel him force his temper down. *"I'm* not the one who's friends with the Rousseaux. That's you, remember?"

"Screw you. I'll find my own way out." I turned to the wall, feeling for the join between it and the barrier.

I had no warning. Jason moved *that* fast, yanking me around and pinning my shoulders to the wall. "Hyacinth, listen to me! I know you're pissed—you have every right to be. But if we work together, we have a shot."

"Then *help me,* for God's sake!"

"I'm trying to! But you won't tell me who you are, or what the fuck you're doing!"

He released me and took a step back and I sagged against the wall. I'd felt so safe with him, so protected. Now everything was quicksand in an earthquake.

"I've been patient," Jason continued. "But if you won't tell me the truth, I can't help." He had that earnest look, and his voice was so *reasonable.* He *exuded* trustworthiness.

"Drop it. I *know* how good an actor you are. Or maybe you've been using your magic on me this whole time. Is that what you did to the girl at the library? Used your Demon Arts?"

"We don't have time for this—when your friends get back, they're going to—" He stopped, like he didn't want to finish the thought.

"What? Kill us? Nice try. Whatever they do, I'm sure you'll help."

"Jesus fucking Christ—I am not one of them!"

"But you *are* with the Dioguardis!"

"Damn right! They aren't all what you think."

Fear fueled my rage until, like Eric, I was about to pop.

Eric.

I shoved Jason in the chest. "Where the hell is Eric?"

"Fuck that—*who* the hell is Eric?"

He glared down at me, doing his towering routine. I had too many other things scaring the crap out of me, though, to let him intimidate me. Taking a deep breath, I closed my eyes and tried to *feel* Eric.

Nothing. Not even a frisson to tell me where they'd put him or if he was safe. In fact, I couldn't sense *anything* outside myself, other than Jason breathing down my neck, his heat almost unbearable. I should have pushed him away, but my concentration was so deep, I didn't want to disrupt it. Besides, in a very junior high way, I didn't want him to think he mattered.

I opened my mind, trying to recreate what I'd done at the Plutonium. There, Eric had started out nearby, and we'd already established a connection. Wherever he was now, it must have a ghost-proof barrier, since

Eric could dematerialize through "normal" walls and escape.

Why Jason couldn't—or *wouldn't*—just magic us out also crossed my mind. Was he really *not* a demon? But he'd admitted it…

Focus.

Beyond this room, the house was…black. Muffled, like soundproof walls surrounded us. I pushed harder, sending a thread of thought into the void.

Eric—where are you? I'm here—I'm not going to leave you.

Nothing.

Nothing-nothing-*nothing.*

While I was at it, I tried calling Michael down, but the thought felt like it landed in cotton, absorbed before it left the room. However Claude had sealed us in, he'd done it well.

My shoulders sagged, and I opened my eyes to find Jason watching me, which pissed me off even more. I couldn't beat Claude up, but Jason was a—relatively—safe alternative.

"Stop staring!" I said and shoved him in the chest for emphasis. Childish, maybe. But not any more so than his response, which was to snatch my hands and grip them tight. I wanted to cry with frustration, which only fueled my determination more. I closed my eyes, shutting him out, and sent another tendril into the void, drawing on everything I had, and then—

There.

A pulse, pure and true, reaching through the blackness. *Eric.* I caught the thread with my own, testing it. Weak, but seemingly undamaged. Then—dear *God*—he put a sense of *irony* in it. I gave a half-sob, half-laugh, and started to send a pulse back, when Jason jerked back and dropped my hands. My eyes flew open to find him staring at me in shock.

"What the *fuck* was that?"

Something was off here. I mean, really off, not just *trapped-in-a-demon-villa-with-another-demon* off. Why was Jason—a *demon*—upset that I sensed a dead guy in another room?

"That was Eric."

"I got that—I meant what you did. What in God's name was *that?"*

Jason breathed hard and fast and his eyes were coal-black. What had Claude said? A demon's eyes go black when their shield goes down? I didn't know what a "demon shield" was, but evidently, Jason had dropped his.

That should have scared me, but I didn't have time to let it. "None of your damn business." I closed my eyes again, trying to reconnect with Eric.

But no matter how many tendrils I sent out, I got nothing back. Not a damn thing. Feeling lost and shaken, I tried to remember what I'd done—how had I reached him? What was the key?

And then it hit me and I opened my eyes again. "Give me your hands!"

Jason looked at me in confusion, but I grabbed his hands and held on tight, then closed my eyes. Instantly, my thread grew, glowing bigger by the moment. I thought of Eric—sent my thread out—and just like that, his thread appeared. Jason's hands jerked, and I gripped harder, concentrating, *feeling* him. Whatever he had was different than Eric—hot and bright, but not exactly evil. It burned, strong and sure, and I took it and joined it to my thread, then flung it forward, searching for clues to Eric's situation.

"It *was* you," Jason said in a low voice. "On Malta—the farmer—*you* saved us."

The truth hit me, and my eyes snapped open. "You lied. You knew all along he wasn't a Dioguardi, didn't you?"

Jason shook his head. "He was a demon. I didn't have my shield up. Stupid of me. I should have known, but the stones blocked him, and I didn't realize until he attacked."

I dropped his hands, suddenly needing distance again. "So he *wasn't* after me."

"No." He cleared his throat. "I tried to put my shield up, but I fell, and then…I felt you. I know it was you—but I don't know what you did."

"Neither do I." I couldn't help the admission. He was close, and I'd trusted him for so long, and whatever he was, I needed him to find Eric and get out of here. "I thought at first he was trying to hurt me, and you and Geordi were just in his way. I didn't think, I just saw a barrier, and tried to make it stronger."

"That was my shield. You saw it?" I nodded, and he sucked in a breath. "You saw my shield—and you *helped* me with it. Jesus, Hyacinth—*what are you*?"

I shook my head. "I don't have time for this. How do we break the barriers?"

He opened his mouth to argue, then shook his head and scrubbed a hand over his face. "We can't. We need someone on either side."

"We've got that. Us—and Eric."

A muscle in his jaw twitched. "It would be better if your…friend…wasn't trapped also. Hyacinth—please.

At least tell me who he is, or how you can communicate with him. Give me *something* to go on."

I hesitated. Screw it—I couldn't even feel Eric without his help. "He's dead. I met him the night all this started. It was his car we took to the docks."

He jerked back. "Jesus. He's been with us the whole time?"

"Mostly. Look, I need to get him out, and I need to get to the Rousseaux. Just tell me how to break the barriers—*please.*"

"Tell me first—*why?*"

"I tried to tell you before. The Rousseaux took something, and if I don't find it by sunset, I have to…leave. I can't—I have to help Geordi. No matter what you say, I'll never believe the Dioguardis are good for him."

Seconds ticked by, before Jason nodded slowly. "Maybe you're right. We aren't *all* bad." His mouth curved in a sad half-smile. "But…some of us are worse than you'll ever know. As for Geordi…I just don't know if he's better off with you—or safer where he is."

He wasn't going to return him, then. I blew out a breath. It wouldn't matter if I didn't get the rock back. I needed Jason to get out of here, but I didn't need him to get to Colossae. *If* I succeeded there, I'd hunt him down until I found Geordi, or Michael made me stop, whichever came first.

"Show me," I said. "Show me what to do, and I'll show Eric."

Jason shook his head, as though not believing what he was about to do. He took my hands in his, then hesitated. His eyes were dark, but not fully black. "I have to let my shield down the rest of the way. To use my 'demon magic,' as you call it, I can't shield it at all."

"Okay. Go for it."

"Hyacinth—whatever you feel while we're doing this, or whatever happens afterward—it's not *me*. No matter what you think, I'm not like the Rousseaux."

His words made no sense, but I didn't have a choice, so I said "Okay, I get it. I'm ready."

"No. You're not," he said, and squeezed my hands.

And the room shattered. No. My mind shattered— black and sharp and shiny, like Jason's eyes. They hurt to look at and I shut mine in self-defense. But that opened my mind to him more. The tentative threads that were Eric and me twisted, tore apart, rejoined with something I knew came from Jason. Something so terrifying and powerful I wanted to run, to hide and never come out, but there was no escape. The threads wove together and grew, bulging into a light so blinding, the blackness burst into clear crystals that pierced the backs of my eyelids.

Whatever had happened on Malta was *nothing* like this. Then, I'd unwittingly helped Jason put his shield up, reinforcing whatever blocked his demon-ness. Now, everything was loose—his powers or magic or essence—it roiled in waves, pulsing, throbbing through me, boiling hot, like a million needles jabbing me from the inside out.

Jason let go of my hands and instead wrapped his arms around me, and I threw mine around him—the one steady thing in a world exploding with chaos and annihilation.

"Pull him out!" Jason shouted. "Use me to pull him out!"

Through the black-red haze, I saw the threads and twined them into a rope until they writhed together, pushing against the chaos, forcing it back like snakes from a torch. And then all at once I lost control of it—the rope flailed away—the blackness surged forward, shiny-sharp and eating into my soul. Jason stumbled, then sagged against me, and I screamed silently.

No—you have to hold on! Help me, damn it!

There was a *pop!* followed by a roar of air, like an airplane's roof ripping off. I felt the wind—hot, sucking at me, pulling me away from Jason. Everything tunneled—I was losing them—losing myself—the threads slipping through my grasp, like hot oily ropes.

Then the thread that was Eric separated, reaching out to me, and I grabbed it, held on for dear life, clinging to Jason's body and Eric's soul and my own sanity. And then Jason's energy was there, pulling us to him, and I grabbed on with my mind as well as my arms, feeling him like a magnet, keeping me close while I guided Eric as he rushed toward the physical me, stronger, surer, as he had at the Plutonium, momentum building, faster and faster, until he was in the hall, outside the door, pounding at it.

Jason pounded back. I don't know what they did, or how they did it. Now that Eric was here, Jason took control of the threads. He shuddered, and I felt him harnessing…*something*, so horrifying in its sheer strength, his earlier power paled in comparison. It hurt like knives in my bones, my whole body ached, but I couldn't escape. Clinging to him, I tried to stay out of the way as they fought the barrier, squeezing it, pressing and pressing until with a sonic *boom!* louder than the one on Malta, it imploded into a million particles of dust.

Eric burst through, falling to the floor at my feet, and Jason let go, staggering back. I dropped next to Eric, took him in my arms, held him tight.

"Mon ange…" His hold was weak, but it didn't matter, because he was *here*.

"Thank God—are you all right?"

"I am fine. Truly." He managed to sit up and looked toward Jason. "Him, I am not so sure about."

I turned. Jason lay crumpled on the floor, eyes closed, white-faced, sweaty and shaking. Even though he was a demon—*and* a Dioguardi—I ran to him and checked his forehead. Cold as ice. I started to look for a blanket and his hand shot out, gripping my arm. His eyes opened, just barely. They were pure blue, and when he spoke, the words came out on a rasp.

"*Go*—they'll come for me. You have to go."

"I can't leave you—not like this."

His grip tightened. "You don't understand. Demons—can sense other demons—when unshielded. The Rousseaux know what I did. If you don't leave, they'll trap you again."

Eric said, "I am afraid he is right."

I turned to him. "They can't come now—they have to send the rock to Satan at sunset."

Jason moved convulsively, and I turned to see him trying to sit up, eyes wide. "Fuck, Hyacinth—this has to do with *Satan? Are you fucking nuts?"*

"It's a long story. We have to get you out of here and get to Colossae."

He shook his head. "Leave me. I'm…drained. Get me near Satan, and I'm a goner."

"Mon ange," Eric interjected. "We must depart,

with or without him."

He was right, but every little bit of knowledge might help me. Telling myself one more minute would be okay, I said to Jason, "I won't go until you tell me— what *are* you?"

The burst of anger had restored his color, and he no longer shook. I saw the struggle warring on his face before he accepted that, to make me leave, he'd have to give me an answer.

"I'm not a Demon—a full-blood—but I have demon blood in me. There's more of us than you'd think, especially in the Dioguardis. The short version is that eight hundred years ago, a priest made a pact with Satan. In exchange for an infusion of demon blood, he would do certain things, force good people into committing heinous acts that would damn them to Hell."

"Why?"

"Power. Wealth. His own evil army. But he made a mistake and used the blood all at once, and it spread unevenly among his children. Then their children received even less, and so on. It's pretty diluted now, like a recessive gene that some of us get, and some of us don't."

My throat closed with dread. "Nick...?"

"No. He was a God-awful bastard. But that was all him, not demon blood."

"How can you be sure? Couldn't he have shielded himself, or whatever you call it?"

"It comes out, in spite of our efforts. You saw what happened on Malta. And here—it's my fault the Rousseaux caught us. I lost control, and they sensed me. Also, it usually manifests in puberty—like pimples or your voice changing. There's no hiding it, until you can shield."

"But what if Nick was a late bloomer?"

"Never *later* than puberty." He hesitated, glancing at the window, then back at me. "In extremely rare cases, the blood is so strong, it shows up in infancy, in which case another demon has to shield the baby until it's older. But that wasn't the case with Nick."

Thank God. At least Lily hadn't married a demon.

Eric moved impatiently. "*Mon ange,* I know your desire to learn the truth. But if we hope to get to Colossae, we must leave now."

"He's right," Jason said. "You have to get out of here."

If I wasn't sitting, I'd've fallen down from the shock. "You can *hear* him?"

"And see him. Since we pulled him out. I told you I had to unshield completely. Being here, with my shield down—it's like an addict with a loaded needle. I had to open myself up to some of the Rousseaux's power, in order to get him out."

I stared, horrified. "You mean by helping me, you made yourself *more* a demon?"

He shrugged. "I don't actually know what the long-term effects are. But yes, I took some of the powers the Rousseaux left behind and added them to my own. It's…changed me." He searched my face. "I've never met a human who could talk with ghosts. Usually, that's only Demons—full-bloods, not partials."

"Which is why you thought I was a demon."

"Partly. Plus, I smelled Claude on you after you met him at the shop that first time, and I sensed him when you walked past my apartment. The higher the demon, the less they bother to shield. I had to wonder if Nick brought him around—or you did."

Eric jerked back from the window. *"Putain.* We have to leave—your demon friends are not back, but they sent their helpers."

I jumped up and ran to the balcony. Eric was right—two of the Rousseaux's thugs were just disappearing into the house. There was another balcony below us, and below that, a three-meter drop to the ground. I heard feet pounding somewhere inside, getting closer by the second.

"Can you stand?" I asked Jason, and he pushed himself up.

"I'm fine." He still looked a little shaky, but the time we'd spent talking had clearly helped him recover. "I can stand, and I can run."

"Great," I said. "How do you feel about jumping?"

Chapter Twenty-Three

"I will ransom them from the power of the grave;
I will redeem them from death."
                    ~The Bible, Hosea 13:14

Jason insisted on going over first, saying that since he was taller, he could help me. The drop to the balcony wasn't too bad. The drop from there to the ground was worse, but Jason did manage to break my fall, staggering a little on impact, though from my weight or his own weakness, I wasn't sure. I was still freaked out over the whole "open myself up to some of their power" thing he'd done. I didn't want to question his abilities, human or otherwise, too closely.

Meanwhile, Eric simply floated over, the first time I'd seen him attempt anything like it. My impression was that whenever he did something "special" or "ghostly," it required more energy than doing it the "normal" way. For instance, once he neared the ground, he let himself drop the rest of the way, and then proceeded to run alongside Jason and me as we headed across the yard to the back fence.

The gate was locked again, and there was another keypad on this side. "We'll have to climb it," Jason said. A wheelbarrow sat in front of a nearby shed. Jason dragged it to the wall while I glanced back at the house.

Incredibly, Claude's goons hadn't followed us over

the balcony. Could they be running down through the house instead?

Jason saw the direction of my gaze and said, "They're pets." He climbed onto the wheelbarrow and made a stirrup out of his hands. "Demon pets. Mindless, loyal, good at following instructions. Not so good at thinking on their feet. Hurry—climb on."

I stepped into his hands, and he lifted me up. With his height plus the wheelbarrow, I easily reached the top of the wall and grabbed on. "You mean they aren't going to follow us?"

"Oh, they'll follow. But it'll take them awhile to figure it out. Either Claude underestimated you, or he didn't have time to tell them what to do if they got here after we escaped. We have some leeway, but not much."

He gave me a quick push and I flung my free leg over the wall, then dropped down on the other side. A moment later he followed suit, and I saw that Eric had either floated over or dematerialized through, and already waited for us.

The sunlight had dimmed considerably in the last several minutes. The "pets" might not be hot on our heels, but I didn't have time to waste. I turned and ran down the alley, Jason and Eric close behind.

As we rounded the corner and neared the car, Jason panted, "Keys...?"

There was no way I'd hand them over—to a Dioguardi *and* a demon. He might have saved Eric and me, but he'd also lied, betrayed me, and kidnapped my nephew.

"I'll drive," I said and unlocked the doors.

"I know. I just wanted to make sure you still had

them." He turned to Eric. "Get her to Colossae—help her with whatever the hell she has to do."

Fear clenched my gut. "You can't leave us here!"

"Can, and am. You don't want me along on this—trust me. I just stole powers from High Demons, *in their own home,* for God's sake, then shattered several of their best spells. I'm open to them—completely raw and vulnerable, no way to stop them from using me for whatever they want. Besides, they'll know I'm coming from miles away."

"Won't they sense me—or Eric?"

"Not as fast. And—no offense—they won't care. You're hardly worth their notice. With their powers in me, I'm like a dog in heat. They know *exactly* where I am, right now, and what I've done enrages them. But unless I force myself on them, they'll wait and deal with me later."

Merde. What could I say to that? "But where will you go?"

"Can't tell you."

"You mean *won't.*"

"Yep." He turned back to Eric. "If you let the Rousseaux or Satan or anyone else hurt her, I'll hunt you down and send you to Hell myself."

Eric inclined his head. "And if *you* hurt her, I will do the same."

"Agreed."

A sudden certainty flooded through me, and I stared at Jason. "The Dioguardis—you contacted them the night Lily died. They're the ones who cleaned up the scene."

Jason gave one of his lopsided smiles. "Someone had to see that your sister got a decent burial. And

Nick," he added as an afterthought.

A lump rose in my throat. For all I cared, Nick's body could rot in the morgue, while his soul rotted in Hell. But it had bothered me to think of Lily being manhandled by the cops. The Dioguardis might be mafia to the core, but they'd never leave their only grandson's mother to lie in unconsecrated ground. At least, the non-demon ones wouldn't.

"And Geordi's passport?"

"Paolo came back and dropped it on the ground for me to find. He said he jogged past your car while you and Geordi were sitting in it outside the shop."

"That was *Paolo?* Nick's *cousin?* How the hell do you know him?"

Jason's smile widened. "He's my cousin, too."

I stared, open-mouthed. "But…"

"*Mon ange,*" Eric cut in. "We do not have time— we *must* go."

"One more question—I promise." I faced Jason. "Why didn't you take Geordi to the Dioguardis that night?"

Jason shook his head. "I'd like to tell you. Really, I would. But Eric is right. You don't have time." With surprising speed and strength, given his previous condition, he reached out and pulled me close. "I'm sorry for everything. Except this."

He kissed me then, fast and hard, and just as fast, released me and ran off down the hill toward Denizli.

****

By the time Eric and I got to Colossae, the sun touched the horizon, and I still didn't know where the ritual would occur. I parked the car on the side of the mound near the river and we got out. There were more trees than I remembered, and with the late afternoon shadows, everything looked different.

"Which way?" Eric asked.

"I don't know."

Oh, God, I really didn't know. Think. I had to think.

Find the bend in the river—that was the first thing.

I put the water on my right, the mound on my left, facing roughly west. Michael had said to find the spot where the river poured into the sun. It didn't look that way here, so I moved forward, stumbling over the uneven ground. It felt like forever but took only a few minutes before I rounded a bend and was blinded by the sun shining right in my eyes.

I turned and looked to the south. There, between two trees, I saw a lump on the side of the mound. A tumulus, like the underground graves at Hierapolis.

Of course. I just had to find the entrance, and the Rousseaux—with the rock—would be inside. They *had* to be, because I was out of ideas and time.

"This way," I said to Eric, and hurried toward the hill.

Unbelievably, it was hotter now than at midday. The closer we got to the mound, the more the heat rolled over me, and by the time we reached it, I was sweaty and out of breath.

"Mon ange—you must rest a moment."

"I can't! I have to find the rock, before they send it to Satan."

"Can you not sense it?"

"No—it's blocked or something." Oh, God. I fought down the nausea. "We're too late—they've started. *I'm going to lose him*—I'm losing Geordi!"

Eric gripped my shoulders. "*Non.* You will not give up—*tell me what to do.*"

The order cut through my terror and I gasped in a breath. "Look for a hole, entrance, anything."

He nodded, and we split up, him taking the eastern side, me the west. It was cooler here, and the farther I went, the cooler I got, even after I rounded the side into the lowering sun again.

It crawled below the horizon—*I wouldn't find the rock in time*—Michael would take me away—*Geordi*— *the Dioguardis would get him.*

I would not let that happen.

I forced myself to pause, to breathe in the cool air. Tried again to sense the rock. *Nothing.* Eric said something from behind me, and I turned to face him, but he was too far away. I took several steps toward him and warm air washed over me, contrasting with the cool at my back.

Warm air.

Heat.

From the first, I'd noticed the heat rolling off the Rousseaux. The rock was warm, too. *And Jason.*

I broke into a run, faster and faster, moving east toward Eric. Hotter air filled my lungs—I let it guide me—past Eric, who stepped out of the way in surprise, then ran after me.

There. Barely large enough to squeeze through, hidden under a clump of grass, the opening to a narrow dirt tunnel.

Without stopping to think I dove in, worming my way into the earth, the heat almost unbearable. Eric dove in after me, but my focus was on whatever lay below. It was pitch black but there was noise up ahead, a rush of air that grew to a roar as I rounded a bend in the tunnel and it opened up, spilling me into the tumulus' large inner chamber.

I stopped in the nick of time, jerking back into the shadows. Then I assessed the situation.

The chamber was large, maybe thirteen meters across, and domed at the top. Torches burned in wall sconces all around, giving off a fiery hellish light. Whatever corpse had occupied this place originally was long gone, but the room was far from bare. Lush new carpets covered the stone floor, with fancy furniture and ornamentation everywhere. I guess if you're a High Demon, you might as well make yourself comfortable.

Speaking of demons, the Rousseaux stood facing the far wall of the tomb, oblivious to my presence—so far. No doubt they'd notice me eventually, but for now, they were thoroughly engrossed by something in front of them. Off to the side stood my old pals the chauffeur and the truck driver, as per usual, staring into space and awaiting their masters' instructions.

The tunnel was wide enough for two at the entrance, so Eric squirmed in next to me just as Claude and Jacques stepped away from the wall, turned, and raised their arms toward something suspended mid-chamber, above the center of the floor.

The rock.

It floated, turning slowly, its pyramid inverted, the top pointing down. I looked below it, then sucked in a breath. Where the shadow of the rock struck a bare spot on the floor, a chink formed. It grew, then divided, then divided again, until a spiderweb of cracks split the floor, popping the rock slab, forming a jagged pentagon. Jacques raised his left hand and flicked his wrist, and the rock spun faster. The fissures vibrated, like a million twisting snakes, then the slab shook and dust choked me as part of the floor heaved and groaned and imploded downward.

Beside me, Eric blanched, and I swallowed back the bile. That sure looked like an opening to Hell—who knew how close the Rousseaux were to completing the ritual.

Not stopping to think about the consequences, I sent a thread out to the rock, trying to sense it, to tease one of its own threads back out. The Rousseaux had blocked it—I got nothing.

I turned to Eric. "Help me. Try to pull on the rock, the way we did at the Plutonium."

He nodded and threw his thread in with mine, instantly making it stronger. We pushed together, toward the rock, testing, while I begged silently, *Please, please, please let this work.*

I was almost ready to give up when I felt the tiniest motion in the atmosphere, the smallest vibration. *Thank God.* But it wasn't enough—whatever the Rousseaux had done was too powerful.

The hole had widened to two meters across, and broken, sharp boulders heaved all around it. The opening was so dark it went beyond an "absence of light," the black a physical cloud rising from below. Then the bottom of the cloud began to glow, yellow, orange, then fiery red. The black cracked and split, the constant roar in the room rising to an ear-shattering crescendo.

Jacques lifted his hand higher, and *something* far-far below rumbled.

Desperately I closed my eyes, shutting out the

terrifying scene. But like Vadim's edict against cameras, now my mind could "see" what was happening.

At first, everything was a jumble of white-hot light and shadows, confused and chaotic. Then my thread and Eric's, still twined, became more distinct, and I realized the rest of the energy came from the Rousseaux. It must be their "threads," though it pulsed so strong and blinding that it was more a heavy cable, putting our combined tiny effort to shame.

I thought of Jason, of how he'd helped me pull Eric to safety. *Use me,* he'd said, and I'd grabbed his thread and added it to my own, just as I did now with Eric. What I hadn't known then, but did now, was that Jason *also* had supplemented his powers—with the Rousseaux's.

I didn't have time to think—to process—to wonder if I *could* do this, or if I would survive it. In the fraction of a second between understanding and action, Eric realized my intent, and his hand shot out to my arm.

"You cannot—it is too dangerous!"

Too late. I pulled our threads close to the flaming light-void that was the Rousseaux's energy, then grabbed a strand, intertwining it with ours until I had a rope of light. Not as big or strong as theirs, but much more robust than what I'd had before.

Then, fast as I could, I flung it toward the rock.

There was an instant of shattering light, sparking and splitting into a million pieces, and then the rock's own thread burst forth and joined with ours.

My eyes flew open. Jacques stumbled, falling to his knees at the edge of the pit, and Claude looked startled, glancing in our direction. I pulled on the rock, and it moved toward us at the same moment that something happened in the chasm below. The rumbling grew louder, followed by a sound like thousands of teeth gnashing.

Claude shouted something at the pets that I could barely hear, in a language I didn't recognize, and they turned as one and moved toward us. The rock was halfway between me and the center of the pit, near its edge but not close enough to physically grab it. The more I pulled, the more I felt whatever was in the chasm pulling it back. I couldn't think about what—*who*—was down there. Satan couldn't leave Hell, could he? Or did his banishment only apply to Heaven, not Earth?

In a few seconds, the pets would reach us, and he wouldn't need to come out. I'd be thrown down to him, along with Eric and the rock. I pulled harder, Eric pulling with me.

The dual forces, ours against the one from Hell, created a vacuum. The pit was growing, the chamber's walls shook. A piece of stone fell from the ceiling, smashing into the truck driver's skull. With a surprised look, he toppled to the ground. I just had time to realize he could still die, when suddenly, there were two of him, one lying down, the other standing.

No—his corpse lay on the floor. It was his soul I saw next to it. He looked down at his body, then at me. With a roar of rage, he ran toward us and I jerked away, almost losing my hold on the rock, then snatching it back just in time.

"I will take care of him!" Eric shouted. I felt him fling his thread at me, giving me total control of it, while he pushed out of the tunnel and rushed to meet the dead driver.

The other, not-dead pet paused uncertainly, looking down at his friend's corpse, and I remembered what Jason said about their inability to think under pressure. Apparently, death released the enchantment, because the enraged truck driver now seemed perfectly able to think on his own. Eric met him at the edge of the pit and they grappled. I tried not to watch—if I did, terror for Eric would make me lose what little advantage I'd gained with the rock.

It was so close to the edge of the pit. If I could just reach it—

Claude shouted at the chauffeur, who resumed his plodding toward me, hampered by the heaving floor and the crashing rocks. Jacques, who'd been kneeling, seemingly in a deep trance, jerked upright and raised his arms higher. The pit swirled, the stones shifting and melting, molten lava that crawled up and out, spilling onto the floor, over his feet and Claude's, not seeming to affect them at all, nearing Eric and the truck driver— so hot, any other heat I'd felt before, demon or otherwise, was nothing in comparison. My skin sizzled with it.

The truck driver had a grip on Eric's neck, pulling him toward the lava. It crawled over the driver's own foot and he screamed—the part of his form touched by it flared bright. Then with a tremendous *crack!* his whole leg from the knee down vanished. He shrieked, his rage and pain seeming only to increase his strength, and he twisted and hopped on his remaining leg, yanking Eric with him toward Hell.

"NO!" I screamed. I couldn't wait—I launched myself at the rock, just beyond the edge of the lava. My

toes were inches from the searing heat—hands stretching out—grasping—

I had it! The rock was in my hands—I yanked it to me, toppling back. Earth crumbled, stone shattered, my ears split, the whole chamber shook and erupted all at once. The chauffeur fell over, a jagged stone piercing his back, and, undeterred, crawled toward me.

I realized I still held the threads in my mind and let Eric's go, feeling it slide back into him. He twisted free from the truck driver's grip and shoved him backward into the lava. The driver shrieked in agony, popping and cracking as he dissolved and was sucked down to Hell.

Eric turned and sprinted toward me. *"Run!"*

I still held the piece of the Rousseaux's power in my mind. From across the pit, Claude's gaze met mine. He knew. He saw my dilemma and smiled, and the power felt so good. Surely, I could keep it—just a tiny bit. Jason had demon blood in him. Why couldn't I take this, a teeny drop of demon power, and use it for something good?

Eric grabbed my shoulders and shook me. "Let it go—you *must* let it go!"

Claude sent a pulse into my mind. Subconsciously, I tried to step toward him, but Eric blocked my way. Something about that confused me, as did the rock in my hands. How had it gotten there? Why on earth would I want a boring old rock, when there was a perfectly good pit in front of me, into which I could toss it?

The chauffeur reached us and grabbed one of my ankles, pulling on it. Eric kicked him in the head and turned me toward the tunnel. Either the floor was sinking, or the lava was rising, or both. Jacques was more than half-covered by it. Claude, farther from the pit, had it up to his knees.

I half-turned, looking longingly at Claude across the chasm.

And then Eric pulled me away again. Leaned close to my ear. Gripped my shoulders tight. Said, *"Geordi."*

I shot forward, away from the Rousseaux and the pit of Hell. Claude made a noise like a million souls wailing and yanked on their thread, dragging me back. I released it and it whipped back into him, knocking him over with its force. It coiled, slithered, arced, then merged with the fire in the pit, pulling him down until he vanished below the lava.

Jacques' eyes snapped open. His gaze flew to my face and he regarded me steadily. But without rancor. I was a curiosity to him—like he wondered how I'd stolen his power and taken the rock, then vanquished his brother, but he felt he had plenty of time to work it all out. He shook his head once, then walked forward. Not to me. Into the pit, moving slowly downward, holding my gaze until the lava covered him with a soft, satisfied, sucking *pop!*

The walls began to crash in around us, and Eric shoved me into the tunnel. I was vaguely aware of the chauffeur crawling along behind us. I'd half hoped Eric's kick had finished him off and he'd gone to join his buddy in Hell, but apparently not.

And then, like the barriers at the Rousseaux's villa, the chamber imploded into billions of particles of sharp, hot dust, and I scrambled for dear life back up the tunnel, choking on the stench of burning death. An instant later I burst out of the tumulus onto the side of the mound, Eric and the chauffeur right on my heels.

Behind us, the tunnel entrance collapsed, filling with dirt until no sign of it remained.

The sun was just vanishing below the horizon.

And the rock was safe in my arms.

Chapter Twenty-Four

"For death begins with life's first breath,
And life begins at touch of death."
                    ~John Oxenham (1852-1941)

Eric sat up and crawled to me, and I said, "Go! Get out of here—I have to call Michael down, and if he sees you, I don't know what will happen." He opened his mouth to protest and I cut him off. "Listen to me—I have to give Michael the rock, so we can go find Geordi."

I thought he'd try to argue, but at last he blew out a ghost-breath. "This is not poaching." He pulled me into his arms, solid and real, and with a sob of gratitude, I clutched him back.

"Mon ange," he murmured against my neck, and then he pulled away and scrambled around the hill toward the car.

The chauffeur still lay on the ground a few feet away, stunned but apparently unaffected by the smoke and debris that clogged my lungs. I ignored him. Without the Rousseaux to command him, he wasn't a threat. I took a second to clear my head, and then I thought, *Michael.*

Nothing happened. Both times before, he'd come without asking. Maybe I wasn't doing it right. *Michael,* I thought again, harder this time. *I've got it—come down, damn you.*

"You really should be careful who you damn," said a deep voice a few feet away, and I turned to him, relief washing through me in wave after wave.

"I've got it," I said, shoving the rock into his hands. "Here it is—I satisfied our bargain."

He stared at it, astonishment writ large on his face. "Hyacinth Finch—you amaze me. I did not truly expect you to succeed."

"Gee, thanks."

He grinned, then paused as though searching for something in his mind. "Ah, it is so. The Rousseaux—I felt them leave. Whatever you did to them, they have gone back to Hell, to recuperate." He shook his head in wonder. "Extraordinary."

He saw the chauffeur then, and his expression became the calm, reassuring one he'd used with Lily. He moved to stand in front of the man, and said, "You may get up now, my son."

To my amazement, the chauffeur slowly pushed himself up to a sitting position, looking around in confusion. His gaze landed on me. *"Tu peux m'aider?* Which way should I go?"

I don't know who was more surprised, Michael or me. But the man looked at me so searchingly, so hopefully, that without thinking, I said, "You're dead?"

"I…suppose I am. Can you help me?"

Of course he was dead. I'd seen the broken stone stab him but assumed it hadn't killed him. Now I realized—Eric had kicked him, which was only possible if he were a ghost. His corpse must have been obscured by all the falling rocks when his spirit left it.

Michael watched me curiously. No point in trying

to keep my secret from him any longer. I turned to the chauffeur. No matter how hard I tried, I couldn't see him going to Hell. As with Monsieur Lebeau, everything in me suggested he should go up, not down.

"What's your name?" I asked.

"Jean. It was Jean, before…" He looked at me helplessly, as though unwanted memories flooded back. "Claude Rousseau—he came to the bank where I worked. To recruit me, he said, as a financial advisor for him and his brother. He took me to dinner—that's the last I remember."

Was it possible he was actually a good man, who'd been captured by the Rousseaux and turned into a pet against his will? I looked uncertainly at Michael.

"Well, child. He has asked for your help. What do you say? Shall he go up? Or down?"

I shook my head. I didn't want this—it was too much responsibility. Surely Michael wouldn't just do whatever I said. He expected me to say something, though. I opened my mouth to state the obvious, that a demon pet belonged in Hell. But I couldn't do it.

"He should go up. This better not affect our deal, because I know how crazy it sounds. But…I really think he should go up."

Michael stared at me for a long, long moment. "Incredible. Have you always been able to speak with the Dead?"

"Only since you sent me back down."

"And…do you always sense whether they should go to Heaven or Hell?"

I thought of Eric. "Sometimes. It hasn't come up that often."

He stroked his chin, while Jean waited silently,

watching us. At last he said, "Hyacinth, I believe we had a deal. You have fulfilled your end of it, and then some." He paused to look lovingly at the rock, which fairly glowed with happiness in his hands. Then he raised his gaze to mine again. "Therefore, I grant you your wish. You may stay on Earth long enough to find a home for your nephew."

Hope soared, rushing through me, glorious and strong. Geordi would be safe—I'd find him and take him far away from the Dioguardis, and make sure he was safe, safe, *safe.*

Michael raised a hand. "There is one condition, however."

His words sank like a stone in my gut. "Condition? You can't do that—we had a bargain!"

"True. But this is an unusual situation, and you have an exceptional talent. *Two* talents, both of which I find necessary to help me."

I drew in a breath, trying to calm my temper. We might have had a deal, but he was an archangel. It didn't necessarily follow that he would keep his word, if something he deemed important enough changed things. "What condition?"

"While you are on Earth, and until you find a home for your nephew, you will work as my assistant."

"Assistant?" I couldn't have been more shocked if he'd demanded I grow a second head. "What in the world can I do as your assistant?"

"Two things. First, continue to help me search out more pieces of the rock."

"How do you expect me to do that? It was a fluke that I found this one!"

"And the one at the Plutonium. Once is a fluke.

Twice is a pattern. Either you are very good at sensing them, or they seek you out. Either way is useful to me. And due to your, shall we say, unique skills, you have connections to those who covet this very type of artifact. You can keep your eyes and ears—*all* your senses—open, and if you find anything, return it to me. Perhaps if we find enough pieces of our own, Satan will give up his plans to find them himself."

I could see his point, and stopping Satan sounded like an excellent plan. Just not if I was the one doing it. "And the second thing?"

"As I've said, there are many-many newly dead, and guiding them takes much of my time. There may be some that I miss, here or there."

The breath caught in my throat—did he know about Eric? His tone held no suspicion, though, so I kept my mouth shut and waited.

"If, in your travels, you come across a soul in need, you will act as my gatekeeper, helping them along their way."

I stared, open-mouthed. Me? Guide souls? For *him?* He was the *Angel of Death.* "But…the Dead hate me!"

His laugh roared out, and Jean watched us curiously. Michael turned to him. "My son—do you hate this woman?"

Jean shook his head vehemently. "She released me from the Rousseaux. I am eternally grateful."

Michael turned back to me. "There, you see—the Dead, like the Living, are complex. But I've no doubt you've angered quite a few throughout your career. Perhaps this will give you a chance to atone. The final decision will be mine, of course. Your job will be simply to guide some of the newly Dead, should I not find them first. The choice is yours. If you wish to stay, you will do so as my assistant. Otherwise, you may come with me now as I take Jean away."

What could I say? It seemed I'd find myself in Hell after all, if he literally meant I would go the same direction as Jean. But either way, I couldn't leave Geordi, and Michael knew it.

"Okay," I said at last. "It's a deal. But I won't do *anything* until I get Geordi back."

"Agreed."

"And I get as long as I need, to find him a *good* home. Not just *any* home."

His eyes narrowed. I don't know if he suspected I wanted to stay on Earth forever, but he merely nodded and said again, "Agreed."

They were small victories, and might have been granted anyway, but I felt like I'd won something. Michael was fair. He had his own agenda, and he'd use me for whatever he could, but I'd get something out of it, too. Something so precious and wonderful, I'd do anything for Michael in return. Which he knew.

"Go," he said now. "Find your nephew. I will be in touch."

"Wait. One more thing. Before you sent me back to Earth, you told me you couldn't do anything about the Dioguardis because they're only human."

He nodded. "Yes, I recall."

"But…" I wasn't sure what to say. His expression was guileless. Did he really not know of their demon blood? He'd said often that he wasn't omniscient. Hell, he hadn't even known either rock was found until I told him. But it was his job to deal with Satan. Wasn't keeping track of demons, full or otherwise, a huge part of that?

Should *I* tell him?

If Michael knew about the Dioguardis, what would he do? Could he do anything? Or as "half-bloods," were they too human—too alive—for him to intervene? Was the blood really so weak that, as Jason claimed, they weren't even truly demons?

Moreover, what did I *want* Michael to do? Annihilate them? Even supposing he could, it occurred to me that might not be in my best interest. The Dioguardis were my only excuse for sticking around to keep Geordi safe. If they went away, there went my reason to stay.

Okay, that was the most cowardly reason ever to allow demons and Mafiosi to wander the Earth. I wasn't proud of it, but not so ashamed that I told him. In the end, I just didn't have enough information. Nick was a bastard, but not a demon. Jason *was* a demon, but had done nothing but try to help me, ever since I'd known him. Other than kidnapping Geordi, which he'd only done to protect him.

Michael waited expectantly, and when I didn't speak, asked, "Was there anything else?"

I thought, *Yes. Millions of questions. Like why is Eric still here, and how can demons walk the Earth, and how do I get my nephew back?*

All I said was, "No."

"Very well." He turned to Jean and took his hand. "Come, my son. It is time."

Jean's face lit with the same trust and hope that Lily's had when Michael led her away. He turned and met my gaze, his own overflowing with heartfelt gratitude. *"Merci beaucoup."*

Michael also looked at me. "You are correct, of course. He should go up."

Then they were gone, leaving me alone on a hill in Turkey, wondering what the hell I'd gotten myself into.

"Tata Hyhy?" said a small voice behind me, and I whirled, and incredibly—impossibly—*wonderfully*—Geordi stood near the bottom of the mound.

I raced to him, falling to my knees, pulling him close, crying so hard I could barely speak. "Where—? How—?" I pulled back, checking him over, hardly believing he was real and in my arms again.

He looked exactly the same as when I'd seen him last—was it only a day ago? He appeared to be unharmed, dressed neatly, backpack on his shoulders. In one hand, he clutched the scarab Nadezhda had given him. In the other, a paper lunch bag.

"Are you okay, sweetie? Did—did anyone hurt you?" I almost asked if Jason had, but I knew he never would. Dioguardi Demon he might be, but beyond a shadow of a doubt, he would never, *ever* hurt Geordi.

"I'm okay," Geordi said. He held out the bag. "This is for you."

I opened it, then laughed through my tears. Inside were two cold cheeseburgers and a large order of lamb kebab. "Thank you, sweetie. But—how did you get here?" I craned my neck to look behind him, expecting to see Jason coming down the hill, but there was no sign of him.

"Jason brought me." He pointed to the top of the mound. "We waited up there until the big man with the beard went away. Then he told me to come down."

Jason must have seen me with Michael and waited

for him to leave, before sending Geordi down the hill. But where was he now?

I grabbed Geordi's hand. "Let's go find him, so I can thank him for bringing you back."

Geordi came willingly, but he shook his head. "He's gone, Tata. He said he couldn't stay, but he wanted to make sure I got back to you okay."

Something in me cracked with a pain so sharp, I almost fell. I was furious with Jason for taking Geordi, but I understood why he had. I'd imagined finding Geordi, taking him back, then duking it out with Jason like we'd always done. And like he always had, I'd expected him to get over the anger, and stick around. Instead, it looked like he'd finally given up on me.

I ran to the top of the mound, pulling Geordi along. Though the sun was long gone, enough light lingered for us to see that, sure enough, the place was empty as always.

I turned to Geordi. "Did he say where he was going?"

Geordi shook his head, fighting the tears. I wasn't the only one Jason had abandoned, and it made me want to kill him even more. At least Nick had never led Geordi on.

"Oh, sweetie," I said. "I'm so, so sorry."

"It's okay," Geordi said bravely, swiping his nose. "He said to give you the food, and to make sure you ate it." He gave me a fierce look that was so much like one of Jason's own, I wanted to cry myself.

"I promise," I managed solemnly. "We'll go to the car, and I'll eat as soon as we sit down."

Geordi nodded, and we started to walk toward the road. Eric would be waiting for us. He at least wouldn't desert me. The Rousseaux were back in Hell for the time being, and as far as I knew, the Dioguardis didn't know where Geordi was. I didn't think Jason would have given him to me if they did. I didn't know what had changed his mind—why he'd suddenly decided Geordi was safer with me. But I was eternally grateful for it.

As for what we'd do next, I had no idea. Even if I could remember how to drive Vadim's boat, we couldn't go back to Marseille. At least, not right away. Maybe the harbormaster in Marmaris would sell the boat for us. That would give me enough cash to get us out of Turkey.

Maybe we'd go to Switzerland. There was still Lily's and my bank account, which I could tap into. We could take a little time to recover before I started my "temp job" as gatekeeper to the Angel of Death. At some point, I'd have to face the monumental task of how to stay on Earth. But maybe not right away. Maybe, for a little while, we'd get a reprieve.

We reached the bottom of the hill and stepped onto the road. The car was still pretty far away, but I saw Eric lounging against it. He saw us and straightened, relief evident in his every aspect. I would have waved, but I didn't want Geordi to think I was acting crazy again.

Suddenly, Geordi stopped and looked up at me. "I forgot—Jason said something else. Right before he left."

Hope soared—maybe he hadn't ditched us after all. Maybe he'd told Geordi something to help me find him, or to give me a clue about why he'd left. "What is it, sweetie? What did he say?"

Geordi thought carefully, like he wanted to get it just right. "He said to tell you…I have it, too. The thing he has, but Daddy didn't—I have it, too."

My heart stopped and my blood froze and I stared at my sweet, angelic little nephew, with his black-black hair, and his blue-blue eyes, Jason's words roaring through me.

Rare cases…blood so strong…
Demons can sense other demons…
Someone has to shield the baby…

Somewhere deep inside, I shook. And immediately, I felt Eric's presence, reassuring, offering his strength, even when he didn't know why I needed it. I was glad he was there—glad I didn't have to face this alone.

"Tata Hyhy," Geordi said solemnly, "am I going to be like Jason when I grow up?"

Oh, God. I didn't know whether to hope he wouldn't…or hope he would.

I dropped to my knees and dragged him close.

"I don't know, sweetie. I just don't know. But no matter what, I'll be here with you. I will never, ever leave you—I swear it."

A word about the author…

Kerry has been a writer since before she could read. Her father used to copy down the stories she dictated, most of which involved princesses who got bored with their princes and ran off with the dragon instead.

To this day, she likes surprising her readers. And she still likes dragons! She's fascinated with the "other"—ghosts, psychic powers, mythical/mythological beings—and with human relationships and interactions. She loves history, and how it connects with and influences our present and our future, and she also loves a good mystery. And science! But most of all, she loves stories—hers or someone else's, telling them, listening to them, reading them. Which is why she's thrilled to be here, writing them for you to (hopefully) enjoy!

She has a degree in Comparative Literature (French and Middle English—think Rabelais, Flaubert, and Gide, side by side with Chaucer, Geoffrey of Monmouth, and the Welsh Triads) from U.C. Berkeley, and a Master's in Teaching English and Mathematics from the University of Portland. She lives in the gorgeous Pacific Northwest with her husband, two "kids" in their mid-to-late teens, assorted cats and dogs, and more hot pepper plants than anyone could reasonably consume.

To connect with Kerry, visit her website at https://kerryblaisdell.com, or go to http://bit.ly/KerrysVOML to subscribe to her Very Occasional Mailing List (to win free books and learn about upcoming releases).